the
FALL

T. GEPHART

THE FALL
T Gephart
Copyright 2016 T Gephart

ISBN-10: 0-9944759-7-7
ISBN-13: 978-0-9944759-7-8

Discover other titles by T Gephart at Smashwords or on
Facebook, Twitter, Goodreads, or tgephart.com

Cover by Hang Le
Editing by Perfectly Publishable
Formatting by Max Effect

For you.

I needed to write something different.
For better or worse you followed me here,
so this is for you.

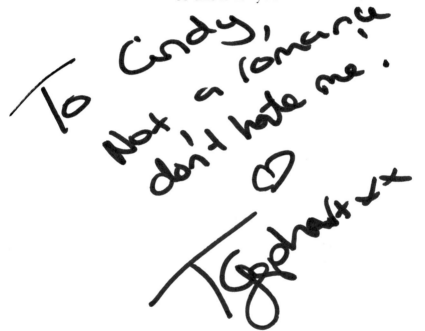

la

Xmas?

that I don't hate me?

Regards x

PROLOGUE

"**P**lease."

An anguished scream ripped through the night as the rain pummeled against the thick stained glass. The heavy splat against the windows was not unlike the streams of unrelenting tears that rolled down her face.

Darkness had come, and with it the howling wind battered at the doors, stirring at the unrest. The fat white candles that littered the room were the only source of illumination, a lightning strike killing the power an hour or two before.

The sisters had gathered, huddled together as mumbled *Our Father's* competed against the sound of the storm, fearing the Devil himself was knocking at their door.

It wasn't just the gale and torrential rain that crackled in the dark. Evil was dense in the air, rolling in like an all-encompassing fog—heavier than the thickest winter coat.

Another scream pierced through the sound of the weather. The very voice tore from her throat like a soul desperate to leave its earthly vessel.

There was no hope. It was the sound of death.

"Please," she begged. The accumulation of fear and pain weighted in that one word made the sisters' skin goose bump like the cold that had yet to breach the room. "Please, save him."

Labored breaths dragged in air behind her chattering teeth.

"Please."

"Save."

"Him."

It was more than a plea, and there was no mistake it would be the woman's last request.

"Mother?"

Sister Catherine's gaze rose to Mother Superior from her place on the floor. Her knees had been cemented to the very spot for the last ten hours, but not for prayer like the others. She waited for direction as blood stained the cold blue stone rock around her. Both the mother and child were closer to meeting the heavenly Father than the dawn was to the new day.

"Mother, we're losing her."

Mother's eyes closed as she drew out a long, deep breath—Sister Catherine was right—the end was coming quickly.

"We will do all that we can, child. Be at peace." Her hand brushed against the damp forehead of the expectant mother.

They had been the only words of comfort Mother could offer without betraying the cloth. She couldn't lie to her. Not because of the promise she had made when she had accepted the habit, but because her very eyes watched as mortality slipped from the blessed child on the floor, the gray pallor of her skin already making her look like a corpse.

"One more push." Sister Catherine's attention was refocused, her actions determined to keep Mother's promise. "I can see the head, but you need to help me."

Sister Catherine's hands worked swiftly, her fingers doing their best to work with the limited knowledge she had. Her calling had come during her second year of medical school; the important things not yet learned. But she was young, just barely having accepted her final vows, and her determination to serve was stronger than her fear.

This was not how she'd imagined her vocation, but one did

not question when it came to serving the Lord. She would do whatever she needed to do, and tonight it was the experience of her pre-cloistered life that was desperately needed.

There were no further words, not from Sister Catherine nor from the woman who lay in front of her. The last gasps of energy were needed if the mother was going to be able to birth her child, and only the Lord himself knew if either of them would survive.

"Agh!" The mother fell back, the rock beneath her biting into her skin but she no longer felt pain. Not from her body at least, her agony had long been numbed. It was the heaviness in her heart that was her only emotion.

Just a little more.

She wasn't sure if it had been Sister Catherine's urging or her own internal thought that spoke those words, but it had been enough to keep her going. Her face strained from the effort as she bore down through the constant contractions. It would have to be enough. She had nothing left.

The child she had carried for nine months slipped from her body, finally making his entrance as she whispered her offering to the Father. That offering being her own sacrifice.

Take me, she prayed. *Let him live, take me.*

Her eyelids closed as Sister Catherine delivered the son, but there had been no cry. Not from the mother and not from her child, the eerie silence settling into the room as she accepted her fate. In fact, there had been no sound as she took her last breath, her eyes not having the luxury of gazing on the boy she'd been so desperate to save. Whether or not she'd succeeded, beyond her control.

"He's breathing, barely." Sister Catherine's hands swaddled the boy with her own veil, his entrance into the world only a few moments before. "He's weak, but he's fighting." She hoped it would be enough. They had already lost the mother; losing the boy would surely be too much.

"A fighter. Yes, we shall call him Michael." Mother genuflected beside the altar, offering quick word of thanks before she rose to her feet. There wasn't a lot of time; they needed to get the child to the hospital and fast.

"Blessed child, Michael." The tiniest drop of holy water rolled off the infant's forehead. Mother's hand hovered above it, her lips moving quickly as the sacred words of baptism spilled from them. It was the best she could do without a priest, but at least she'd given him hope.

"There's no time for an ambulance. Sister Mary, bring the car around. I will keep him breathing if needed." Sister Catherine's resolve kicked in. He would live. He would not die on the cold stained floor of the church.

"Go." Mother clutched at the crucifix that hung close to her breast and slowly removed it from her neck. "I will care for the mother." The gold chain placed gently upon the lifeless body of the mother who would never know the child she had birthed.

Sisters Catherine and Mary wasted no time; the boy's breaths shallow as they ran out of the church into the courtyard toward the old used sedan. The rain soaked their clothes in minutes, the doors closing quickly behind them as the engine roared to life. Thankfully the hospital was not more than a few miles away.

And while it had been Sister Catherine's previous expertise that had kept Michael alive, Sister Mary's reputation for her lead foot was exactly what they needed now. The church and the convent quickly faded in the rearview mirror as they sped away.

Catherine and Mary's attention had been about reaching the hospital, while Mother knelt beside the woman whom she hadn't known nearly long enough, but had loved like her own child. She remembered the very day she had come to them, the day they had accepted her as one of their own.

She had been so brave; even as the end came her strength had not waned. Fearless, even in the face of her own death. She was safe now, seated with the Father, free from pain and sorrow. The Lord would protect her and do what Mother had been unable to do. God forgive her, while it had been Sister Catherine's hands that had been bloodied, it had been Mother's who had worn the biggest stain.

Had her vow of silence been responsible for the death?

"Should we call the police?" Sister Bridget offered, her bright eyes blinking away tears they all felt welling. "Mother? What would you like us to do?"

It was a question Mother had been contemplating for weeks. What she would do when the time came and the child was born. Had she done the right thing? They should have taken her to a hospital. It was insanity to try and handle this within the walls of their sanctuary, and yet it was exactly what she had promised. No one would ever know about the child. Not how he came to be in this world or who his parents had been, his existence hidden by not only her resolve, but that of her devotion to the mother.

No. No one could know.

The plan was set.

The boy was to be reported as abandoned, left in the church's vestibule with no indication of who the mother was. It was a lie and one she would take to her grave. Her father would judge her, but when that time came she knew he would understand.

"No. No police." Mother's voice was hoarse as she removed the veil from her head and covered the body. "Our sister is gone. We will see that she is buried with the faithful at the back, but there can be no record."

"Mother?" There was a collective gasp, the very fabric of

their lives called into question as she told them her plan.

"We must honor her. We must give her the peace in death she was unable to gain in life. I have prayed on it and it is the only way. In this you must trust." Her voice maintained its steely resolve, even if underneath her heart was breaking.

Did she do everything she could?

God help her, she couldn't be sure she had.

"Save him." Mother's eyes rose to the crucifix mounted on the wall, the words more a prayer than a request. "Please, Lord. Save him."

Her thoughts returned to the boy, his mother giving her own life so that he might live.

Only time would tell whether it had been enough.

ONE

MICHAEL
Thirty years later

D^{**rip.**}Drip.
Drip.

The blood hit the cement floor one drop at a time. The slow rhythmic splat not in any way gratifying as I watched the asshole cry in front of me like a little girl.

Oh, and look at that. He'd pissed his pants. Fucking awesome. At this rate it would take him a year to bleed out. And if I had to listen to his whine any more, I was going to stab myself.

The thug routine was *not* my favorite.

Despite my willingness to play it on a usual rotation, tying up grown men and watching them beg for their life didn't get me off. Actually, it disgusted me. Seeing them tap out the minute any real pain was inflicted was embarrassing, and half the time I had to fight the urge not to slice their balls off purely because they didn't deserve them.

Pussies.

All of them.

Tough talking douchebags with shit for brains who couldn't man up and take care of their end of the deal. Whatever that deal was. Like this asshole whose love for the ponies saw him get in twenty-five large with a less than honorable bookie. Of course, the dude who ran numbers didn't like to get his hands dirty which is why he hired me.

Me, and my lack of give-a-shit, meant that I'd cut off a finger or a toe if it secured the payment. Earned me quite the reputation and a steady stream of business, which is why I was sitting in the downtown storeroom of *Lou's Meats* while Lou's arms and legs were secured to an office chair with cable ties.

"Please. I'll pay. I just need a few more days." He gave me the line I'd heard so many times before, his eyes wide like it made a difference if he was being sincere or not.

No, really. Did he honestly think I gave a shit? If he paid or he didn't had no effect on my bank roll, so why these assholes felt the need to give me the song-and-dance was beyond me.

"Don't care." The smile I had no hope of suppressing spread across my lips. "I'm not here to set up a payment plan. So, either you give me the full amount or your wife gets you in a body bag. It's that simple."

Maybe I'd hand deliver it too just because I'd seen the hot piece of ass who happened to share his last name. She was real model material, big tits with a coke habit that would put Whitney Houston to shame. Which was exactly my type. Maybe I'd visit her either way. I doubt this piece of shit had the ability to still get it up, so she could probably use a decent fuck.

"Okay, Okay." The asshole's head shook as sweat rolled down his face, more tears forming on the outer rim of his bloodshot eyes. "There's a warehouse on the Southside. I have it there. I'll take you. Please, let me go and I'll pay the money." The sucking in of air split his sentence into more parts than it needed to be.

I guess the piece of shit also missed the newsflash that I wasn't interested in a scenic tour or playing chauffeur. *He* wasn't taking me anywhere. And unless he suddenly developed a case of shut-the-fuck-up, he was going to end up in a body bag anyway. My patience was dangerously close to the end of my rope, and I didn't subscribe to channeling my inner peace.

"Give me the address," I spat out, already bored with the dickless wonder in front of me.

Lou nodded as he slowly stuttered out an address in Armour Square. "The money is in the safe. The combination is thirty-two, seven, eighty-five. Turn the dial at least four times to the left and then stop at the first number. Then—"

"You think I haven't worked a combination before?" I cut him off before he completed his idiot's guide on a spin lock. "Please, you're already skating on thin ice, don't insult me even more."

"I'm sorry, I'm sorry." He lost whatever battle he'd been fighting with his balls as his head fell forward and he continued to cry like a baby.

"And there better not be any surprises," I warned, wondering if I wasn't going to be walking into a situation I'd rather not.

I assumed there would be some kind of security system—nothing a few cuts in the wires couldn't fix—but a bunch of assholes packing assault rifles was not my idea of a good time. He didn't seem like the type of low life who could afford armed guards, but I hadn't survived my thirty years by leaving shit to chance. So if the place was occupied, I'd rather know about it sooner than later, give me a chance to smoke them out without wasting rounds. Not because I was scared, in all honesty the smell of carbon got me hard. But because this job was already taking longer than it should, and I wasn't getting paid enough to expend the bullets.

"No. No surprises." The sweating piece of shit shook his head, his eyes front and center in an effort to convince me.

"Well." I unsheathed the machete from its holster under my shirt and pushed the blade deep into his forearm. The cut was deep enough for the blood to trickle out at a steady pace. "Just in case." I smiled pushing it a little deeper into his skin before yanking it out.

The deep red stream crawled along the length of his arm while I dragged the blade against his pants to wipe off the blood. No point getting my threads dirty.

His screams fruitless as I shoved the same dirty rag back into his mouth that I'd used when I'd dragged him in. If I had to listen to his voice anymore, I was probably going to stab him again.

"Looks like you've got a nasty cut there." My head tilted to the gash on his arm. "Now, I'm not a doctor but I'd assume that if you don't get that taken care of in the next few hours, you'll probably bleed out. It would be a shame if your own stupidity ended up getting you killed, wouldn't it?"

His mouth strained against the rag. Screams—or cries, I didn't care enough to decipher which—kept muted by the cloth I'd shoved in his mouth. He was still making too much noise for my liking.

"Shut your hole." My fist slammed into his gut, sending his body ricocheting against the back of the chair. Thankfully that helped turn the volume down on account that he was more concerned with filling his windbags with air rather than screaming.

"Good, so now that I have your attention." The blade of my machete angled at the fleshy part of his thigh—the part that had an artery or two that would cause more of a mess than the scratch I'd just given him.

"Blink twice if the warehouse is clear." I waited as his lids gave me the open and shut times two before I moved my hand away.

"Well done, asshole." My machete slid back into the leather sheath against my skin. "Now for your sake, you better hope I don't hit traffic on my way." I straightened out to my full height, my feet settling onto the hard concrete floor.

"And assuming you aren't full of shit and there is the money in the safe, I'll call 9-1-1." My eyes locked onto his. "And you'll be thankful. So thankful that you are alive that you can't remember me or what happened here, right?"

My eyes tracked the slow defeated nod before I continued. "Because if you suddenly feel the need to talk, and I have some unwanted heat following me. This conversation will happen again. Only this time, it will be with some extra participants. That wife of yours will be first, followed by your sister. And we'll just keep going until you get so desperate you beg me to drive the knife in your heart, we clear?"

He and I both knew it wasn't an idle threat. The only value human life held for me was the number of zeros I got paid to give a shit either way. But killing someone who squealed, that would be purely for pleasure. Which is why, even though I'd been hauled in by Chicago's finest more times than I could count, nothing ever stuck. No one saw shit, and what do you know, my alibis were always rock solid.

Lou gave me another nod, this one a little slower than the last just to make sure there were no misunderstandings. Clearly not as stupid as I'd first pegged him which might just have saved his life.

Without bothering with a goodbye, I unlocked the door and strolled into the deserted butcher shop, the glow of the streetlights coming through the glass giving me enough light to move around without having to hit the switch.

And just like I had slipped into the building, I was out, my feet moving quickly to the back alley where my latest ride was waiting. Not my black Camaro—the car I actually enjoyed driving—this was some five-door piece of shit Mazda that had been parked on the wrong street at the wrong time.

Boosting a car or two was easier than risking my ass being hung out to dry, which is why I operated as a ghost, taking what I needed so I could remain under the radar. And to-morrow morning, Sally Jones—or whomever the car belonged to—would be getting her rusty shit box in one piece. Maybe parked a little further up the road so she'd question her sanity, but devoid of any DNA or fingerprints that could tie me to it.

I didn't return the car out of some misguided morality. Ha. I didn't believe in karma, for me it was about keeping my ends nice and tight which didn't happen when you started holding onto shit you didn't need.

The Mazda roared to life, its four cylinders getting a bigger workout than they were probably used to on account of my boot punching the gas.

Lucky for Lou, traffic was light and getting to the shitty warehouse didn't take long. And assuming the moron had been on the level, as soon as I busted the lock and retrieved the cash, I'd call a meat wagon so the asshole didn't bleed out.

Or not.

I couldn't make myself give a shit either way except for the fact Damon wanted his return business. Dead men couldn't borrow cash. Which meant in about six months I'd probably revisit the loser, earning me more green.

I eased the car around the back and killed the engine. This wasn't the kind of area I'd expect any neighborhood watch peeking through their drapes, but wasn't the kind of guy who took chances either.

It was dark. The overgrown grass and weeds littered the backyard, obscuring the rusty door on the old brick building. The faded sign above the door pointed to a failed import/export business venture, the padlock keeping out unwanted visitors needing nothing more than a pair of bolt cutters in place of a key.

Pulling the bag off the passenger seat, I unzipped it and checked I had what I needed, grabbing the flashlight and an extra clip for my Glock before busting the lock.

And just like that, I was in. The musky air of the building filled my lungs as I shined a flashlight through the dusty space, the gutted-out interior making it crystal clear that whatever purpose it had served in the past had long been retired. The building itself was probably worth less than the money I'd been sent to recover which didn't look promising. Now, to find that safe.

My phone buzzed from the front pocket of my pants; it had been vibrating for awhile, but I'd chosen to ignore it. Damon had the phone habits of a sixteen-year-old girl and I expected the previous missed calls had been from him.

Why I chose to fish out my phone and take the call is not something I understood. Possibly because I was already bored with this job and enjoyed playing Russian roulette with Lou's life. *Or* maybe because I, like any contractor, never knew when the next big job was coming. For whatever reason, I hit accept and pulled the phone to my ear as I walked to the rear of the warehouse, trying to find this illusive safe.

"Yeah," I barked into the cell, my current burner not having enough numbers to warrant checking the caller ID.

"You're a tough man to get a hold of," the voice rumbled on the other end of the phone.

It had been a few months, but Jimmy Amaro wasn't the kind of man you forgot. Neither was the gravelly rattle that came out of his voice box every time he spoke, gifted to him from about forty or so years sucking on the Marlboros.

"I'm in the middle of something." Neither of us bothered with friendly introductions.

"Yeah, well get out of it. I have something that requires your attention." He wheezed into the phone, the details of the *something* noticeably absent.

"Well, it will get my *attention* when I'm ready." I didn't do too well with demands, especially unspecified requests from a bastard who'd buried more men than AIDS.

"You're still the same pain in the ass." Jimmy laughed, the disruption of air supply inducing a lung-rattling cough. "Meet me at the place. Don't keep me waiting."

Ordinarily that kind of invitation would have received a two-word response—*fuck* and *you*. But turning down the self-proclaimed king of Chi-Town wasn't what many men lived to regret. Besides, Jimmy was a lot of things—cheap bastard wasn't one of them—which meant my pockets would probably be a little heavier just for having the conversation.

"I'll be there in two hours."

"Good. Don't be late."

The call ended in the same no-fuss way it began. No names, no places, no details. Too many ears, and phones—even unregistered ones—couldn't be trusted. Thanks to Bin Laden and the Patriot Act, the only way serious business was done these days was face to face, which suited me just fine.

It would have been easy to call Damon and tell him I was walking. Lou was probably already buying time with the reaper, and I still had yet to locate the safe. But I didn't like leaving jobs half done—call it a personal grievance—which meant I needed to haul ass.

With my cell shoved back into my pocket, my flashlight did another sweep of the warehouse. And there, sure enough, along the back eastern corner of the space was a matte-black box that was remarkably clean considering the rest of the landscape.

Bingo.

Then it was just a case of a few twists left and right and it was giving it up quicker than a cheap hooker in West Garfield Park.

And what do you know—it was empty. Color me surprised that a sackless POS with a gambling addiction didn't have any actual cash. Sucks to be him. Well, at least it was no longer my problem.

I palmed my cell and dialed Damon's digits, he could decide whether or not he wanted Lou dead or alive—my end had been taken care of.

"Mikey, taking a little longer than usual." Damon's Irish lilt crackled on the line.

"He's dry, and close to lights out." A quick scan of my watch giving me the heads up he'd probably lost consciousness by now. "Your call."

"Well, that's a damn shame." He let out a long sigh. "Still, it's my wife's birthday today, so maybe I feel like giving out a present or two. It's amazing what some newfound perspective will do. I'm positive Lou's *situation* will change in the very near future."

Translation, he was feeling charitable and was hoping now that Lou knew playtime was over he'd come up with the cash. No money to be made from a dead man, I guess.

"Yep. Understood." I ended the call without so much as a goodbye.

Gathering any evidence of my visit and tossing it into my duffle bag, I pulled out a second burner and got my fingers working fast on the keys.

"Hello 9-1-1, what's your emergency?"

I doubled timed it out of the warehouse and back to my boosted ride. "Need an ambulance at Lou's Meats, West Lake Street. Near West Side." The call killed before they could ask any more questions.

No doubt they'd trace the call, not that it would yield much. But just to be sure, I pulled out the SIM and let the heel of my boot get cozy with it before tossing the lifeless phone over the fence.

No point taking chances.

Now I just needed to dump Sally Jones' Mazda so I didn't have a police escort to my meeting with Jimmy. And here I was thinking the night was going to be boring.

TWO

MICHAEL

Jimmy Amaro might sound like he had a foot in the grave, but he was still razor sharp. Standing around six-two, with shoulders that would put most of the Bears defensive line to shame, his expensive suits earned their price tag keeping his big frame under wraps. And while he was happy to hang an American flag outside his door, it wasn't the red-white-and-blue that had his allegiance. The self-serving bastard's ties to the Old Country might have been a couple of generations removed, but it did nothing to loosen his stronghold on the family business. And by business I meant anything and everything the black market moved. Drugs, whores, guns, people—whatever there was a demand for, the Amaro family dealt in, which earned out more dollars than most small countries GPD.

A call from the man himself meant two things. The job was personal and the payout would be substantial. He had enough thugs and lowlifes in his crew that he didn't need to outsource, so if he was—well, it couldn't mean good things.

The *place* was an old speakeasy on South Dearbourn Street, on the south side of Chicago. It had been in the "family" since the Amaro Grandfather stepped off the boat, and while it seemed like a harmless old bar, the underhanded shit that passed through its doors would give Al Capone a fucking hard-on. It had been raided a couple of times, and every time—whether it be Feds or local PD—they left empty handed with their tail between their legs. No one knew how they pulled it off, and if you were smart, you didn't ask.

After returning the Mazda—the busted ignition sure to give poor Sally a case of the heebies—and wiping it down for prints, I retrieved my own set of wheels and made it to the meet with barely a few minutes to spare. It seemed the running theme, the tight schedule not unusual when running more than one job at a time. But it was being on Amaro's turf without so much of a clue rather than my full agenda that was giving me the scratch.

"You carrying?" Sal, Jimmy's personal bodyguard greeted me at the door. The bastard grinning like he already knew the answer as he met my eyes.

Standing six-four, there weren't a lot of guys who gave me the eyeball without tipping their chin. Sal was no exception as he readjusted his stance.

"No, I was walking around town with my dick in my hand." I rolled my eyes as I slid up my shirt to reveal the forty-five in the small of my back and the nine strapped to my chest.

"You can't take those." Sal smiled, a nod of respect thrown my way.

"Well, then we have a dilemma don't we?" I made no attempt to unarm, my shoulders squaring off as I lowered my shirt.

I hadn't called the meeting. So if Jimmy wanted a sit down, he was going to have it with my Glock and Heckler and Koch joining the party. I could just as easily walk out the door, and as much as Sal was a nasty SOB, he'd never shoot a man in the back.

"You make a move that is in any way hostile, you'll be dead before your body hits the floor," Sal warned, delivering his threat with a smile.

"Are we done with the theatrics now?" I folded my arms across my chest, his *friendly* advice not needed. "The old man called me; I've got better things to do than watch you jerk each other off."

"Ah, Michael." Sal chuckled. "You amuse me. That's rare my friend, but don't think for a second it makes you indispensable. We all have expiration dates."

Considering the guy had been a suspect in his wife's homicide, I didn't doubt for a second that he'd pull a trigger on anyone if needed. Unfortunately for Mrs. Sal, she'd been caught fucking her daughter's drama coach—the irony. And there was only one thing valued higher than family in these circles— loyalty.

Fortunately for me, I had no family so I didn't need to make the distinction. Everyone was a traitorous bastard, and I was just biding my time until it was time to have my earthy sleep.

"Jimmy ready?" I gave Sal my second let's-move-this-along, knowing the old man was probably watching the whole exchange on his intricate security system.

"Yeah, follow me." Sal turned and led me through the main part of the bar, the place still full of drunk-ass wastes of space even though it was well past midnight.

The old wood-paneled walls hadn't changed in over fifty years with any upgrades keeping with the old-time feel of the joint. And although there was a stage, no one came to hear a band. Most of the clientele were either unsavory characters who treated it as a one-stop-shop of excess—drugs, drinks and pussy. Or they were adrenaline-chasing assholes who got off on dipping a toe into the scumbag pool.

Moving to the back of the bar, we hit a set of stairs that led to the basement. And unlike its above ground counterpart, had been completely gutted and renovated.

My heavy boots echoed off the reinforced steel stairs that had replaced the original wooden ones, descending until we landed in a room so pristine you could probably do surgery on its floor. Chances were, it probably had seen a stitch job or two.

The two meatheads at the entrance gave Sal a nod as they turned and followed us like obedient Rottweilers, our little adventure apparently needing an entourage.

We continued further down the hall to a set of doors. The overhead LED's flooded the space with so much light it was hard not to squint, Sal doing the honors and beat his fist against the large metal door.

Unlike my initial welcome, we weren't greeted at the door. A dull metallic thud signaling the lock had been disengaged was the only sound as Sal pushed open the door and stepped aside so I could enter ahead of him. His eyes tracked every step I took as he and two of his 'roid loving friends joined us in the modern office space.

"Michael." Jimmy didn't make any moves to stand, instead tipping his head to the vacant chair in front of his desk. His trademark version of a *hello and take a seat.*

"You called?" My ass lowered onto the fancy armchair I'd been offered; its patterned cloth fabric looking out of place in the testosterone-filled room.

"Yes, I have a job for you. It's of a *sensitive* nature." Jimmy didn't bother insulting me with the idle small talk, getting to the point on why I had been summoned.

It wasn't the first time I'd been offered work from Jimmy. While he was fully decked out with his own heavies, every now and then he needed an outsider to handle *sensitive* issues. I didn't ask questions, which he liked, and the payout always made it worth my while. It was a win/win for everyone concerned which is why I guessed he was a return customer.

"My gentle touch is legendary." I smirked, my tightly balled fists resting on my knees. Just because I was smiling didn't mean I was relaxed. I never did well with company, preferring to be alone rather than chilling with a crowd. "What's the job?"

"I need you get a girl, keep her out of sight and alive." Jimmy eased back into his chair, zero emotion in his voice or on his face.

Well, this was new. I'd done a lot of jobs in my time, most of which involved breaking a few bones. None had ever involved keeping anyone safe. Not my gig, that's for damn sure.

"I'm not the babysitting type, Jimmy." I did my best not to insult the motherfucker, because he was clearly out of his mind. "You best shop around for someone else." My boots shifted on the floor as I rose to my feet.

"Sit down." Jimmy tipped his chin to the chair just as he had when I'd walked in, his voice no louder than it had been. "You haven't heard the price yet."

Money for a man like me was a big motivator. In fact, it was the *only* motivator, and the reason why I did what a lot of others found unsavory. I wasn't bound by the same rules as everyone else. Morality, family, religion, conscience—all met a dead end when it came to me.

My ass lowered back down, hitting the seat as I waited for a figure worth sticking around for.

"One hundred." Jimmy smirked, the additional clarification on *thousand* not needed.

Okay, so now he had my attention. "That's an interesting amount of zeros." And given I had no idea how long the gig was going to last, I was still undecided on whether or not I wanted to commit. "How long?"

"A few weeks. Just until I find a better solution." Jimmy's eyes dropped down to the sealed envelope sitting on top of his otherwise meticulous desk before snapping back to mine. "Not so quick to leave now, are you?"

A hundred K for a few weeks work was too good to be true. And in my experience, lottery wins didn't exist. So unless Jimmy had decided he was trying on a red suit and giving the fat man a run for his money, this spelled out bad news.

"This isn't just a baby sitting job, is it?"

I didn't usually get chatty. In fact, the less I knew the fucking better, but something about this seemed off. Too many unanswered questions. Like why a man like Jimmy fucking Amaro, who had more money than the douchebag who owned Facebook and infinite resources, wouldn't put this girl on a plane and have her chill in the Bahamas. Or hook her up in one of his undisclosed properties; the ones that made the Pentagon look like a freaking Wal-Mart.

"You don't usually ask questions." Jimmy's brow rose, my need for elaboration unprecedented.

"And you don't usually hand out favors." Nor was I in the habit of accepting them. "So if you're tossing out those Benjamins, I'm expecting I'm going to be earning them. I'm not going in blind. What's the catch?"

"She's my daughter and not so thrilled with my way of earning a livelihood. Children, they really are sent here to test us." He gave me a tight smile before continuing. "She recently has been making more noise than usual, which might suggest she has actually found something. And her vendetta has extended to people who aren't so friendly and who aren't so tolerant. And I promised her mother that no harm would come to her at their hands."

"There's a price on her head." It was a statement, not a question and the look in Jimmy's eyes gave me all the confirmation I needed. The large stack of bills he was offering suddenly not so big. "Who?"

"Take your pick." He waved his hand dismissively, his poker

face slipping slightly as he eyed the other men in the room. Our audience had wisely remained tight-lipped, but I was sure this hadn't been the first time they were hearing it. "She's a cop and she has very few friends in this world. There are some who will do it for free. Which is why you are here."

Great.

She was a cop.

Nothing could chill a room a few degrees more than the mention of law enforcement. Especially when her father's rap sheet looked like a Pablo Escobar's greatest hits. And let's not forget that every asshole in Chicago would probably be out looking for her. Wanting to either collect the cash or the notoriety of putting her in the ground. Jimmy's kid and a cop—fuck, that alone would be worth seven figures.

"How do you know I'm not going to flip and kill her myself?" Considering what I was up against, it would make sense. Bigger pay out, less hassle and we'd already established my need to please was non-existent.

"Because, despite all that you are, you have never flipped. It's why you're in such high demand in a city full of shady individuals." Jimmy smiled in appreciation, the respect I'd earned a result of years of keeping my word. "But just to be sure, I'm going to give you more than just the money."

"What?" I laughed, wondering what the bastard could offer me that would be worth more than money.

"Your mother's identity." The words fired out of his mouth like a double-barreled shotgun. The name of the whore who'd spawned me obviously housed in the envelope he'd been fingering since I'd walked in.

It was no secret that my lack of give-a-fuck had evolved by my less than stellar upbringing. Dumped at a hospital a few hours old, barely hanging on to life. No fucking clue as to who my parents were, and if not for a couple of nuns who thought saving me might earn them a higher place in heaven, I'd have been six feet under before my nightmare began.

For years I'd wished they let me die. Because, unless you were in a Hollywood movie, orphans didn't get a happy ending. Thrown into the system that farmed out kids to fucktards who shouldn't be trusted with a dog, much less a kid. And boo-fucking-hoo, poor me ended up a punching bag for a piece of shit drunk who liked to sneak into my bedroom while "mommy" worked nights. No, he didn't fuck me. The limped-dick asshole couldn't have got it up even if he tried, so instead he used my back as an ashtray, holding lit cigarettes against my skin until I screamed.

He was the first man I'd killed.

I had already left. Running away from home when I was fourteen, much to everyone's delight, only to return a couple of years later and slit his throat while he slept. The police investigation was inconclusive, his murder chalked up to a botched robbery, and for the first time in my miserable existence I'd felt empowered. I no longer gave a fuck who my parents were or what cards I'd been dealt. That light at the end of the tunnel wasn't coming unless I climbed down there and lit the fucking thing myself.

Which is what I did.

Self-made asshole, at your service.

"You think I give a shit about some crack-infested slut dumb enough to get pregnant?" I couldn't help but laugh. "Let's just make it two hundred, and you can keep your bedtime story to yourself."

While I couldn't give a rat's ass about my family ties, for an extra hundred K I'd take care of his problem. Especially if it meant we could stop talking.

"She wasn't on drugs, or a slut. Quite the opposite actually. She was young though and not from around here." He leaned forward in his chair, baiting me.

"Still don't give a fuck." I answered with no more interest than when we'd first started talking. "We agreeing on the price or what?"

"Fine, two hundred." He consented with a complete lack of surprise, his initial offer obviously being a low-ball opener he'd expected me to counter. "And I'll give you this as well." He slid the envelope across the desk.

"Unless they are the details of where your daughter is and an accompanying photo, I'm not interested." My hands repelled, the contents and the information no longer needed in my life.

"I really thought you were smarter, Michael." Jimmy eyed me up and down. "You should never turn down information, especially when it's about you. You never know when you are going to need it."

It was exactly the sort of rhetoric that would make most men flinch, the handshake with one hand while a knife hovered at your neck with the other. But I didn't play in anyone else's sandbox, so they didn't get to make up the rules. And what I knew or needed to know was on the list of shit no one else got a say in.

"I'm not here for a pep talk, and considering what you are asking me to do, you might want to keep your unsolicited advice to yourself." My voice didn't waver; neither did the eyeball I'd shot him across his desk, which I hoped got my point across. He might own the town, but I didn't come with that bill of sale. My attitude frowned upon as his hired guns twitched at my side.

"Easy boys, Michael just forgot his manners." Jimmy smiled; his narrow lips uncovered a row of yellowed and crooked teeth. The years hadn't been kind and Amaro wouldn't be winning any awards for being good looking. I shuddered to think what his kid would look like. His three boys had been sent off years ago, earning their stripes on Wall Street or some shit, so I had no point of reference. And the thought of a female *Jimmy* was enough to turn me off sex for a while.

"Yeah, whatever. Details?" The sooner I got out of here and gone, the better for everyone, including the emphysemic asshole seated across from me.

"Details are here." He pulled out another envelope from a locked drawer and rested it on the first I'd refused to take. He really was pushing the issue.

"Thanks." I reached across the desk and retrieved the envelope sitting on top. The beefed-up heavies flinched, making sure my hands didn't breach an undisclosed and invisible line. Their eyes followed my hands as I moved them back into the safety of my own personal space.

They were edgy and trigger-happy but that was typical of Jimmy's men, and while I *understood* the paranoia, I could only handle it in small doses.

"Cash." I stood up and shoved the envelope under my arm. "The regular account." I didn't bother with the extended goodbye, a tip of my chin the only *see you later* Jimmy was getting.

There were few men he would have tolerated leaving before being dismissed, but we'd already established I wasn't one of his lap dogs. He may not like my lack of etiquette, but in my time I'd earned some concessions. Leaving without being waved off was one of them. Besides, his daughter was in the wind like a sitting duck, and the sooner I got to her, the less chance she'd end up in tomorrow's obituaries.

"As you wish." Jimmy nodded as he watched me turn around. "I'll let you know if things change."

"Agreed," I called back over my shoulder, my exit being shadowed by the two dudes who'd been standing by the door.

My escort *out,* the one point Jimmy wasn't willing to bend.

"Good luck." Sal's mouth spread into a grin; our journey coming to an end as we reached the populated part of the bar. "You're gonna need it."

It was hard to tell where Sal sat on the welfare of Jimmy's kid. It wouldn't surprise me if he wasn't secretly hoping she'd end up in a box. The things she probably knew, it would make all their lives easier. Regardless of whether the words were sincere, he wasn't calling the shots. And if daddy dearest wanted to pay me to keep her safe, then chances of her ending up in a dumpster were diminished.

I'd never failed to deliver and I wasn't about to start now.

"I don't believe in luck."

THREE

MICHAEL

The reason why I was so good at what I did was because I was smart about it. There was no smash-and-grab. I went in clean, always knowing my exit route and always with a fucking plan. Of course I'd never had to grab a cop before and hoped some lowlife wasn't hiding in the bushes ready to put a bullet in her head. Or mine. Lowlifes rarely cared about collateral damage and my newfound assignment put a target on my back.

Sofia Amaro had not only turned her back on her family, but also their money it seemed. While her big bros were living large in NYC, she had definitely gotten the short straw.

The modest bungalow downtown she was occupying belonged to someone else, the rental agreement rubber stamped and legit. Her home security was also laughable. Her ADT system requiring nothing more than a few well-placed cuts in wires and it would give anyone access to her house and by virtue, her. All of it genuinely surprised me; I expected more for someone who shared Jimmy's DNA.

I should have asked for more money.

I'd scoped out the place for an hour and not so much as a light had been turned on. So she was either down for the night, or still putting in hours downtown. My hand eased on the doorknob, the action met with locked resistance. I hadn't expected it to be open; that would have been rolling out the welcome mat a little too much. Still, the door wasn't too solid, and other than making sure any neighbors didn't poke their noses where they didn't belong, I didn't anticipate having any issues getting in.

That was until the door I'd been planning to kick in swung open and a nine millimeter was pointed at my chest. Her hazel eyes narrowed showing no fear as she stood in the doorway. "Put your hands where I can see them, slowly." The words so leveled and practiced I'd assumed she'd said them a million times before.

In my line of work, I wasn't surprised very often. I made it my business to work out as many variables as possible so I didn't get "*oh fuck*" moments. But standing in front of me was the opposite of everything I'd been expecting.

Sure, I'd seen a photo of her, but it hadn't done her justice. She had looked like every other dolled-up daddy's girl, face covered in too much shit and hair pulled way too tight. Pathetic. But *this* Sofia was beautiful.

Not in the way you saw in whorehouses or strip joints, but unpolished and completely knock-you-down stunning. Her dark hair was messily pulled back from her face, her skin clear without any makeup. Her body curved in all the right places, the T-shirt and sweatpants doing little to hide what was underneath. She'd looked different from her photo, fiercer and less vulnerable. Her arms were steady as she held her gun. Like she'd be just as comfortable firing it as she would answering the phone. And I didn't believe it had anything to do with being on the force.

"I'm not here to hurt you." I showed her my hands but purposely kept them close to my side. A grab for a gun would take a second, and whether or not I got my hand around it before she fired was all down to how good of a shot she was. I was willing to bet she was better than most.

"No?" Her eyes moved restlessly over my body, looking for the bulge of a weapon. Either that or she was sizing me up for a suit. "You think you're the first thug to come to my door?"

There was an edge to her voice that I couldn't help but enjoy. That she wasn't the helpless weeping mess I'd expected to find made me hard.

And that was rare.

Not that a woman turned me on, but that *this* woman turned me on. The one who was essentially my meal ticket, at least for the next few weeks.

"You look smart, so why don't you lower your weapon and invite me inside." My head tilted toward the doorway she was still standing in.

"You're right, I *am* smart which is why my gun is staying right where it is." She didn't even flinch; the business end of her Smith and Wesson M&P 9 aimed at my chest.

"I'm here to protect you. You need to get out of town because the next person who knocks on your door isn't going to be so friendly." My head did a whip around to survey the surroundings. Every second we were out in the open could mean exposure—for me and for her—so it was either bag her and GTFO, or talk her down. And fuck me, did I hate talking.

"Do I look like I need protecting?" If she was scared, she sure as shit wasn't showing it. Little did she know that I wasn't the problem. Of course, if she didn't comply in the next minute or two, *she* would be.

"I was wrong about you. You're fucking stupid if you think one person is going to stop the rainstorm of shit that is about to land on your doorstep."

"You threatening me? I'm a cop."

No shit and yet the clock was still ticking.

"I know who you are. Your father sent me."

It was the first time the cool exterior she'd been wearing cracked. Her eyes widening as her mouth dropped open. Not a lot, but enough for me to notice. The gun in her hand lowered too, not intentionally, but it was no longer rock steady as it had been.

"I don't speak to my father."

"I really don't care."

It was as long as I was going to wait. I raised my jacket slowly, careful not to spook her and risk ending up full of holes, as I showed her my weapon. Her eyes dropping to my flank where my loaded forty-five was chilling.

"I can grab my gun and we can have a showdown on your lawn. *Or* you can invite me in and we both will probably make it through the night. But I'm not standing out here a second longer with my ass flapping in the breeze. So make your fucking choice, and make it now."

"So you think you're just going to turn up on my doorstep in the middle of the night and I'm just going to take your word? Now who's stupid?"

"Sofia." It was the first time I'd used her name as I moved closer to her. "Don't think for a second just because I have given you the illusion of choice that you actually have one."

My feet continued to move forward, and despite having no good reason to trust me, I wasn't filled with lead either. Whether she wanted to admit it to me or not, she knew she was in danger. I could see it in her eyes. The way her pupils dilated as they tried to stay on me and scan the periphery.

"Invite me in."

It was the last time I was going to ask.

"Fine, but keep your hands where I can see them and move slowly." She backed away from the door, facing me as she reentered her home. Her gun and eyes stayed on me as she made her backward journey inside.

"If I was going to shoot you, I would have done it already." I followed her in, my arms relaxed by my sides. "You need to pack. Make it quick and drop the gun; it's starting to piss me off." My hand pulled the door closed behind us.

"You are in my house, I have no idea who you are or even what your name is. And you accuse me of pissing *you* off? You must be a friend of my father's; only someone who consorts with him could be so arrogant and abrasive."

"I'm not your father's friend. I'm here because he paid me to do so. And trust me, if he paid me to walk out the door right now even though I know you'd probably be dead by morning, I'd leave just as easily. So don't think this is personal, sweetheart, your feelings aren't high on my list of give-a-shit."

My words were sobering. Both to me and to her. I didn't give a fuck about her feelings—that part was true. But if she wasn't a job, I wouldn't necessarily walk out the door either. She was interesting, the kind that makes your pants tight in your crotch, which would definitely warrant a moment or two consideration before giving her a see-ya.

"What makes you so sure I'd be dead by morning? I'm still the one holding the gun." She tilted her head to the nine still in her hands in case I'd suddenly developed blindness and missed it.

"If you were so sure of that, you wouldn't have let me in your house *and* you would have fired already. Don't insult us both by wasting time and crafting bullshit we both know isn't true."

While my knowledge on Jimmy's daughter might have been limited to what I'd been given in the file, I was quick in getting a read on a person. The streets will do that. All those years with nothing but gut instinct and bravado will sharpen the senses of even the dumbest asshole. Either that or be killed. Watching men die has also contributed to my education; they let go of the mask and you see who they really are.

Which is why, no matter what was coming out of Sofia's mouth, she had to be at the very least concerned that I was telling the truth. And the enemies she'd attracted weren't the ones who left unfinished business. If her family were lucky there would be a corpse, but most likely no one would ever really know what happened.

"Why now?" She lowered the gun. My eyes followed its path as she brought it down by her side. It was the first time since we'd met that she'd put herself in a position of vulnerability.

"Lots of reasons. Poking your nose in places where it doesn't belong would be my first choice, and the fact that despite your family name you seem hell bent on being the thorn in your father's side."

"Do you know what he does?" She looked at me incredulously, like I could have no possible idea of the inner workings of the *family* business. "I'm sure you're a criminal of some sort, but whatever you've done is small potatoes compared to him. I saw it. Grew up around it. Felt its shame on my soul." Her eyes narrowed, either disgust or anger making her face harden. "There are consequences for everything and for me the only redemption was trying to stop him. Bring justice for those who have suffered."

Great.

Redemption.

Because we weren't dealing with enough bad shit tonight. She had to bring up that we were in this mess simply because she was trying to balance out karma. Like it was a real thing, and there really was someone upstairs who listened to all the miserable crap people prayed for.

Ha. Well I knew better.

"There is no soul, sweetheart. You're just a shell like the rest of us, and bad shit happens all the time. Best you can do is get out of its way when it comes. Which is why I'm here. Pack a bag, we're done talking."

She looked like she was going to argue, her mouth opening and closing a few times before settling into a thin line. I guessed the conversation wasn't done, but she either knew it would be a waste or clued up that things were time sensitive so she shelved it for another time. And hopefully if she got the urge to bring it up again, it would be when I wasn't around and forced to listen.

Instead, she slid on the safety and shoved her gun into the waistband of her sweatpants, my quest to get her to pack a bag—so we could get gone—finally given the attention it deserved. Thank fuck.

"Give me a few minutes." She moved toward what I assumed was a bedroom. "I need to get a few things."

"You have two. Make them count." I walked toward the window and pushed open the drapes as I peered out into the street.

It was quiet. Too quiet.

It made me uncomfortable, the heat prickling at my neck as I listened to Sofia get whatever it was she needed before we ejected. I couldn't see her coming back here anytime soon. Death threats didn't disappear until the job was done. And what she didn't realize was she was kissing this house—and her life as she'd known it—goodbye.

"One minute." I let the curtain fall as I un-holstered my forty-five.

I never anticipated an easy exit and tonight was no different. And only time would tell if the face-off was happening here or at another time, but sooner or later it would happen.

Amaros meant trouble, and Sofia was no different.

FOUR

SOFIA

I **knew this day would come.**
The wolf at my door demanding payment for the sins of my
father.

No one gets away for free, and the things I'd seen were
enough to banish anyone into hell for an eternity.

But I'd broken free. My last-ditch effort to bring some
balance. And I was doing everything in my power to make sure
men like my father would feel the weight of their actions.

My mother had cried when I'd left my family home, and
then tried to kill herself when she found out I was joining the
force. Her way of cutting out the middleman I guess, thinking
eventually my actions would kill her.

Or me.

My defection was seen as the ultimate betrayal; the
unforgivable sin that would affect us all.

Even my brothers had stopped talking to me. With the line
in the sand drawn, they sided with my father. And while they
maintained they weren't in the *business*, they would never turn
their back on a man they idolized. Their love for him ultimately
meant they couldn't love me too. I hated it but I understood,
and everyone needed to make their own choice. Time would
tell if my father would draw them further into his deceitful
web.

For years I'd been looking over my shoulder, fully expecting someone to gun me down before I'd even graduated from training. But by some miracle, I'd been spared. I'm sure my father had greased a lot of palms to secure my safety; either that or he'd hoped that someday he'd be able to use my position for his gain. Perhaps he believed I'd flip. Become a corrupt cop that we all knew existed. It wasn't coincidence that he'd never done time. Or that despite the amounts of drugs, weapons or other imports he moved into the city, we'd still lacked any tangible evidence to satisfy the DA. Maybe he was on the take too. It wouldn't surprise me.

What *did* surprise me is that he'd sent someone to protect me. His parting words to me were if I walked out the door, I was on my own. I'd expected it. Knew if I needed help, he would be the last person I'd ask. Which is why when a thug landed on my doorstep claiming to be my savior, courtesy of my father, I was doubtful. But he hadn't killed me yet, and if there was one thing criminals lacked, it was patience.

I might have had the advantage, the sensors hidden at the front of my house alerting me to his presence, but he had yet to pull his gun. He was either extremely cocky, playing the long game or—and I was still wondering if I wasn't completely stupid—actually here to help me.

While my head told me I should run, go out the back door and get as far as I could while he was distracted, I knew I wouldn't get far.

I wasn't submitting. Far from it. But by going willingly, I maintained some semblance of control. Men like the one in my house didn't leave before finishing the job they'd been sent to do. I'd seen it with my own two eyes, their unwavering commitment to their cause. And as strong as I liked to think I was, overpowering him would be next to impossible. It was either shoot him and make sure he stayed down—which would make me no better than my father—or go, and hopefully he wouldn't gag me and toss me in the trunk of his car. He hadn't tried to take my gun, and as long as I got to keep it, I'd let this play out a little more.

He was tall, well above six feet and even with clothes on I could tell he was strong. The curves of his chest against the fabric of his T-shirt hinted he visited the gym in between turning up on doorsteps and waving guns around. Old habits died hard as I mentally catalogued his profile. The color of his eyes: brown, estimated weight: two twenty-five easily, and hair: golden brown that was slightly longer on top, parts of it dropping across his forehead whenever he moved. I hated that I noticed that he wasn't completely unattractive, even if the handsome lines of his face were sharpened in contempt.

"Where are we going?" I bundled the packed overnight bag over my shoulder as I stuffed my extra gun and ammo into a duffle. I had no idea how long we were going to be gone, but something told me that clothes were going to be my last concern.

"You'll find out when we get there. The less you know the better. And stop asking questions, it's giving me a headache," he grumbled, grabbing the overnight bag off my arm and turning around toward the door. "I go out first, come out behind me. Have your gun ready and don't shoot me in the back."

He didn't converse. He barked out orders. His social skills were abysmal and he had even less compassion, but I doubted he wanted to kill me. At least not at this moment. But I wasn't stupid enough to think being alive was a sure thing while I was in his company.

"If you don't want to get shot then I'd suggest being a little nicer. It wouldn't kill you to not be an ass." The words fired out of my mouth with little to no thought. It was more terse than I usually was, but then it wasn't everyday a strange man walked into my house and started bossing me around.

"Actually it would, and I'd rather be an *ass* than be dead. So shut your mouth, get that gun out you're so fond of, and let's bail. We've already been here longer than I'd wanted."

He was all business, his focus continuously moving even when he was talking to me. He might have been attractive if the weight of death wasn't bearing on his shoulders. Those eyes of his— those endless dark pools—had probably seen a lot. Like he'd lived a life before this one. Both of them, unforgiving.

Even though it was night, the streetlights and security lights from nearby houses made it virtually impossible to hide in shadows. It had been one of the reasons why I had picked the rental. My dreams of living life outside of my family name had come at a price, but I wasn't going to make it easier.

It also meant our short walk to his car was more conspicuous than I would have liked. The bags and drawn guns broadcasting to whoever might be watching that I wasn't leaving to go on a vacation. Still, the late hour would afford us some privacy. Not enough it seemed.

My escort—I still had no idea of his name—stopped in front of me. His head snapping to the left like a German Shepard catching a scent.

"What's wrong?" Even looking in the same direction, I saw nothing unusual. Unless the haphazard placement of trashcans that lined the sidewalks ready for the morning's collection bothered you.

He didn't answer, ignoring my question as he pointed to the matte-black Camaro parked a few feet away—his I assumed. Whatever had spooked him didn't seem to give him much more concern, his feet moving purposely to the car as I followed behind.

"Get in." His hand squeezed the keyless entry. The locks clicking open as he moved to the driver's side, his eyes staying on me until I opened the door and slid inside.

My body lowered onto the cloth seat, the duffle I was carrying with extra firepower placed at my feet while he tossed my overnight bag into the backseat. No words were exchanged, the process taking less than a few minutes before he started the car and pulled out onto the road. I had barely gotten my seat belt fastened, pulling the cloth strip across my chest.

He hadn't bothered with his.

I checked my weapon and flicked on the safety, resting my gun on the bag between my legs. It was close enough to get to in a hurry without being overtly visible. Not that he seemed to have the same concerns about not drawing attention to us.

"You should put on your seatbelt," I said, not bothering to hide my annoyance.

He didn't answer, his eyes remaining on the road as he put distance between us and my house.

"Your gun?" My head tilted to the forty-five that was resting across his thigh, closest to the driver's side door. "Is that registered?"

Again, no answer.

Not even an additional blink giving me any indication he'd heard a word I'd said.

"I'm just saying that, if you are trying to not arouse suspicion, driving around without a seatbelt isn't smart. Traffic cops are working this beat all the time. You get stopped for a minor infringement, and they search your car, I'm sure they are going to find more than just one loaded gun."

Not even a flinch as I took a breath and continued.

"And assuming they *are* registered—which I'm guessing that they're not—you would also need to be licensed for concealed carry. Which I'm also assuming you aren't. So at the very least you should put on your seatbelt and try and keep close to fifty-five."

"No one in this town does fifty-five." He gave me a quick sideways glance before his eyes returned to the road, the needle on the speedometer edging closer to eighty. "And I don't need handy hints from a cop." The distaste on the last word not missed.

"You know, you could drop me off somewhere. I could leave by myself and we can each go our separate ways." I looked through the windshield before turning over my shoulder to look at the rear window. "It doesn't look like anyone is following us. No one saw me leave, and as you pointed out, I'm a cop so I know how to cover my tracks."

I'm not sure why I was trying to bargain with him. This wasn't a date that hadn't worked out, and he was being polite by seeing it through. He'd either been, or would be paid by my father to take me somewhere. Jimmy Amaro had most people either on his payroll, or scared of him. And if I had to guess, I'd say he wasn't going to give up the payout.

Silence.

"How much is he paying you?"

I knew I was pushing it. That the last thing the man beside me wanted was a conversation, but I really didn't care. I needed to find out as much as I could about my current situation. And I was on a steep learning curve. "I'm curious as to how much I'm worth."

Nothing. Didn't even move a muscle.

He just continued to drive; the lights passing us in a whirl. Even at this time of night there were cars on the road, and while their presence should have made me feel less isolated, instead it made me more uncomfortable.

Was someone watching us? Waiting until we pulled up at a

stop sign before they tried to ambush us? Was I unjustifiably suspicious and was this all just a major ploy by my father to terrorize me into submission? Was this just the calm before whatever unknown storm came and engulfed me in it? The feelings weren't new and something every officer had to face when they went out on patrol. Add in my last name, and I battled an almost constant case of paranoia. What I didn't usually have to deal with was not knowing the intentions of the person beside me and how they aligned with the dangers outside of the car. So on top of all those variables, I didn't even have a partner to back me up.

My nerves buzzed with every part of me hypersensitive, the lack of information bothering me as I looked to his impassive face. A complete locked vault of emotion.

"Nothing? You're going to sit there and tell me nothing?" I glared at him in frustration, reducing me to behaving like a teenager being grounded. I wasn't sure which I hated more—the silence, or the feeling of insecurity that was creeping up inside of me.

He didn't respond, the hum of the engine the only sound. Not a music lover I assumed, the stereo as mute as he was. "At least tell me your name." *So I can tell you to fuck off properly*, I finished in my head.

He hesitated, seeming to field some internal debate on whether or not to tell me. From the display I'd seen earlier, social skills probably weren't his forte, so it was no wonder he had yet to introduce himself. That, and I'm sure the less anyone knew about him the better.

"Michael."

One word.

That's all he gave me, the full stop to my endless questions. And for now, just knowing his name would have to be enough.

Michael.

We drove the rest of the way in silence to the Far West Side, the Camaro easing off the road into a back laneway and pulling up to an old red brick garage. The structure separated from the main house.

While the building might have been old, it had been updated with an electric roller door, its metal panels lifting with the touch of a button. The remote I'd missed Michael retrieving from the console—my eyes too busy scoping out my surroundings—was tossed back as we entered the dark garage. The door rolled back down behind us as the car submitted to stop with the turn of a key.

Keeping to form, there was no announcement of where we were. Or if this was our final destination. I didn't even know if I was supposed to be getting out of the car except he had already opened his door, and I'd be damned if I was sitting in a dark garage with no way to see what was coming.

"Are we staying?" I grabbed the bag at my feet—the one with my extra ammo, gun—and palmed my nine. The overnight bag that was packed with everything else could stay on the backseat for now. A change of clothes was the least of my problems.

Michael didn't answer—*shocking, I know*—shutting the driver's side door; the thud shaking the body of the car slightly as I exited from my side of the vehicle.

We crossed the dark backyard, the backdoor of the house visible. It looked to be an old rundown Brownstone, the moonlight illuminating the brick double story.

"Is this your place?"

I'm not sure why I persisted. It was obvious getting details from Michael was like extracting blood from a stone, but it made me feel better. And considering I still had no idea what I was dealing with, I was all about making myself feel better.

"Yes. Get inside." Michael inserted the key and pushed open

42

the door.

I didn't do well with orders, my father could attest to that.

"Look, you need to start giving me some answers." I hesitated in the doorway, the darkness of the house doing little to invite me in.

His eyes narrowed, doing a quick scan of the area before pushing me into the dark entrance. I'd barely had time to react, my feet stumbling as he followed me through and shut the door behind us.

He didn't reach for the light, just stood there in silent darkness as my eyes blinked trying to adjust.

"I don't give anyone answers." The words fell from his lips, each one weighted with a slight pause between. "And if you have any self-preservation at all, you'll stop asking."

The door wasn't locked, instead he walked away leaving me standing uncertain in the hallway. His heavy footsteps taking him away as his boots echoed on the wooden floors.

I could run.

The idea bounced through my mind as I reminded myself I was unrestrained, armed and right near an escape route. Despite feeling out of control, he hadn't kidnapped me. I was here of my own free will, even if I was questioning my sanity. Even if what he was saying was true, I had resources at the Chicago PD that should be able to keep me safe. There had to be other options. Ones that didn't have me questioning the character of my company, or making me feel like I was on the wrong side of the law.

My hand went to the doorknob; my fingers gripping it tight as I twisted and felt the lock pop open. Was it some kind of trap? Did he want me to run? None of this made sense.

I pulled open the door, the cool air of the night hitting my skin as I peered out into the backyard we'd just walked through. The trees gently blew in the breeze as I stared out into space, my mind unresolved about what I was doing and why.

This wasn't like me; I always had a plan. But as I stood there silent, my feet undecided on whether to step forward or backward, I drew a complete blank. I had no idea what I should do or who I should trust.

"You would have left already." His hot breath tickled the back of my neck, his approach so quiet I couldn't be sure he hadn't appeared from thin air. "Close the door, Sofia and come inside."

He didn't yell nor did he sound angry, his voice kept low and steady. He didn't reach for me either, his body so close but not even his hands touched mine. Nothing, just his looming presence at my back holding me like an invisible shackle.

He was right.

If I were leaving, I would have gone already.

"Okay." I turned around; my fate feeling like it was slipping from my fingers. "What's the plan?"

FIVE

MICHAEL

My instructions were to get her, keep her safe and sit tight.

Not as effortless as it sounded.

It would have been easier to knock her out, tie her to a chair and lock her in a room. And as long as she wasn't hurt, Jimmy wouldn't question my methods. He had to have known she wouldn't come quietly.

Ironically, I had managed to get her to do *exactly* what I wanted without resulting to my old bag of tricks. It was either curiosity or fear that motivated her, and I hadn't worked out which.

And why make my job harder than it had to be? Because I could tell if this shit had gone down any other way, she wouldn't have come so easily. She might wear a badge, but it was still Jimmy's DNA running through her veins.

"Bedrooms are upstairs. The bathroom is too."

I didn't bother with a tour. She had eyes and a decent sense of direction, and part of me was a SOB who liked keeping her on edge.

"Am I going to die?" Her feet stayed rooted in their place as I went to walk away. The complete lack of panic in her voice made me freeze in place.

Usually when I heard those words it was emotional. The

person on the other end begging for their life, but as I looked into those large hazel eyes I didn't see the anxiety I was expecting. She wasn't falling apart, or if she was, she was smart enough to keep it locked down.

"We're all going to die," I answered more honestly than I usually would. "And you will be no different."

Her eyes flickered, blinking as she looked at me. "Are you trying to scare me?"

The space between us wasn't more than a couple of inches, and if my proximity to her was making her uncomfortable, she wasn't showing it. But she wasn't as solid as she was pretending to be. While she had talked a good game up until now, I could see the crack in the mask. It was small but undeniably there, its reveal giving me more pleasure than it probably should.

"You're already scared." My lips curled into a grin as I watched her eyes widen.

"Fuck you," she spat out, irritated her face had betrayed her, her legs moving quickly toward the staircase as the bag slung over her shoulder bounced off the wall beside her.

I watched her go, taking the stairs two at a time until she disappeared around the corner and I heard a door slam. And I didn't need to be a fortuneteller to know she was probably going to cry. At least she'd been smart enough to do it in private, save us both the indignation.

A breath slowly pushed out from between my lips, my head rolling from side to side as my neck relaxed. There would be no sleeping tonight. At least not until I had my own intel on what I was dealing with. I didn't trust Jimmy's sources, and if someone was coming for her I wanted to be prepared. Hearsay didn't mean shit unless you had some fact to back it up, and those fucktards who ran the city gossiped more than a bunch of old women.

A quick trip to the garage retrieved the overnight bag she'd left on my backseat. Obviously, clean panties weren't as pressing as the need for the firepower she'd packed in the other. Either way, the last thing I needed was for her to go out exploring in a few hours if she got the urge to change her bra.

Before heading back inside, I pulled open the zip and did a quick search of the overnighter, my hand hitting the hard surface of what felt to be a cell phone just before I hit the bottom.

Great.

Let's make it easier for the bastards to find us.

I shook my head as I pulled out the SIM card and snapped it between my fingers. The battery was also removed as I turned her cell into a glorified paperweight. I'd been sloppy in not searching the bag, the phone enough of a breadcrumb for whoever was out there to track her down.

Cursing under my breath, I went back inside. And with the bag in my hand, I climbed the stairs and dumped it in front of the only bedroom door that was closed.

Mine.

Not sure if it was defiance or purely to piss me off but, out of the three available beds, she'd picked *that* one. And as much as knowing she was in my personal space was giving me the scratch, I wasn't giving her the satisfaction of a reaction. Besides, I'd already decided I wasn't sleeping.

Ignoring the closed door—and the person behind it—I went back downstairs to my living room. The area I'd set up as my command center.

While my Brownstone looked like it was ready for demolition from the outside, I had gutted it and refurbished the entire place when I moved three years ago. Contracted out all the technical BS, but other than that had done a lot of the work myself. The less people who knew my address, the

47

better.

Inside it was modest but modern, and although I had no need for lots of furniture, the computer system I had set up in my living room was a Steve Job's wet dream. Amazing how quickly you can gather life skills when you need them, and computer programming in these times definitely classed as a life skill.

Sadly I wasn't advanced enough to hack into main frames or snoop around in government websites, but I could bounce my IP around the globe a few hundred times so my activity was untraceable. I had also found a group of bored frat boys who could do all of the above and liked to balance their 4.2 GPA with a side of illegal online activity. No names, no questions—just a few payments to an offshore account and those kids could get me anything I needed. *Who says customer service is dead?*

There was no noise from upstairs as I made myself comfortable in my leather office chair, the two monitors in front of me lighting up as I hit the mouse. I needed to dig a little deeper.

Jimmy and his crew boasted they were anti-technology, with most of those bastards switching phones like they changed their underwear. But I doubted the tech-ban extended to email. And if there was any electronic chatter out there regarding my new houseguest, I wanted to know what was being said and by who.

A few keystrokes connected my ICQ window. The no-longer-popular chat system was the most reliable method of communication for people who liked to keep their identities under wraps, and I was all about keeping my name off the grid.

My fingers got busy, tapping out Sofia's full name and social, all of which had been provided by her dear old dad. That was all that they needed, my back easing against the leather as I waited to see what pinged back.

It didn't take long for the benign shit to flood my screen. LinkedIn page, graduation information, address and phone number. Most of which I could have gathered myself without too much effort.

I knew it would take a little longer to get to the juicy stuff, so I got out of the seat and walked to the kitchen to grab a beer before settling back in and getting comfortable.

Okay assholes, let's see what we're dealing with.

SIX

SOFIA

I knew it had been his room.

The bedrooms had almost looked identical, a box spring and mattress directly on the floor with almost no bedroom furniture. Except for one room that still carried his scent.

It gave me a twisted sense of satisfaction to be in his room, a space that, if not for a messed up comforter, looked barely lived in. This was where he slept, where even *he* was vulnerable. And I was in it.

Tears had stung my eyes as I slammed the door. But I managed to hold my breath and choked down the sobs, only allowing silent rivulets to trickle down my cheeks.

He didn't get to see me cry.

I wouldn't give him that.

I kicked off my sneakers, letting the bag on my shoulder fall beside the bed as I sat on top of the mattress. My head pounded, like my forehead had developed its own heartbeat as I lowered my body, allowing my head to rest on the pillow. It was the same one he favored I assumed, as a mix of body wash and cologne wafted through the fabric as my head moved against it. It smelled the way he looked.

Powerful.

Strong.

Fearless.

Hard.

He was stone—cold and unyielding—and I was stuck here with him.

I closed my eyes, trying to shut out the nightmare of my uncertainty knowing full well I wouldn't be sleeping. How could I? Instead my mind flicked on like an old-school projector and replayed the night's events in slow grainy flashbacks. The memory of his eyes locked on mine made me gasp as I sat up in bed. The weight of his stare wasn't something I could easy shake off, and I'd faced cold-hearted killers. His eyes had something infinitely more unsettling— what that was exactly I didn't know—and if my racing pulse was anything to go by, I didn't want to find out.

Damn it. I was totally freaking myself out, conjuring up hypotheticals about who he was. *He was just a man* I told myself, the room just as empty as when I'd closed the door. My thumping heartbeat now matched the headache I had going on as I drew my knees up to my chest. I wondered if he had any Motrin hiding in his bathroom cabinet; surely even criminals needed pain relief once in a while.

My feet dropped quietly to the floor, wincing as I tried to make as little noise as possible. I wanted the chance to explore without his attention, padding on my tiptoes to the bedroom door, hoping to make it to the bathroom without running into him.

The overnight bag I'd left on the backseat of his car had been dumped in front of the doorway, my feet almost tripping over it.

"Fuck," I whispered, regaining my balance by grabbing onto the doorjamb. I managed to right myself onto my feet and pulled it into the room.

Shit. My cell phone.

I had completely forgotten I'd buried it under my clothes,

not willing to give up a link to the outside world when I'd left my house. My hand plunged into the overnight bag, the idea of finding it and putting it somewhere safe weighing heavily on my mind. I didn't have to look too far.

Sitting on top was my disabled Samsung Galaxy, the casing still split into two pieces.

He'd found it and killed my phone.

My fists balled tightly as I tossed the useless pieces back into the bag, my only method of communication stripped from me. I should have carried the bag up myself. Shit. It had been stupid to leave it behind.

Ignoring the slight setback, I moved back outside the doorway and silently walked past the stairs. The faint glow of light floated up from downstairs as I made my way to the small bathroom at the end of the hall.

Like the rest of the house, it had been redone. The light reflected off the shiny fixtures and clean walls as I hit the switch. My face looked back at me, courtesy of a mirrored medicine cabinet, and God did I look like hell.

My eyes were red and puffy and my hair was a mess, all of which was tossed aside as I pulled open the cabinet door and hoped like hell he at least had some Tylenol in there. Jackpot. Advil. It would do.

Turning on the faucet and using my hands to cup the water, I swallowed a couple of pills and prayed they'd kick in soon. My eyes closed for a minute as I shut off the water. Just the sound of it running down the sink made my headache worse and I needed a minute to be still. My lids slowly lifted, the movement at my side making me jump.

"Shit. You scared me." The back of my legs hit the tub as I instinctively moved away.

His head tilted toward the partially opened cabinet door. "You need something?"

"No." I brushed him off, not bothering to tell him I'd already found what I needed. "No, I'm fine."

"You should get some sleep. We'll probably be moving in the morning." He folded his arms across his chest, stepping out of the doorway so I could leave.

"Going where?" my mouth asked without thinking.

His eyebrow rose in a sarcastic taunt, the you-really-think-I'm-going-to-tell-you not needing to be spoken.

"You broke my phone."

"GPS chip makes you traceable, I took care of it."

"You don't think that when people can't get ahold of me, they aren't going to be worried? When I don't show up for duty tomorrow, it's going to raise some questions." I wouldn't be surprised if it was my own Captain who filed a missing person's report. I'd never failed to show up for work, not even called in sick. People would be wondering where I was.

"So you suddenly developed a case of the flu." He'd lost the jacket he'd been wearing earlier. His arms flexed on either side of him, the bulge of his weapon poking through the fabric of his shirt. Even inside he was armed. I wasn't sure if it was me or there was someone else he didn't trust, but I was guessing he was more comfortable with steel against his skin than without it.

"There's a burner phone downstairs. Make the call; tell them you expect you'll need a couple of days and hang up. Don't try to be a hero or tip them off, and keep the call under five minutes." His dark eyes warned that he'd be standing by to make sure his criteria would be met.

"And what happens after a few days?" My mouth continued to speak at will despite knowing it was irritating the hell out of him. Probably *because* I knew it was irritating the hell out of it.

"Jesus, do you ever stop asking questions? Like ever?" His head shook, his hand scrubbing the side of his face as he kept his eyes glued on me. "You have to know by now I'm not going to answer them."

He didn't like to show emotion—or converse—both of those things had been kept to a minimum since he showed up on my doorstep. But as he stood there looming over me, I thought I saw a crack in his usual passive brooding. I couldn't tell if it was bewilderment, like perhaps he was more used to people laying down and accepting his way, or if it was amusement. Much like a cat toying with a mouse they have trapped. There was no need to guess as to which of us was the mouse.

"If the situation was reversed, would you just go quietly? Not ask questions?" I'm not sure why I was trying to appeal to his humanity, or why I continued to push. It hadn't gotten me anywhere, but it was the only thread of sanity I had left.

"I would never be in your situation," he answered coldly, the distaste either for me or *my situation* dripped in each word. "Go to sleep. And in case I didn't make myself clear, that wasn't a request."

He didn't wait for a reaction or a response, turning on his heel and vacating the space. The heavy footfalls of his boots echoing down the stairs as I stayed rooted in my place in the bathroom. He was so fucking arrogant, bossy as hell and I had already decided I hated him. But even with all of that, my gut instinct told me to stay. Lord knows why. Whatever trouble he thought I was in wasn't the kind that could be solved in a few days. And I knew it was only a matter of time before I'd be deposited somewhere at my father's bequest. Like an errant runaway being returned to their family. The thought made me want to be physically sick.

I wouldn't go.

Even if it meant dying, I wouldn't go to him. I refused to see the look of satisfaction on his face when he would see me, no doubt reminding me that there would never be a way out. That even though I tried to deny it, I was damned because of the family I'd been birthed into. But I was done with all of that, and no matter what my birth certificate said, I would never be his daughter again. Never.

My stomach churned uneasily, the possibility of vomiting becoming less of a hypothetical the more I thought about it. I pushed down the urge, refusing to allow the bile rising up to travel any further as I opened up the faucet and took another mouthful of water. I was stronger than this; I mentally chastised myself as I concentrated on the air I was sucking into my lungs.

Breathe, I repeated, my internal pep talk hopefully enough so I could get a handle on my nerves.

Breathe.

I would be okay.

Whatever *this* was, it wouldn't be what claimed me.

I had no way of knowing that for sure. In reality everything pointed to the opposite, a bad outcome. But in my heart I believed I would survive this.

With my breathing slowed and the danger of me being sick minimized, my hand eased off the faucet. The room was as it had been when I walked into it. Empty and sterile—me, the only person in it.

Michael hadn't returned, and that made me feel uneasy. I didn't want to see him, hating the weight of those cold dark eyes on me. But not knowing what he was doing was almost worse. Wondering if he was in the wings watching me, reveling in all of this. It was the not knowing that made it hell.

The minor freak out in the bathroom had gone on long enough I'd decided, my hands shaking off any excess water before hitting the light switch and walking back into the hall. I didn't bother closing the door, or trying to be silent as my bare feet padded against the floor. I didn't care if he heard me or not, but as much as I hated to admit it, he was right about one thing. If I was going to get through an entire day of uncertainty tomorrow, I would need some sleep. My instincts would be sharper after a few hours rest, and as much as I would love to pretend I was a machine, the need to power down hinted I was very much human.

As I reentered his room, his lingering scent once again invaded my nose, and it didn't matter I was alone, he was right inside that room with me.

It should have sickened me but it didn't, the thrill tingling against my skin as I slid in between *his* sheets. My act of defiance meant I would sleep in his bed, even if it was the last place on earth I wanted to lay.

I pulled the covers over myself, cocooning within them as I closed my eyes. *I would get through this.* I would be okay.

SEVEN

MICHAEL

Sofia Amaro had been a busy girl.
Leading the charge against organized crime, she had made it her personal mission to fight what most of us knew was a losing battle. There was no cure for a disease that continued to regenerate, and criminals had a knack of evolving faster than the tactics employed to stop them. And it hadn't been just her father who had felt the pinch. If you believed the propaganda circulating from the Chicago PD, every thug in the city had a target on their back.

Which was bad for business.

Everyone's business.

It meant every lowlife worth his salt would be coming out of the woodwork trying to end her. I completely understood why they'd be gunning for her ass too, and it wasn't just to collect the bounty either. This was about their livelihood, their ability to do business in the future, and it was about their fucking pride.

Within hours I had at least twenty to thirty instances of internet *chatter*, her name pinging left and right, with all kinds of suggestions on what a better use of her mouth would be. Here's a hint, most of them involved the use of a cock. Whether she'd be alive when they shoved it in there was still open to debate. Some argued they needed to take some restitution first and necrophilia not being their thing. Can't say I ever understood the appeal of fucking a corpse, but I didn't really give enough of a shit to be disgusted by the behavior either. And as long as it wasn't my dick, who the fuck cared? What I did care about was collecting my paycheck, and for now that meant keeping her breathing. So my mind wandering over uses for her mouth while interesting weren't helpful, especially when getting her out of her neighborhood wouldn't be enough.

I'd been careful last night. Checking the rearview to see if we were getting tailed, but nothing had given me reason for concern. Just to be sure, I took the long way, adding a few extra miles before lapping around.

Whether or not she returned to the piece of shit rental after I handed her over to her father was none of my biz, but while she was with me she wasn't going back. That would be stupid.

And stupidity seemed to be a theme that continued too, with the sunrise bringing a variable I hadn't counted on.

When she'd packed up her shit last night she neglected to mention the off-duty detective work she had been compiling while moonlighting. Because being a cop wasn't bad enough, clearly. Instead she'd taken it upon herself to compile shit while she was off the clock as well. And the thumb drive that had held a database she was putting together wasn't the sort of thing you wanted lying around. Especially if that shit fell into the wrong hands. And I didn't mean the cops. So much for not going back to her place.

She looked rested as she stared at me across the room, my bed giving her the respite it hadn't given me last night.

"Just tell me where the fucking thing is."

Taking her to her house in broad daylight wasn't an option, especially not after I'd successfully evact'd her. Going back in was a whole bunch of complications, not to mention the stupidest move ever.

"I can come with you. I'll be in and out quicker because I know what I'm looking for." She checked her nine, sliding an extra clip into the pocket of her jeans.

Man, she was a pain in the ass. Firstly, that she'd be so stupid leaving that shit behind, and secondly thinking she was *coming with me.*

"Here are your options." I was quickly losing patience with this shit as I held up my hand. "You either tell me where it is and I go in cleanly, or I lock you in the basement and tear your place apart and find it myself. Neither of those scenarios involves you moving your ass from this house. You got me?" I pointed to the chair she'd lifted her ass out of, our morning meeting not going to plan after she fessed up about the fucking computer files.

"You aren't locking me in a basement." Her eyes got wide, not looking convinced that it wasn't where she was going to end up. "I'm still holding a gun." She held it up like I needed the reminder.

"I don't give a fuck if you are holding a rocket launcher, the fact is remaining unchanged. If you hadn't been so stupid in the first place and left it behind, we wouldn't even be having this discussion. And I have a very low tolerance for stupidity and conversation, you might do well to remember that."

I should have asked for more fucking money, if only to cover the truckload of freaking Advil I was going to need for the headache. Seriously, what the hell was wrong with shutting the fuck up and letting me do my job?

"You're calling me stupid?" Her eyelids peeled back in surprise, obviously not having entertained the thought. "You gave me barely any time to pack. It wasn't the most pressing thing on my mind," she spat back defensively. "It's in a locked drawer and the files are password protected. No one besides the two of us even knows about it, there is nothing even hinting to its existence on my hard drive."

"You're staying here." I took a couple of steps closer, my body looming over hers. I was done with negotiating. "Tell me where the fuck it is."

"The bathroom cabinet, the bottom left drawer." She folded her arms across her chest finally conceding defeat. "The key is—"

"I don't need the key." I waved her off; the key was the least of my problems. I was more concerned about her need to make things difficult. I didn't need the bitch suddenly developing a feeling of empowerment and deciding to follow. And *that* kind of surprise wasn't happening.

"Now let's get you downstairs so I can get this shit taken care of."

There was no need to elaborate; the flick of fear in her eyes was enough of clue that she knew where my head was at.

"I told you where it is." Her words might have sounded confident but her body told me otherwise, her feet taking a step backward.

"Downstairs, Sofia." I didn't yell, there was no need to, the words crystal clear there would be no further argument.

Those pretty hazel eyes narrowed, her slim body throwing off attitude even though she was far too small to be anywhere near intimidating. And I could tell she wanted nothing more than to take that loaded nine from her waistband, aim it at yours truly and pull the trigger. But she wouldn't, more to the fact I *knew* she couldn't. She wasn't like me, she needed a good reason to take someone's life and as of yet, I hadn't given her enough of one.

"Keep your gun loaded and don't argue." I motioned to the stairs, ready to get this show on the fucking road. "And anyone other than me comes through the door, shoot first and ask questions later. This isn't the time for you to have a conscience."

"When this is over, I'm going to make sure you burn in hell like the rest of them." She released her arms, taking a tentative step forward.

"I don't believe in hell, sweetheart." My lips curled, my laugh unable to be contained. "But you go ahead and tell yourself whatever you need to."

Her mouth goldfished, the words she'd wanted to say not making it out. I didn't care if it was to cuss me out or try and convince me I was wrong, nothing she said mattered to me. I wasn't the kind of man who could easily be swayed by words. And I was beginning to think that deep down she knew she was better off saving her breath. I watched as she moved to the stairs, her eyes roving constantly as her hands twitched at her sides.

She didn't speak, she didn't cry and she didn't argue. Her feet stepped steadily down into the basement with me behind her. And as much as I was a cold-hearted bastard, not even I could deny how well she was handling all of this. I'd seen men twice her size and double her age fold like a pack of cards, and I hadn't even seen her chin wobble. Or at the very least, she had enough mental fortitude to keep that shit to herself.

"I'll be back soon," I said, surprising myself with the explanation. "Stay out of trouble."

She didn't answer, her eyes locked on mine as I closed and secured the door with her behind it.

I didn't like people in my personal space, especially women. And the one who was currently locked in my basement was no exception. The sooner I could wrap it up and get her out of my hair, the better. Not to mention the additional heat it would undoubtedly send my way.

Thanks a lot, Jimmy, you piece of shit.

So, rather than contemplate how much I disliked socializing, I locked up the house and armed the security system. I had it rigged to remotely notify me if some asshole even breathed an inch over my property line, so at least there was that. And with my ass in my car, I was back on the road, not excited at the prospect of getting to know her neighbors.

Like the night before, I took a few unscheduled turns and detours on the off chance I had someone on my ass. As far as I could tell there was nothing suspect as I stopped a few doors down from Sofia's residence. Not so far that I couldn't access a quick getaway, but not advertising where in particular I had business either. The place looked even more rundown in the light of day.

I couldn't help but shake my head, still pissed the trip was needed as I made my way to her front door. I didn't bother asking for the key. I'd managed just fine without it, preferring my way of doing things. And with my hand rake and pick, the lock popped open with little effort. It was a talent. I'd been able to get myself inside doors before I'd known my times tables, although my tools were a lot better these days.

Once inside, I didn't bother wasting minutes, double-timing to her bathroom and retrieving the tiny silver thumb drive that had caused the headache in my frontal lobe.

Then, before I left, I made some adjustments to her house.

She'd raised a good point last night. Her boss would probably come sniffing around wondering sooner or later, and we had enough fucking problems without attracting the Chicago PD.

It was a risk. My actions would no doubt invite some kind of investigation, but I hoped that the chaos would burn in on itself. Ironic really, considering my methods.

No one would really know what happened to her. Not with any certainty, and that's all that we needed for now. Plus the confusion could possibly chill some of the others' attempts. These guys hated attention and it was harder to kill a person when she was the leading news story.

And before *I* became part of that leading story, I got back into my ride and left. The trip back to my place took a little longer on the return on account of the fucking traffic.

Even though Jimmy hadn't given me any sort of direction, my plan had been to relocate her somewhere else today. There had been no good reason for it other than a feeling I got that shit wasn't right, but then decided against it. Moving in the daylight would be stupid at the moment. Unless there was reasonable intel to suggest anyone knew where we were, the best thing would be to stay put, at least for the next few days. And there was no way in hell I was doing anything during the day.

The house was quiet when I opened the back door. Honestly, I was surprised. I wasn't sure what I expected, but compliance wasn't it. The door down to the basement had been bolted from the outside, so unless Sofia had X-Men powers I didn't know about, there was little chance she'd been able to get out. But it didn't mean she wouldn't try. Possibly smash something against it.

"I'm back." I pulled open the door, allowing her to walk back up the stairs and into the main part of the house.

She looked pissed. Like her time down there had marinated her bad mood, the attitude amplified as she stepped into the living room.

"Wow, thanks. Couldn't have worked that out on my own." The sarcasm dripped from every word, as did her displeasure. And I couldn't help the smile that crept across my face, enjoying both.

"Change of plans, we're staying here for the next day or two. I'll evaluate then." I didn't bother giving her the particulars. Partly because I hadn't decided when we'd mobilize, and partly because I enjoyed pissing her off. Besides, the less anyone knew the better, less chance of someone fucking it up.

"I need to call my boss. My shift starts in less than an hour." She ignored my statement completely, disregarding my plan for laying low as she held out her hand for my cell. "You said I could call."

It was a statement, not a question.

"Yeah, I changed my mind." I folded my arms across my chest, my smirk getting wider. "Figured it was better you didn't say anything."

In all honesty, I couldn't trust her. And while she had been compliant up till now, I couldn't be sure she wasn't biding her time. She still had her piece and ammo, and that was as big of a concession as I was going to make. The risk of a tip off far outweighing any concerns her boss might have. Besides, by the time her shift started, it was no longer going to be an issue.

"That isn't smart," she snapped, unable to keep her annoyance under wraps. "They'll come looking."

Ignoring her, I walked over to my computers, the monitors coming to life with the flick of the mouse. She followed close behind despite the lack of invitation, her mouth no doubt not done with whatever she needed to say and I didn't care to hear.

"I have a gun. I could easily shoot my way out of here." She barely took a breath before continuing. "And if this is about my safety then surely I should have a say in it. I'm trained, I'm not a liability."

She watched as I sat at my desk, my fingers twisting the knob of the small handheld scanner that sat beside the monitors, the static pop making her flinch as I adjusted the volume. The garble slowly formed into coherency, the efficient yet impassive voices of dispatchers tossing words back and forth with units in the field.

"That's my address." Sofia's focus bored into the scanner, like eyeballing it would give her any further clues. Her hands gripping the back of my chair so tightly, the leather creaked in protest.

"Hmmm, sounds like it." Cue my lack of surprise as the word *suspected explosion* and *fire* were attached to the current description of the property. The state of the occupants had yet to be ascertained.

"What the hell?" Sofia's hand moved to her mouth, the sharp intake of air whistling past her lips.

"Sounds like there was some kind of fire. Huh. I guess that negates any questions that will be asked. It will take some time for the fire department to comb it for a body." My eyes moved to hers, the lids had peeled back to maximum.

It's not how I usually liked to operate, a little sloppy if I was honest. But I had limited time and even less resources, so a trip to Wal-Mart was not in the cards. So I worked with what I had, the result a little messier than I would have liked, but no less effective.

"What did you do?" She blinked back in disbelief; her head shaking like that would suddenly make it less real.

I didn't bother lying. No reason, besides it was probably going to be on the next news bulletin anyway—the blast rocking surrounding houses.

"I pulled your gas line from behind your stove. Then it was just a matter of cranking your heating and waiting for either the spark from the thermostat or the pilot light to ignite. Hard to know which it was. Gas is unpredictable when it's pissing out. Good thing you weren't in there." I shrugged, slowly turning to face her. "I hope you have renter's insurance," I said coolly, the edges of my mouth cranking a little higher.

65

"You bombed my fucking house." The words spat out of her mouth as her fists white-knuckled at her sides. "You bastard! You could have killed someone. I have neighbors. What if—"

"You've forgotten I don't give a shit." I quickly ended her list of possible scenarios I hadn't been paid to care about. "You think I give a rat's ass if your dumbass neighbor got toasty? Newsflash, they aren't my responsibly."

I wasn't stupid, unless there were bone fragments, teeth— anything that could yield DNA, all I'd done was buy us some time and leveled her house. But it was a hundred percent the right call.

On paper it looked like madness, drawing attention to her and by virtue to me. The arson/suspected murder investigation sure to throw her name into the spotlight. Add in she was a highly respected member of the force and whose daddy happened to have a questionable employment history. And that was the kind of story that Matt Lauer jerked off to at night. So why paint an even bigger target on my back? Easy. Nothing like hiding in plain fucking sight, the mayhem giving me just the kind of cover I needed. Every asshole on both sides of the line would be stalled trying to gather details while we ghosted. Oh, and detonations gave me a hard-on.

"I hate you, you son-of-a-bitch." Her right hook came closer than I would have liked, my fist catching it before it made contact with my jaw. "I hate you and my father." Her voice dripping with so much venom I was surprised she hadn't gone for her gun.

"Once again, sweetheart." I forced her shaking hand away from my face, the resistance hinting she'd thrown some conviction behind it. "I don't give a shit what you or anyone else thinks. And I'm not here to help you sort out your fucking daddy issues either."

"Yeah, well right now I'm not sure who I'd rather see dead,

him or you." Her jaw was so tight the words barely got out, her hand shaking loose from my grip.

"But *I'm* the bad guy, right? Maybe you are more like me than you think." I laughed, pointing out what a fucking hypocrite she was being. "I'm a lot of things, Sofia, but I'm not pretending to be something I'm not."

She wanted to walk away; I saw it in the way her body twitched. Her response the usual when it came to me. Run away. Fast. But she didn't. Her feet planted in place refusing to budge.

"You tell yourself whatever you need to, *Michael*." She said my name in place of *bastard* or *asshole,* but we both knew she wasn't being polite. "But we are *nothing* alike."

The stare competition could have gone on for hours. Maybe it did, I didn't bother checking my watch as I met her eyeballs with my own.

I felt the loathing, her repulsion.

I welcomed it.

Liked it even.

And it jacked me up so tight my balls ached.

This was as close to foreplay as I had ever gotten, the pure disgust giving me a hard-on.

Most men wanted the game. Their ego stroked followed by their cock, but I didn't prescribe to the BS. I didn't want the lie, or a woman to call my own. Sex—well that was necessary, and I preferred it uncomplicated and emotion-free, which is why I usually paid for it. At least with a hooker there wasn't a pretense. And let me be clear, when it came to women, you were paying one way or another. My way was cheaper.

Even hookers were smart enough to know there was more to me than met the eye. Sure, they were all I'm-so-wet-for-you-baby while I fucked them, but I could sense their fear. I watched them struggle with the instinct to run, even though I'd given them no reason. It wasn't my face that scared them off, some of them getting turned on by what I had to offer, nope it was my lack of connection to anything with a heartbeat. That's the kind of emotion you couldn't fake and more importantly, I didn't want to. But everyone wants to get paid, so they pushed the urge down and gave me what I wanted.

Sofia was different.

Not just because she wasn't a whore, but because it wasn't fear that was prickling her skin.

It was fury in her eyes, her distaste.

And that lack of fear is what got me hard.

Still, there wasn't a chance I'd bury my cock into the woman in front of me. Not because she couldn't get me off. Fuck knows that tight ass of hers and those perky tits would be enough of a reason. And it wasn't out of some sense of morality or decency —we both knew I had neither. No, the reason I wouldn't take her was because I *wanted* it, and that feeling unnerved me more than anything.

Neither of us spoke.

The silent showdown not one either of us was willing to concede.

In the end it was my fucking phone, the piece of shit vibrating wildly from my front jeans pocket that broke the stand off. The iPhone was answered as I continued to keep my eyes locked on her.

"What?"

No one calling me was going to expect anything more; I wasn't the have-a-chat kind of guy.

"Is she dead?" The words were level, unemotional. Jimmy didn't bother with small talk, the news of his daughter's house going bye-bye obviously reaching his ear. Had to say I was impressed, it had barely been an hour.

"Checking up on me?" I cracked a smile; Sofia shifting her

weight on her feet able to only hear one side of the call. "Not sure if I'm touched or offended."

"Stop jerking me off," he huffed into the phone impatiently, "was that *your* handy work or someone else's?"

I didn't like someone looking over my shoulder, or expecting to hold my fucking hand. Their payment got them a result; the method was mine to decide. And whether the job was Jimmy's kid or not, it didn't give the bastard a free pass. No amount of money gave him a say in what or how I did it.

"Mine," I barked back, my spine steeling. "And I don't appreciate your tone."

"More balls than brains." Jimmy laughed, I'd assumed relieved he didn't have to decide whether it was lilies or roses that would be placed on top of his daughter's casket. "You might want to watch it, son. You just bought yourself a bunch of eyes on you."

"I'm not your *son*, asshole." I felt the need to remind the POS on the phone that my allegiances weren't to him. "And if you're looking to lodge an opinion, you might want to try the People's Choice, not here."

My thumb killed the call regardless of whether Jimmy was done or not.

She wanted to ask. I could see her lips pressed into a thin line to stop her from opening her mouth. At war with her need to know who I'd been talking to, and her desire not to give me the satisfaction.

"Your father." I decided to play nice, figuring my less than predicted response would keep things uneasy between us. I didn't want her comfortable or being able to anticipate anything, especially not my mood.

"He well?" She tilted her head to the side in faux concern.

"Didn't ask." I laughed with genuine amusement. "It's been at least four years since you've seen each other; I'm sure it's going to be one hell of a reunion when the two of you get back together." Part of me wishing I could watch the fall out.

Oh, I wasn't interested in their family politics. Couldn't give a fuck if they had a happily ever after. But something told me watching Sofia hand her father his ass would be worth seeing.

EIGHT

SOFIA

To have your fate in the hands of someone else was unnerving. Having that person not *care* about your fate—an unhinging of the cruelest kind. That's where I found myself, forced to trust someone I didn't, and unable to know if I were better or worse with his help.

I hated it.

I hated him.

And I hated my father for putting me in a position where I no longer knew who the good guys were.

Blissful ignorance faded quickly as I grew older, and as much as I loved my family I couldn't ignore what was going on around me. My body was wracked with guilt as I took communion at Sunday mass, Father Thomas giving my family an extra blessing for our generous donations.

He had to have known where the money came from. He frequently came to our house, my mother working herself into a tizz at the honor of a personal visit. The best china and silverware were laid out as he ate baked ziti with my family. He knew. They all knew. And it killed me that the lines were no longer clear.

The chain of the gold crucifix around my neck choked me under the weight of the sin. I was too young to be damned and yet the fires of Hell licked at my heels even as I knelt at the pew.

It was ironic that I found myself there again. Feeling like that fourteen-year-old with eyes as big as saucers, my too-thick hair unable to be tamed, on my knees praying for a way out.

"We need to lay low until I'm ready. Then we are out of here. *Permanently.*" His voice pulled me from my thoughts, thrusting me into the present.

That wasn't something that surprised me, him blowing up my house and destroying everything I owned was pretty final. Going back wasn't a possibility even if someone *wasn't* trying to kill me.

I pulled my gun from my waistband, where it had been the entire time. The arrogant son of a bitch didn't even flinch, watching as I leveled it against him. He thought I didn't have it in me to pull the trigger; truth is I wasn't sure I did either. But there was an ugly feeling deep in the pit of my stomach that stirred. Something new I'd never felt before and for once, I wasn't sure I would do the right thing. Even as I lifted the barrel higher and my finger flicking off the safety, he didn't move. That smug grin on his face, ever present.

"I have done everything you asked." The air came out of my mouth in a rush as I held my arm steady. *I could do this*, if it came to saving my life, I could do this. "I haven't resisted. I haven't tried to escape. I told you about the files."

"And what? You looking for an applause?" He smiled like this was some kind of a joke, but I saw his hand lower, hover at the side where he had his forty-five holstered.

"No, I don't need your approval." And most of all, I didn't want it. I'd rather turn the gun on myself than be the kind of person *he* would be proud of. "But I won't allow you to make decisions about what happens to me without my input." Every word past my lips made me braver, stronger, more determined not to back down. Something inside me had clicked and there was a different part of me taking control.

"Or what? You going to shoot me?" His head angled toward the gun I had yet to lower. I was so close to him. Just a few feet. Even a blind man could pull the trigger and hit his heart— assuming he still had one. So he had to have known that with my experience, I wouldn't miss.

"Or maybe," he drawled, his voice lingering over every word sadistically, like he was enjoying the threat. "You're hoping *I'll* shoot *you* and end all of this for both of us."

No. That was his fantasy, not mine. But I would rather die than spend another night unsure of what would happen to me in the morning.

"I won't be a passenger in this." I did my best to keep it unemotional, not entirely succeeding. I hated how helpless I'd been, but I wasn't going to allow it to continue. Not after he'd taken almost everything. My home, my freedom—I wouldn't let him take my life as well. Not without a fight.

"I don't play well with others. Guess you can call it a character flaw." He arched his neck first to the left and then to the right, the conversation clearly annoying him. "I'm done talking about it."

Well, I wasn't.

He infuriated me. His casual disregard for anything I had said was causing me to slowly become unhinged. And I wasn't sure if it was anger or my need for survival that made me unpredictable.

"I want the drive back." I held out my left hand expectantly while my right hand stayed aimed at his chest. "You don't need it. Or know how to access the information."

His jaw tightened, annoyance moving to agitation. "You aren't getting shit." His voice was barely a whisper, and somehow that made it worse. "You know, you shouldn't aim a gun at someone when you have no intention of pulling the trigger. This is the second time you've done it, and I can assure you, I won't allow you a third. So here's what's going to happen." His arm stretched out, his fingers wrapping around the barrel. "You are going to lower the fucking gun or you are going to shoot." His hand didn't even wobble as it held my Smith and Wesson.

"Don't think you know me." My hand stayed locked; my decision whether or not to pull the trigger still not made. *I could end it, end it all right here.*

"I don't, and I don't want to."

The words were cruel, the kind that usually you would snarl at someone in order to hurt them. But he hadn't done that. They lacked any weight when they'd left his lips, no emotion, no sting. It was simply the truth as he saw it.

I didn't want to shoot him and I wasn't sure if that made me relieved or angry. "Have you ever known anyone?" I asked before I had a chance to stop myself, my voice quieter than it had been as his hand lowered my gun without resistance.

Something inside me told me I knew the answer. The coldness wasn't an act. I'd seen men hardened by time, used bad choices as an excuse for crime and some who had shown no remorse. But the longer I looked at Michael, even with only a few words spoken between us, I saw that he was presenting himself honestly. This was the only way he knew how. I hadn't wanted to see it, but out of the two of us, he was the one being authentic.

"We'll leave soon." He avoided the question, nothing betrayed in his words or his eyes. "I'll tell you when."

He turned, the large expanse of his shoulders my new view as heavy footsteps took him out of the room. I assumed the drive was with him, possibly in a pocket. He hadn't even confirmed he'd retrieved it, the whole subject sidestepped completely. Maybe it had burned with the rest of my house.

It was weird. How he was able to speak and say so little. Not just with words—his body, his face—a locked vault. And nothing was really confirmed or denied. No black, no white, just an endless stretch of gray.

"I need to eat," I said loudly, even though I was the only person left in the room. "You might be able to live on air, but I need food."

It was probably more than just an empty stomach that made me alter my thoughts. It was easier to deal with something tangible like food rather than the minefield in my head. And last night's dinner had been hours ago, with nothing more than some water, the Advil and a cup of coffee going into my belly since. Adrenaline would only allow me to ignore biology so long. I'd slept because I needed my head in the game, and I had to eat if I was going to be able to stay standing.

"You want to eat, make yourself food," he called from the other room, not bothering to give me the courtesy of a face-to-face. "There's no room service here."

No shit, asshole. I flipped him off even though he couldn't see it, the childish reaction making me feel marginally better. My quest for food was going to be a solo venture.

When we'd arrived last night, I hadn't gotten a chance to really explore the layout of the house. But this morning before I'd been marched into the basement and locked up like an animal, I'd done my best to get a feel for where everything was. You never knew when your life might depend on knowing where the closest exit route was, and which wrong turn would back you into a corner. I committed to memory each window, each door—every single detail of each wall and crevice in case some day it might be relevant.

The Brownstone had been heavily renovated in its interior, the spacious rooms on the bottom floor more open than a house of this vintage would have otherwise been.

My feet moved mechanically to the back of the house, completely ignoring Michael as I made my way to the kitchen. It had been updated, just like the rest of the house and the modern appliances looked untouched. The thinnest film of dust covered the oven door, the only hint that it wasn't as freshly installed as it looked. He didn't spend much time in here, and if he did, I was guessing the microwave saw most of the action.

His refrigerator didn't wear the same signs of neglect. While not old by anyone's definition, the double stainless steel doors had some minor scuffmarks, their sheen matted in certain places from handprints.

Pulling open the large French doors, I was expecting to find an array of condiments and beer. Sure, it was a typical bachelor stereotype, but he hadn't given me much else to work with. Instead I found the clean interior shelves lined neatly with Tupperware containers. Each one contained fresh vegetables, fruit or lunchmeat.

I blinked, half expecting the carefully lined containers to disappear, but they didn't, my hands reaching for them as my stomach grumbled. I was hungrier than I'd thought, the smell of roast beef wafting up my nose, making my mouth water as I ripped open the first lid.

Placing the makings of a sandwich on the kitchen counter, I pulled open the pantry doors in the hopes of finding some bread. Like the fridge, the shelves were neatly lined. Items stacked with military precision with all the labels facing outward.

It was so meticulous. Even in his personal living space, everything was *exactly* how he'd placed it. It was so strange that a man who seemed to live his life in chaos would be afflicted with what looked like a severe case of OCD.

My hunger overrode my need to continue my psychological evaluation of Michael, locating a loaf of bread on the third shelf and carrying it over to the counter with the rest of the food. Plates and cutlery were easily found; a cabinet here, a drawer there—and I had everything I needed, assembling my sandwich as I went.

It tasted even better than I'd expected, my teeth biting into the pillowy softness of the bread as an unsuppressed moan escaped my lips. I didn't care if he heard me, taking another mouthful of food while I stayed standing at the counter.

In any other circumstance, I might have asked if he was hungry, or made something for him too. After all, I was already making something for myself, so it wouldn't be any extra effort. But I didn't. Partly because I thought he would see kindness as weakness, but more importantly, because he hadn't deserved it. It made me feel better that I was able to make the distinction and more importantly make the choice.

When I'd finished and cleared my dishes—even though I didn't have the same neat freak tendencies, I played nice—I retreated back to my room. Which was actually *his* room, and just the space I was currently occupying.

There was nothing to do. Nothing. No internet, no phone—no link to the outside world. Just the walls and my own thoughts.

Did everyone think I'd died?

Did my father tell my mother I was safe? My brothers?

Or was I being mourned?

The truth was I couldn't be sure. Part of me was gutted that I could potentially be wiped from existence and no one would really miss me. I couldn't think of anyone who would even be sad, and certainly no one who would cry at the loss. Instead their lives would continue without little interruption.

My own thoughts were torturing me more than being

confined within the four walls. And it was utterly ridiculous that, considering the kind of trouble I was facing, I was sad about not feeling loved. And despite all of that, I still held hope that I had the ability to love. If not, then what was all of it for?

I had been in a few relationships, but something always felt off. My dedication to my job was blamed, my single-eyed focus on my career, with most guys checking out after a few months. One even made it an entire year, but like the others, he felt he never had my full attention.

I'd hoped someday to find the right person. It's what we all wanted deep down, I think. To know that there was someone out there who would love us with every fiber of their being.

"They were right," I said, even though there was no one to hear me. I had never really given myself to them. "They hadn't been a priority."

As the hours melted into the next, I stayed in the room. Not because I had been instructed to, but because I had nowhere else to be.

A couple of times when I needed the bathroom, I'd glanced down at the stairs. There had been virtually no sound, nothing more than occasional shuffle of fabric to indicate he'd moved.

He didn't come upstairs.

I didn't see him eat, or drink or sleep. Nothing. Just the constant low hum on his computer screens, which I had to strain my ears to even hear.

It was much later when I'd realized it was no longer day. The small stream of light that cut through the tiny crack between the drapes was no longer there, the sun setting without me stepping one foot outside.

My hands fumbled against my neck, my fingers finding the gold crucifix I'd always worn. And I closed my eyes and prayed as I did every night. Only tonight I wasn't exactly sure what those prayers were for.

"Help me, Lord," I whispered as my fingers lifted the cross to my lips. I wasn't sure if I'd said it out loud, or if it had been part of the continual silent litany. And I wasn't sure if it was because of the words or the routine, but I felt calmer, my body slowly rising off the mattress I'd been sitting on for most of the day.

My feet tiptoed over to the window, pulling the drapes aside as I rested my hand on the cold glass. The glow from the nearby streetlight illuminated the view—the back garden, the garage and the back alley.

The even thuds of heavy boots echoed from the other side of my door making me jerk my head around. Each of Michael's footfalls was weighted and steady as I heard them move closer. I waited, my eyes glued to the wooden rectangle that separated us, but he didn't seem to stop. The sound remaining even as he walked past, the noise dimming when I heard a door close.

Without heading out into the hall, there was no way to tell where he'd gone, and it was only after I heard the spray of water hitting tile that I was able to pinpoint his location. The bathroom. His need to shower reminding me he was in fact human, even if he didn't act like it.

As the water ran, I didn't bother leaving the room. The simple act of him getting clean could have been a test, seeing if I would go and search for the drive. Then like some B-Grade movie he'd catch me in the act, rifling through his drawers when the whole time what I had been looking for was locked in the bathroom with him. It was too predictable, and he wouldn't make it that easy.

So instead I stayed in the room, my forehead pressed against the glass staring at the blades of grass that moved in the breeze.

The light from the hallway flooding the room was the first

sign he'd entered. Like everything else in the house, doors and windows had been WD-40'd to within an inch of their life so there would be no telltale creak.

His towel was slung around his waist as droplets of water clung to his chest. It looked like stone. Hard lines converged in angles, the corded muscles defined even at rest. His skin was almost entirely bare except for a smattering of hair across his pecs, marks and scars marring what would otherwise be a torso rivaling the perfection of a renaissance master.

And despite all those blemishes—all of which I'm sure he'd earned doing horrible things—with the light behind him, he looked beautiful.

His dark eyes caught mine, their glare lacking any warmth. "I told you to keep away from the windows."

"I don't do what I'm told." I didn't move from my place at the window and he sure as hell he wasn't getting an apology. "Call it *my* character flaw."

I didn't expect the smile. The edges of his lips curled with a genuine amusement, his teeth startling white. And like his body, it too was beautiful. "You're just full of surprises." His arms lowered, his hands anchoring on his hips. "The sarcasm is still intact, even though you've been up here for hours." His eyes darted around the room. "No holes in the walls either. I'm impressed you're not rocking in a corner or begging to get out."

It was easier to ignore that, as he stood before me missing most of his clothes and usual hard expression, he seemed less vicious. Not quite kind, but . . . human. Who knew what brought the change? His moods were so unpredictable. And as much as he probably thought I was a pain in his ass—no doubt hating my endless questions—he seemed intrigued by me.

"I'll never beg, not you or anyone else."

"Pity." His head shook as his eyebrow rose. "I'm sure you

would look good on your knees."

"If that's what you've come in for, you might as well forget it." My hands flew to my hips, my stance mirroring his.

I hadn't forgotten the man was still mostly naked, his purpose for being in the room not yet revealed. And while I had admired his finely chiseled assets when he'd walked in, there was no way I was going to have sex with him. I hadn't completely lost my mind.

No. Way.

"Relax, sweetheart." He laughed. "I don't shit where I eat." He stalked closer to where I was by the window. "And fucking you would be too much work."

Bastard.

It was ridiculous that it stung, but it did; his reassurances laced in another insult. No doubt designed to mess up my already scrambled head beyond repair.

"Then why are you here like that?" I gestured to the towel around his hips, the terry cloth the only thing separating him from nudity. "Hoping I'd blush nervously? You think I've never seen a dick?"

"Don't flatter yourself." He leaned closer and smiled. "But seeing as you picked my room when there were two others vacant, you're going to have to deal when I want clean clothes."

His fingers moved to the edge of the towel—the part that was keeping it together. He watched my eyes follow his hands as it dropped to the floor.

"So deal."

NINE

MICHAEL

Walking into the room—*my* room—hadn't been premeditated.

I'd taken a shower and decided two days wearing the same shirt and jeans was enough. So if she decided to stay in the bedroom that housed my closet, she had no reason to be pissed when I lost my pants.

Her eyes did a quick redirect, snapping up toward my face trying hard to make it seem like she hadn't just seen my dick. And great effort on her part, she spared us both by not doing the whole shielding her eyes BS. And if her cheeks pinked, she'd camo'd that too.

"Don't mind me." I casually walked to my closet, my ass in the breeze with no real hurry as I grabbed a clean pair of jeans and shirt. Then it was another few strides to the dresser up against the wall and grabbed a pair of boxers, turning around before pulling them on.

There was no reason for me to put on a show. Could have easily been avoided by leaving the towel where it was, getting clean clothes and pulling them on elsewhere. But we both knew I wasn't that considerate, and part of me liked making her uncomfortable. Made the fact she was in my personal space a little easier to deal with. Oh, and I was also a bastard who didn't give a shit about her feelings.

"You're still suspected dead." I shoved one leg into my jeans before following with the other. "So we might move before they issue a BOLO. No one will be looking for a corpse in traffic, but we're going to be careful just to be sure." My fingers yanked up my fly.

While originally I had decided to stay put, I reassessed my plan when I'd heard over the police scanner that they were almost positive she'd gone up with the house. That would change in the next few days with the absence of a body, so time was of the essence.

"Where are we going?" She stayed where she was, doing her best to keep her eyes at head level. They may have dipped once or twice but for the most part, they were rock solid.

She was doing a lot better than I'd expected, which was probably why part of me paid her more respect than I usually would. It wasn't because she was a woman; I mistrusted everyone. But I'll admit, her being cool up to this point was making me less hostile.

"I have another place further out of the city." I pulled the shirt over my head, ignoring I hadn't properly dried off and the cotton was sticking to my damp skin. "In an industrial estate near the airport. Not so many eyes out there and a lot easier to see if anything's coming at you. Keeps us off the grid."

"And then what?"

Surprise, surprise. She had questions.

"We wait."

Truth was, I had no fucking idea what we were going to do. My job had been to get her and keep her safe. There hadn't been any talk of relocating or an extraction. I was just supposed to babysit until Jimmy worked out how he was going to handle it.

Not sure how anyone could *handle* it. The people who wanted her head on a plate weren't going to suddenly wake up a few days from now and forget. No, these fuckers had long memories and even longer reach, so short of shipping his kid out of the country, she wasn't going to have any chance of regular life again. I assumed that was his plan, get his ducks in a row and get her out. At the very least out of Illinois, maybe send her to fucking Utah or something.

"Good thing you didn't unpack." My head nodded to her duffle on the floor and the overnight bag beside the bed, all her shit still zipped up inside.

"That's the first time you've spoken to me like a person instead of a prisoner, thank you." Her voice was softer than it usually was, a nod of appreciation shot in my general direction.

"Don't get all Oprah on me." I hoped like hell she wasn't going to pick now to start with the tears. She was right. My mood had definitely thawed and I'd told her a lot more than I usually allowed. But I didn't like that shit pointed out. Or worse, let her believe I was *nice*.

"As you said, you haven't tried to get away and other than being a fucking pain in my ass and running that mouth of yours, you have done what I've asked. But make no mistake," I warned, wanting her to know we weren't going to be suddenly holding hands and splitting an order of fucking fries. "This isn't about me trusting you, or us being friends. It's about hoping you'll be less of a fucking pill."

"You could have just nodded and left." Her fists at her side tightened, the edge her voice that had been missing was no longer MIA. "You don't have to be an asshole every time you open your mouth to remind me how much we're not friends. I didn't develop amnesia. I can recall that all by myself."

"I *am* an asshole, Sofia. It's the only way I know how to be." I moved closer, my feet closing the distance between us. The clarification for her to understand exactly what kind of man I was and remind myself in the same breath. "It's kept me alive, and if you're lucky, it will do the same for you." I leaned forward, enjoying the fact that if she took another step her back was going to be up against the wall with no way out. "So don't think my attitude is for your benefit. You would be wrongly assuming I care about your feelings, in any way."

"When do we leave?" she asked, and to her credit, she held her ground. The only hint that she was uncomfortable was the way her hand reached up and fingered the cross that hung around her neck.

Great, she probably believed there was a hipster who wore a sheet and sat up in the clouds passing out free wishes if you said enough Hail Mary's. Because that makes any kind of sense; that an unknown entity had any power over anything other than scratching his own ass.

Religion.

It killed more men than drugs and was a hell of a lot more dangerous. At least when you injected heroin into your arm you knew what you were getting. Planting your knees on the floor did nothing but prove you believed in fairytales.

"I said, when do—"

"I heard you the first time." I cut her off not needing the replay. "I was just hoping you were smarter than the herd." My head nodded to her hand still up around her throat.

"There is nothing wrong with having faith." She lowered her hand like she had suddenly become aware of it. "Everyone will face judgment. If not in this world, then the next."

I laughed.

I couldn't help it. My body convulsed even more when I saw how serious she was. I thought she had more sense than that, and the hatred I had for those assholes and everything they stood for ran deep. Because blindly believing in something was more dangerous than anything in the world. Giving people false hope that shit would get better. Made you wonder what the fuck you did wrong when that miracle didn't come. There was no one up in the clouds listening, no one who cared and no one who was ever going to give you a free pass. They were thugs, just as much as the next guy. Playing on people's fears to get them to conform. And I would never be intimidated by an institution that didn't care about anyone but themselves.

Yet, she somehow figured *I* was accountable to someone other than myself. And I was going to have to eventually stand in front of some fucktard with a clipboard to see if I measured up.

No wonder the human race was failing; the dipshits believed any lie they were told. Being *saved*, numero uno.

"You have fun with that." I wiped the tears from my eyes, the laugh the best I'd had in a while. "We're rolling out in two hours and we probably won't be coming back. Make sure whatever you need is ready to go, would hate for you to have left a pack of tampons, or your *judgment,* behind."

I didn't wait for a response, walking back to my closet and grabbing out a large black duffle, pulling clothes off hangers and shoving them inside as I went.

She didn't stay and watch, grabbing a spare clip of ammo on the nightstand and collecting her bags. Hefting the straps onto each shoulder—she didn't ask for help and I didn't offer—she carried her stuff out of the room and presumably downstairs. Well, at least she was efficient.

It didn't take me long to be ready to bug out. It was a necessary skill to be ready to go at a moment's notice. But I took a little longer than usual, making sure my head was in the game. As much as I didn't like to admit it, she had gotten under my skin. I didn't like that. Not even a bit. So I needed to remind myself where my focus was. She was just another job and would be gone soon.

Killing the bedroom light with one hand, the other hauling my duffle, I moved out of the doorway and back downstairs.

She was at the base of the stairs, her dark hair pulled off of her face, tapping her foot like she'd been waiting on me. The two bags she had were stacked beside her and next to that she had an old cooler that I kept down in the basement. She must have seen it when she'd spent some time down there earlier and brought it up. Though its appearance with the luggage was still a mystery.

"I packed food and some bottled water," she answered, pulling a mind reader and answering my unasked question. "You suck at remembering the basics and I'd rather not starve or dehydrate."

"Stay here." I nodded, not bothering to reward her initiative, grabbing as much as I could carry and walking past her toward the back of the house.

Any internal thoughts about her or the situation were shelved as I switched gears, my focus narrowing completely on the operation.

The yard was in complete darkness with the security lighting disabled. Not that I had any reason to suspect anyone had been poking around, but I wasn't going to shine a spotlight on my ass and help a fucker along if he was perched sniper-like in a tree.

Once in the garage, I popped the trunk and loaded my duffle and her two bags into the cavity and doubled back to the house, my head swiveling in the dark just in case.

Nothing flagged as strange. A couple of dogs barking in the distance competed with a car revving, the screech of tires and the whine of the turbo happening a few seconds later. I didn't linger, but the hair on the back of my neck standing up for no good reason meant something was off.

A twist of my head left then right didn't give me any

answers; the gnawing in my gut not something I usually ignored. The chill crept up my back and it had nothing to do with the wind. It had been too easy—getting her out, getting her here, the leveling of her house. I didn't believe in miracles or luck, neither did most of the men who would be after her. And yet, not even a whisper in our direction. Whatever happened from here on out, we were far from home free.

As I made my way back to the house, Sofia was doing what she was told for a change without the argument, waiting inside. Hoping she'd continue that theme, I grabbed the cooler and gave her the "let's go," as I eyed her hard.

She got the message loud and clear, her eyes widening, pulling out her nine as she watched me palm my forty.

It had been dumb going out there the first time without my weapon out. Complete rookie mistake. And the fact I hadn't ended up like Swiss cheese meant that whatever was out there was either waiting for a better opportunity or they were biding their time, waiting for me to bring out their prize.

Of course, this was all speculation. I hadn't eyeballed anything to give me that intel, but I was willing to bet my left nut that beyond the fence line there was a hunter waiting for kill shot.

"Stay behind me." I hesitated a beat before stepping back into the yard. "I want you to take even steps, staying as close to me as you can. I'm serious, Sofia, right on my ass like a pair of fucking jeans. Watch your back, I've got the front but don't run, it'll be too easy to trip and then this will all go to shit."

For once she shelved the who-what-where-why, instead giving me a quick nod as my boot hit the night air.

We'd barely made it outside, the sound of a single bullet sliced through the quiet as it narrowly missed my head.

"Get down and keep moving," I hissed as my finger locked around the trigger of my forty-five. That one shot wasn't a single; its friend was already making its way to greet us, fortunately hitting the brick instead.

Lights on either side of us lit up the exterior yards. The dumbasses who happened to be my neighbors, not recognizing that a gunshot is not something you investigated. Maybe they thought it was a car backfiring or some kid letting off a firework. Anyway, not my problem. If they caught a slug from their curiosity, that was on them; I had enough shit to deal with.

I fired a couple of rounds in the direction I assumed the bullets were coming from. I didn't want to empty my clip when I had no real target, but I wasn't going to sit on my hands either. My legs pumped, covering as much ground as I could while keeping my body lead-free. Sofia didn't choke either, sticking to me as instructed; the short walk to the garage exponentially longer when you had some dick trying to give you body modification you hadn't asked for.

It could've been anyone and I wasn't about to stop to ask who. But from the erratic angles of the bullets I'd say it was some cowboy who hadn't been smart enough to go to the Army Navy Surplus and get some night vision. Either that or he—or she, let's face it, it was possible—was a terrible fucking shot.

"Go." I legged it double time the second there was a break in the firing pattern, kicking open the side door, twisting my body to allow Sofia to squeeze past. My hand yanked hard, pulling the door shut behind us, giving us a momentary reprieve.

"Friends of yours, I assume," Sofia whispered, her breaths between each word hard and uneven.

"They must be yours. I don't have any friends." My shoulders rested against the exposed brick wall of the garage, my own breathing a little more intense than I would have liked. "But whoever they are, I doubt they are the patient type. We need to get out of here now."

While most people would be lulled into a false sense of security the four walls gave us, I knew better. We were far from safe. Sure we had some cover, but we were also fucking blind, not able to see who or what was coming until it was too late. And I was almost positive some neighborhood watch hero wannabe had probably already dialed 9-1-1, so we'd have that mess to contend with too. I didn't much feel like wrapping my ass like a birthday present and handing it over, which meant it was time to go.

I tossed the cooler into the backseat. The only reason the piece of shit *Igloo* hadn't been dumped on my back lawn was because I'd used it as cover, keeping the K-Mart special against my chest while avoiding bullet holes. It wasn't Kevlar, but it would be enough to slow the projectile down, hopefully knock it off target and miss any major bits.

"How good of a shot are you?" I cracked open the passenger's side door, beyond pissed I was going to have to make this fucking call. "And I don't want to hear women-can-do-anything-men-can-do shit. I'm talking about *real* shooting, moving targets."

"I'm a cop, of course—"

"Not what I fucking asked," I snapped back, already wasting more time than I would have liked. "I'm looking for precision and speed, not hitting cardboard targets on range."

"Yes. I can shoot," she said confidently, her back straightening in conviction as she moved to the open passenger's side door and sliding into the seat.

"Don't make me regret this." I slammed the door behind her.

Putting her at the wheel wasn't an option. Without recon, I had no idea what we were dealing with out there. I needed to be able to get us out of here alive and put some distance between us while keeping my head on a swivel. This was going to go beyond defensive driving. If I kept pressure on them with my gun as well, I'd guarantee you one of those areas would suffer. Too big a risk. So I was going to have to hope she could at the very least apply some heat. Returning fire, the lesser of the two evils.

"You shoot, I'll drive." I climbed into the driver's side of my Camaro, my forty-five kept at an easy reach on the center consol. If it came to the crunch, I'd have to bring some of my own noise.

"Buckle in. I don't want you messing up my windshield if I need to stop suddenly." I fastened my own seat belt as she was locked in, my hand hitting the ignition a second later.

The V8 roared in the dark—my headlights and interior staying off until we put some distance between us—as the garage door slowly rose behind us. The fucker was taking too long, my foot slamming on the accelerator the second I thought we could clear it.

"Fuck." My jaw locked as the top of the door scraped against the roof of the car, my judgment off by a quarter inch as I reversed out.

Not that screwing up the paint job on my ride was an issue considering as soon as rubber had breached the back alley, a bullet hit my rear side window, blowing a hole into it. The bastard went right through the other side, shattering the glass as we fishtailed in the narrow space.

It was too fucking close and we needed to get gone.

"Give me some cover, Sofia." I gritted my teeth, throwing it into gear as my boot punched the gas, needing to get out of this alley in a fucking hurry. "I don't care if it's a squirrel, if it moves, fucking shoot it."

She nodded, her body twisting in the seat as much as the

nylon strip across her chest would let her. Her nine fired a couple of rounds out of the holes we'd been provided, my back windows history as all glass left in the door frames shook loose with the vibrations as we moved.

"Left side," she hollered, squeezing the trigger as bullets from our *friends* ate into my back left panel.

"Motherfucker." I wrenched the wheel to the right narrowly missing traffic, the ass of my car needing a second before it got on the same page as we slid sideways onto the main road.

And either the trigger-happy asshole was mobile or he had a friend. The minute we passed a streetlight I was able to identify an Audi A8 was on our tail redlining as we both left rubber on asphalt.

"Get them off my ass." I punched it, weaving in and out of lanes as I avoided collecting a car or two as a hood ornament. My feet worked overtime, alternating between gas and the brakes as I took another hard right hoping to get us some clear road in front of us.

"I'm trying." Sofia struggled to get the angle for a decent shot. Unless she could dislocate a shoulder and still maintain enough muscle control to pull the trigger, she wasn't going to be much help.

"This is fucking bullshit." The A8 did its best to shadow me despite me using every single one of those ponies underneath my hood.

There was only one vehicle between us, a silver Yukon that I'd cut off when I pulled out in front of it. It wasn't ideal, but the truck gave us a tiny buffer, the GMC's ass giving me some cover.

My buffer didn't last long, with the Yukon wising up and swerving into the next lane, which unfortunately meant it caught a stray bullet—either Sofia's or the cocksucker's—the driver locking up its brakes and skidding out of control.

Two ton of metal torqued onto its side, sparks flying as the screeching metal cab made contact with the road. Not what I'd planned but one hell of an improvise as the Yukon slid across two lanes of traffic until it hit a guardrail.

"Oh my god!" Sofia screamed, the crash happening so fast. "Are they okay? Did I just kill someone?"

"Get your shit together; they are not your problem right now," I shouted back, my eyes glued to the road as I overtook a couple of cars. Lucky for them the little incident with the truck had momentarily induced a cease-fire. The Audi driver probably using all their effort to stay upright while playing dodge ball with the GMC.

"We've got company." Sofia pointed to a blur of flashing lights in the rearview, the sirens getting louder.

"Awesome, because I needed more of a challenge tonight." I slammed on the brakes and skidded around a bend, smoke rising from the tires as they gripped hard.

No doubt the cops were already calling it in which meant that in a few minutes we were going to be biting off a little more than we could chew.

"We need to get off the road, CPD will call in a helo." She swallowed, her eyes scanning the night sky before she continued. "They aren't going to risk a high-speed pursuit without eyes in the sky."

It was too public; the amount of attention we were drawing was waaaaaay more than I would have liked, which should have been fucking zero. Not that there was any point bitching about it now, we needed to get invisible in a hurry. And not only get away from the fuckers tailing us, but also from the CPD who would only be all too happy to throw us into lock-up. Either scenario would put us in a box about six-feet under, so my vote—and the only one that counted—was that we didn't die today.

"I'm going to get us off at the next exit." My eyes flicked between my windshield and my rearview. "The minute we leave the off ramp, I'm going put us in a spin and you're gonna have one chance to do some damage."

"You're going to do what?" She pitched forward, her eyelids peeling back to maximum like I'd told her we were going to stop in the middle of the road so I could take a piss.

"Don't fucking think!" I yelled, not having the time or the fucking inclination to explain the plan. "The minute I spin, you double-palm your fucking gun and empty as much of your fucking clip as you can into that Audi, we clear?"

"We're going to die." Her head shook, not convincing me she was capable of doing what I was asking her to do. "You're going to kill us." Thankfully sidelining her outrage and pulling out a spare clip to reload.

Great, because we had time for a fucking pep talk. There weren't a lot of other options—in fact there were none—so she needed to get on my level in the next few seconds or shit was going to go bad.

"We are not going to fucking die. Just do as I say." The off-ramp coming into view as my boot stayed nailed to the floor.

"Get ready. Lower your window." The engine roared as we split from the interstate, the tires sticking to the road like fucking champs. The road stretched out in front of us, virtually no cars ahead.

Just needed a little more.

C'mon baby, just give me a little more.

"Now." I twisted the wheel left and then cut back to the right into a full lock as I yanked up the emergency brake. The car screeched in protest as its backend whipped us around, causing us to slide sideways in front of the A8.

View of the Audi cut through the smoke of burnt rubber, Sofia squeezing a few rounds of her nine into the windshield while I kept the steering locked.

What was less than a few seconds felt like an eternity. The bullets sprayed through the front of the A8, glass not so much shattering as exploding into the car.

It truly was a thing of beauty, the timing fucking perfect and Sofia had been amazing. Better than I expected. But our joy ride was far from over. My hands and feet worked in unison simultaneously throwing down the brake, stomping on the gas, the car getting to full power as I cut the wheel back to the left. The backend fishtailed, almost hitting the guardrail; the entire four lanes needed for the Camaro to right itself. The second we were facing the right direction, my boot dropped onto the gas and we were out of there. See ya later.

"They aren't following." Sofia nodded, the slight shake of her right hand hinting she wasn't altogether tight.

"We're not in the clear yet." My foot stayed planted as we moved further down the road;, the Audi stalled out in the middle of the road behind us.

Chicago's finest were also still in the picture. Lights and sirens neon-signing that we had a minute or two before we were going to be spending the night with fancy new jewelry in the city-run Ramada.

We needed to ghost ASAP, and unfortunately dump the car. Man, that was going to piss me the hell off.

"Fuck." I punched the dash, taking a hard right and then a quick left. No real way out of it presenting itself as we continued down the road I'd put us on, the fucking thing narrow with only one lane going each way.

The cops were going to be coming around the corner soon, and it was going to take a little more than a few turns to shake them.

My eyes locked on the road up ahead, a deserted gas station that had been boarded up coming up fast on our left. It was a gamble, but one I was going to take. They currently didn't have line-of-sight, and as soon as that changed we could kiss our chances goodbye.

I downshifted, trying to slow the car down without locking up the brakes as I crossed the centerline and drove on the opposite side of the road. Lucky for everyone involved there was no oncoming traffic.

It was needle threading time, jerking the wheel to the left as I spun into the narrow driveway of the deserted gas station. The pumps passed in a blur as we continued to the back, the overgrown brush doing a number on my paint job as leaves and twigs fell into the backseat.

"Stay down but keep your gun ready." I pulled behind a mound of old tires and cut the ignition, the engine silent as we sat in the dark.

"They didn't see us," Sofia whispered in the dark, the affirmation more for her own benefit I'm sure. "They didn't turn."

No lights or sirens.

But it was too soon to tell.

Not to mention we still had no idea what had happened to the Audi. One thing was for certain; the night was far from over.

"We're not going to wait to find out. Let's go."

TEN

SOFIA

It had to be a dream.
The unidentified shooter, the car chase, trying to outrun the police—it couldn't be real.

It was a nightmare—a *horrible* nightmare—and I just needed to wake up. I tried to will myself back to consciousness, but the heaviness remained. My throat constricted as scattered thoughts flooded my mind.

It wasn't a dream.

It was my life.

"Get it together, Sofia," he hissed in the dark, slowly removing the bags from the trunk of the car while I stood silently beside him. "You did good; don't fall apart now."

"I wasn't. I'm not." I quickly blinked away the tears starting to pool at the corners of my eyes. "I'm fine." My hands moved quickly to the last remaining duffle and pulled it out. "I'm fine."

"Right." The laughter bubbled up his throat, taunting me. "Just *fine*. Come on, let's move."

He was completely devoid of emotion. The coolness in his voice reflected in his steady hand as he strapped a bag on either arm and checked his gun. He didn't bother holstering it, his hand doing a quick slide over its body, almost as if to offer it a caress. It would been easy to have missed it, the subtly of his hand. Its kindness against the steel almost a contradiction to everything else.

The hue of the streetlight spilled its dirty yellow wash just far enough so it wasn't completely black as the smell of gasoline and old rubber invaded my nose. I had no idea where we'd go from here, but I knew that the longer we stayed, the greater chance we'd be found.

"Where are we going?" I tried to push down my panic and get my head back in the game. Like it or not, we were a team and he'd gotten us this far, so I had to trust him. "Do you have a plan?"

He didn't answer, his eyes throwing me the *seriously?* his mouth didn't need to say.

Instead he pointed to the chain-link fence at our back, a dark empty back lot beyond its metal wall. "That way." The two words served as the only indication as to where we were going from here.

I assumed we would climb, heft our bodies up and over the fence and hope to keep the noise minimal. The CPD would surely be doubling back soon, realizing by now we'd shaken them. There wouldn't be that much ground to cover, especially if there was a helo in the air.

"What are you doing?" He grabbed my arm as I repositioned my duffle on my shoulder, my fingers grasping one of the links as I lifted my foot.

"You said that way," I whispered. "Assuming you weren't going to answer any more of my questions, I figured we'd leave." And I was too exhausted to further decipher what he was thinking.

"And you were going to climb over?" His lips twitched at the edges, ridiculously finding something in the situation amusing.

"Well, unless you have a magical teleporter in your bag, the only way to go *that way* is over this fence."

"I don't go over. I go through." He moved to the edge of the fence, pulling out a pair of six-inch side cutters from his bag. "Climbing is too risky, means your hands are occupied and you can't hold your gun." His hand moved methodically snipping through the metal like butter. "Also means your back is either in the direction of where you're going or coming from. Opens you right up for attack." He stopped when he got to the link a couple inches above his head. "Now you can go."

With a steady hand he tore back the fence from the spikey edges the cuts had made, the sheet of curved metal pulling apart like a curtain. His face stayed stoic, watching me as I passed through the gap, not even a hint of the effort I knew he was exerting showing on his body.

I on the other hand, wasn't as cool or collected, my breathing heavy as I replayed the car chase in my head. Seconds. That's what had separated this outcome from something entirely different.

As soon as I was through, he followed close behind. His heavy boots leaving footprints underneath the thick grass. Unfortunately we would be leaving a trail, a roadmap for anyone to find us.

"Follow me and stay alert." His feet stepped forward not bothering to check whether I did actually follow.

Instinctively, we both knew whatever happened in the next few days, I undoubtedly would be by his side. Not because it's what I wanted, but because I had no other choice. Pride was a luxury I couldn't afford. That's probably why he kept moving forward, the unspoken words enough.

He didn't talk any more—which at least spared me his indifference—his large muscular frame moving silently through the darkness. Not an inkling of fear cracked through his rock solid façade with his eyes covering as much land as his feet as we continued to where the vacant lot met the street.

I stayed close behind, the hair on the back of my neck

standing straight up as a single parked blue Nissan Altima came into view. It felt ominous, the dead-end street virtually empty except for the sedan.

Michael stopped midstride, his arm reaching back signaling me to halt. Not that it was necessary, my feet stilled immediately not knowing if there was anyone in the car.

"Stay here," he whistled through his clenched teeth.

"No. It could be an ambush." My healthy paranoia reared its ugly head as I grabbed his arm. Touching him had been more to get his attention without raising my voice because let's face it, he had at least a hundred pounds on me. Holding him back wasn't going to be an option. "If we do this, we do it together. I can be your back-up, I'm not some bimbo who doesn't know what they're doing."

There were a lot of things I never thought I would do. Leaving the scene of a crime would be one—but I'd already done that tonight—while playing partner to a criminal was a close second. Still, I wasn't going to sit and debate my fall from grace when we had no idea what threat lay inside that car.

"Fine, but we do it my way." He huffed out a breath knowing we were running out of time. "Stay low and come up the back. I'll take the driver's side, you take the other."

"Okay." My vision focused beyond him looking toward the parked car.

"Sofia." He snapped his fingers, calling my attention back to him. "If you fuck this up, I'll shoot you myself. I will not die for you, we clear?"

"Yes." The word barely audible as his words chilled me to my core. I doubted there was anyone who would die for me. Maybe my mother before she became an alcoholic with a prescription dependency, but certainly no one now. But I wasn't a liability either and I wanted the opportunity to prove that too. "I won't fuck up."

With a jerk of his chin he signaled our go, our weapons close to our bodies as we closed in, the Altima only a few feet away.

A dog barked in the distance as we quickly closed in, my eyes surveying the area surrounding the car as my feet carried me to it.

My heart thumped in my chest as we split off in different directions, rounding the car with our weapons drawn on either side. My eyes flicked to Michael as we flanked the Altima, my finger resting on the slide ready to move to trigger if needed as I moved to the door.

Nothing.

The interior was dark, the space empty.

A breath I'd been holding slowly pushed past my lips, my finger relaxing a little as I leaned closer to the car. *Always make sure,* I wasn't sure if it was the voice of my father or my training from the Police force that rattled around in my head.

"A little too convenient." Michael dipped his chin to the back windows. He probably had the same thoughts, his left hand dropping to the door handle and giving it a gentle pull.

Locked.

His hand disappeared to his pocket and I was torn between wanting to know what he was up to and keeping my eyes on the car. Asking was out of the question, sure I would get the none-of-your-business he was so fond of.

Whatever he was doing required the use of his gun-hand, his arm dropping from sight for a few seconds before the locks popped open.

"It needs to be searched." The roof-mounted light flooded the interior as he pulled open the door.

While I took care of the back, Michael did a sweep of the front, hitting the trunk release and stepping out of the car.

Once he'd been satisfied the sedan was clean, he tossed the

duffels into the back before returning to the driver's side. "Throw your things into the trunk, we're taking the car."

By the time I'd tossed my bag into the back—the cooler left behind in the deserted Camaro—Michael had pried off the plastic on the steering column and was working the ignition with a wire contraption and a handheld black device. The purr of the engine punched through the silence less than a minute later.

Doors closed on both sides, the slam shaking the body of the car as he eased off the brake and pressed the accelerator. The vacant lot and the gas station it backed into left in the rearview mirror as we pulled away from the curb. Grand Theft Auto added to tonight's rap sheet.

"We need to make sure we aren't being followed before I take you back to the warehouse." Michael's eyes flicked between the windshield and rear window. "Pretty sure the cops didn't get an ID on us other than the car, but whoever sent the Audi is probably going to be looking."

"They'll keep coming." The words fell from my lips before I had a chance to stop it. "I'm not going to go quietly, so they'll keep coming."

I'd been threatened before, but never like this and it scared the hell out of me that I was so powerless. I needed to remind myself it was okay to be emotional.

Michael clearly didn't share my view, rolling his eyes either irritated or bored, I couldn't decipher which.

"We're going to get where we need to be and stay there for the night. It will give me a chance to wipe this car and dump it." He continued without breaking eye contact with the road. "Cops will no doubt find my ride and pull prints and DNA it. Nothing we can do about that. Torching it wasn't an option so your situation will probably get a little more intense when the powers that be get wind that you're alive."

I wasn't sure who he meant exactly—*the powers that be*, it could have been anyone—but the police were also going to be a major complication.

I never thought I'd say that—I'd always been on the right side of the law—but I knew that soon, there was going to be all kinds of attention drawn to me.

After all, my house had exploded, my body not recovered. Which would lead them to believe I had either torched the place myself or fallen victim to foul play. They were bound to find hair or fibers that would place me in that car. Then it was just a matter of connecting the dots. The only thing they wouldn't know is whether or not I was dead or alive. Either way, Michael was going to be a suspect in either a homicide or wrongful imprisonment.

"You know they'll assume you kidnaped me." Which, while initially, wasn't too far from the truth, I had waded into this mess neck deep all on my own. "You're going to be a wanted man."

"You really think like a cop don't you?" He smirked, eyeing me sideways as he kept his hands on the wheel.

"I *am* a cop." I wondered how else I should be exploring this situation. "So they'll find your car." I continued extrapolating out loud, unable to help myself. "Know we were together. Considering we have no connection, it won't be a stretch to guess I hadn't come willingly. Then assuming whoever owns this," my finger waved around the interior, "will discover it's missing and flag it as stolen. We have maybe six hours before we're in even deeper shit."

"They'll place *you* in the car but not me. I'm not worried about the cops."

"Um how do you figure?" I choked back a laugh, finding it difficult to believe he could be so fucking arrogant. "Your plates stolen? Surely the car is registered to *someone*. And I find it hard to believe someone like you doesn't have a record." The last part I hadn't intended to say out loud, but it had slipped out nonetheless. My mouth had a mind of its own at the best of times, and when I was nervous or agitated—well, all bets were off.

"I would have assumed by now you would have clued up." He shook his head, spearing me with a look. "Whatever shit you have in your head, you need to put it aside. Those rules don't apply to me."

"Those rules don't apply to you?" I had been wrong; he wasn't arrogant he was delusional. "Who do you think you are? Jesus Christ?"

"Jesus Christ was a fucking pussy who believed that by allowing himself to die, he'd somehow be saved." Each word dripped in venom. Back at the house he'd laughed at my need to pray but this more than that. It was deep-seated hate he was harvesting. "What kind of fucked-up logic is that? Son of God? He was just a fucktard in a pair of sandals with an identity crisis, and I will never understand how or why people believe that shit. Drink the fucking Kool-Aid if it makes you feel better about yourself, but don't put that shit on me."

His words didn't shock me. I'd heard a lot worse. It was the echo of emptiness inside of them that sent a chill right down to my marrow.

"It must be terrifying to be so alone."

I wasn't sure what I was hoping to accomplish, comforting him hadn't been it. But I couldn't even fathom what it was like to be so devoid of hope, to be so insulated from anything warm.

"You *trying* to piss me off?" There was almost a hint of amusement in his voice. He hadn't known what I'd been trying to accomplish either.

"Probably," I answered honestly. It seemed to be a habit for me, a coping mechanism, and I was still wondering how he was so sure he wasn't going to be implicated in the mess we'd left behind.

"Well don't," was his only reply.

We drove the rest of the way in silence. Navigating the streets until we entered an industrial area. The large monochrome-colored buildings flanked both sides of the large street, their dark empty front lots giving me a serious case of the creeps.

The car slowed, pulling into the concrete driveway that fed directly into the mouth of a huge metal roller door. The heavy door lifted on command, a slight whine as it rose being its only protest as Michael held the remote he had activated in his hand.

As we drove through the opened space into the dark, the door behind us rolled closed. He didn't turn on the headlights, seeming to know the direction on instinct, or maybe he'd driven through those doors so many times he could literally do it with his eyes closed.

"What is this place?" I looked into the dark. And when I say dark, I mean it was completely devoid of any illumination. Like we'd been caught in a vacuum.

"The warehouse," he said, like those two words should mean more than they did. Michael brought the car to a stop, cutting the engine before opening his door.

The warehouse—as he called it—was in a mainly deserted industrial part of town, not far from O'Hare. The wide streets were lined with huge structures, some baring the logos of the companies they represented, some had been just as non-descript as the one we'd driven into.

He didn't bother to wait for me, his door slamming as he walked away. I scrambled out of my seat, partly because I was done sitting in the dark and partly because I hoped I might get more information as to what the plan was from here.

There had to be a plan.

Or at least, I hoped there would be.

The large overhead halogen popped before I had a chance to decide which direction to go. The glow of the blubs blinded me, my eyes needing a minute to adjust even though the lights had yet to heat to full strength. One by one they flickered, brightening in intensity as they lit the complete interior.

The inside was stark, cavernous—large enough to house a 747 comfortably—and yet so immaculately maintained, I wondered if it hadn't been recently repainted. The absence of paint fumes told me no, so I assumed he was either a neat freak or had one hell of a cleaner. I suppose you could find anything on Craigslist.

"There's a living space toward the back." He pointed roughly to the far left corner where drywall had been erected. "You should probably sleep."

"What about you?" I had yet to see him do anything remotely human other than shower. Surely he needed to sleep and eat too.

"I need to find out who was in the Audi first." He turned around, his eyes and voice completely void of emotion. It was something I had grown used to when it came to him but still managed to surprise me. The coldness and detachment so clinical and robotic. Like he'd been born without a heart.

"They will have either collected a corpse or received a report from one pissed off motherfucker." He continued, ignoring my stare. "For your sake, I hope their info is coming in the form of a body bag."

His words chilled me, my skin pimpling as I fought the urge not to shiver.

"You've never killed anyone, have you?" He tilted his head to the side, the corner of his mouth lifting in amusement. He was enjoying it.

"You're wrong. I have." I straightened, not feeling any better that this hadn't been my first time. It was one of the things that most separated me from my father—empathy, and my respect for human life. He hated that about me, saw it as weakness but I refused to see it that way. "I just don't enjoy it."

I had wanted to sound strong, confident, not let him see how rattled I was, but I didn't. The words had wobbled out of my mouth with barely a whisper, and as brave as I was trying to be, taking someone's life would never be something I celebrated. I couldn't. It would make me no better than my father. I had spent a lifetime trying to prove to myself that, even though his blood coursed through my veins, I wasn't him.

"It's life or death, Sofia." Michael's voice surprised me. I'd expected him to exploit my weakness, ridicule it. But he wasn't, his eyes softening from the hard glare I was used to. "Your life means their death, it's that simple and you shouldn't feel bad about wanting to survive. It's instinct, one that is stronger than the need for decency."

"That's surprisingly profound." I shook my head not expecting his kindness as I resisted the urge to thank him.

"Yeah, I also quote Nietzsche on occasion." He smirked, surprising me in what I could only assume was an attempt at humor. "Go get some sleep; I have work to do."

Twenty-four hours ago I would have been unnerved by that smile, convinced there was something more sinister lurking beneath. But as much as I wanted to hate Michael, he hadn't pretended to be sincere when he wasn't. His coldness was mechanical, not manufactured, and I didn't believe he had it in him to be kind unnecessarily.

"Okay." I nodded, knowing I'd been standing there like an idiot trying to analyze the situation long enough. "I'll see you in the morning."

It had been a long day, and as much as I hated not being in control, I was tired of arguing. Every part of my mind and body was demanding I shut down, unable to fully process everything we'd been through. Desperation to hit the reset button was what made my feet move one in front of the other as I made my way to the back of the warehouse, leaving Michael to do whatever he was going to do.

I expected a fold out cot in a corner but what I was confronted with was so surprisingly well thought out. Large planes of drywall had been internally erected to section off an area what I guessed was the living space he'd spoken of. It wasn't fancy, the plaster bare but solid, squaring off about eight feet in the air and framed with wood to create a faux ceiling. A box within a box, the roof of the warehouse looming well above it, the lights swinging from the exposed metal beams.

The atmosphere felt different than the house, and not just because there were no windows. He didn't need to tell me that the space was private, my breath quickening as I twisted the knob and opened the wooden door.

In the house I felt like a visitor, but here I felt like a complete interloper.

Cozy wasn't a word I would usually throw around with my present company but what I was confronted with was remarkably just that.

My eyes roamed over the room as I closed the door behind me, hitting a light switch along the wall so I wasn't in the dark. It was neat and tidy—something I had come to expect—with a large king-size bed in the middle of the room. The bed—like the one back at his house—was a simple box spring and mattress, right on the floor, but it was complete with tightly fitting sheets and a crisp dark blue comforter folded at the foot of the bed. And after everything I had been through I wanted nothing more than to slip between those linens and just forget for a few hours.

There was a door to my left that was closed that might have led to a bathroom, but I was too tired to care, kicking off my shoes and slowly peeling off my clothes until I had stripped down to my T-shirt.

My stomach grumbled, and with the cooler not surviving the journey, I wasn't sure if eating was a possibility. I was too tired to care, refusing to give it much more thought as I pulled up the sheets and slid inside, the cotton soft against my skin.

It didn't take long, my eyes closing involuntarily the minute my head hit the pillow. As much as I wanted to stay awake a little while longer, I couldn't, and all those uncertain thoughts would be shelved. I had to trust I would be safe here and there was nothing more I could do.

Maybe it was the rush of adrenaline leaving my body, or maybe I was just emotionally and physically exhausted, but as I let go, sleep finally came.

ELEVEN

MICHAEL

The warehouse was more of a home than my house had ever been. I'd purchased it for cash off an old Italian guy who spoke little English and cared even less about my purpose for it. I had a feeling we had more in common than not, but both of us knew better than to ask questions. I used one of my bogus identities to register the sale, and as far as anyone knew it was an empty storage location where *Peter Salas* liked to restore boats. I even had parked an old wooden sailboat out front a few times just to keep up the pretense in case anyone was watching.

Though in this part of town most people were doing their own thing, too busy being concerned about their bottom line and keeping their businesses afloat to worry about little old me. Which is why I preferred being here to my actual house. Less eyes on me and I could keep shit locked up tight. With barely any windows and only two doors to man, it was the perfect place to get off the grid. Not to mention store my own personal arsenal.

The computer system was also state-of-the-art, my collection of man-toys almost identical to what I had back at the Brownstone. Truth be told, the house I lived in was purely for appearances; it was here that I felt the most relaxed.

The warehouse was isolated, away from neighborhoods. I

liked when I walked outside there wasn't the need to pretend. No one wanted small talk or looking to see if my lawn was trimmed. And apart from the lack of attention, this place felt closer to what I was used to—what I'd had for years before I'd been able to afford more. The additional *comforts* that the house provided just made it more of a charade. I couldn't let my guard down there, but here, it was a different story.

And while I preferred to spend my time pounding someone's face for having to ditch my ride and being shot at, it seemed like the keyboard was going to be the better option. At least for tonight, or morning, as the case was.

Unfortunately, there was no who's-trying-to-kill-me Google search, so I had to once again enlist the help of my Ivy League quarterbacks. They were getting more of my green than I'd like to part with, but I also preferred to have the upper hand, and information always came at a price. Be it in money or blood.

Sofia had either done us both a favor and listened without arguing *or* was too tired to give me the attitude I'd come to expect. Whatever her reason, she had disappeared into the bedroom space I had tucked away in the back. Good thing too; I could tell that while she'd kept her shit together, she wasn't all cool with the way things had gone down.

People rarely impressed me; I kept my expectations low and even still, in most instances, I still shook my head at the level of stupidity I dealt with. It had been a while since there'd been anyone worth raising an eyebrow over. Sofia was the exception.

It hadn't been just tonight; the whole ordeal had me silently giving her a nod of respect. If she was going to make it out of this somehow intact, she was going to have to dial into whatever shit kept her from falling apart. She wasn't working the beat anymore, and looking into lowlifes behind a computer screen and having one at the end of your nine were two different things.

Speaking of people behind computer screens, it was going to take a while before the Abercrombie and Fitch posse came back with anything useful, so I decided to take some of my own advice and get some sleep.

Of course, at the house I'd crashed in one of the other two rooms, no sweat and no drama. But the warehouse wasn't geared for entertaining, i.e. there were no additional rooms. And while the idea of sleeping next to *anyone* made me want to peel my skin layer by layer, I sure as shit wasn't sleeping on the floor.

Leaving the computers to do their thing, I pushed away from my desk that was conveniently located behind the living space. Then it was just a few steps back around the drywall box I'd constructed and I was at the door.

Before heading in, my hand pulled open the front panel of the black box along the wall and my fingers got busy. I armed the security system on the outer perimeter and made sure all the sensors along the building were on. While I was happy to catch a few Z's, I wasn't leaving any of this shit to chance. And the way I had this place wired, even if a bird took a shit on the roof, I was going to know.

Then without thinking too much more about it, I yanked open the door and stepped inside. If Sofia had been sleeping, she was wide awake now.

"What are you doing?" Her head lifted off the pillow, her eyes peeled back in a sort of panic.

"What's it look like I'm doing?" I pulled my shirt over my head as I toed off my boots. "It's been a long night and I need a few hours." My fingers hit the button and fly of my jeans as I let them hit the floor too.

"Whoa, you're gonna sleep here?" Her voice wavered a little

as she hitched up the blankets closer to her chest, like the fucking bedding was made out of some fucking force field. "With me?"

"You see a guest room?" And I wasn't asking for permission, my hand lifting the comforter on the side of the bed closest to me. "Relax, I'm here to sleep. I thought we already established I wasn't interested in fucking you." My ass hit the mattress, sliding in and laying down before she'd had a chance to respond.

"I wasn't insinuating you wanted to fuck me, I just really prefer to sleep on my own," she mumbled in the dark, my eyes already closed as I tried to ignore her.

"Well, you're shit out of luck then." I kept my eyes closed, hoping she'd take the hint and knock off the noise so we both could get some sleep.

I'd never been entirely comfortable sleeping—too vulnerable—opened you right up to bad things. But I hadn't managed to find a reliable way of getting around the bodily need. Sure, there were drugs I could take. Cokeheads could stay awake for days at a time, but it was also hard to run a reliable business when you were snorting Colombian candy.

"Are we going to be here awhile?"

Surprise, surprise she had a question. Seriously, I'm not sure why I assumed she'd just go to fucking sleep.

"For now."

"Until when? Are you waiting for something?"

"You'll be here until you're not. That's all you need to know."

Truth was, I had no fucking idea how long she was going to be hiding out. All depended on what her father had planned. Originally it was going to be at most a couple of weeks, but if Jimmy were smart he'd get her out ASAP.

And while I knew she was probably churning a million

variables in her head, she did us both a favor and kept them to herself.

It took a while, but she finally drifted off, her breathing evening out and the grip on the comforter loosening. It was only when I was sure she was out for the count that I allowed myself to relax.

It wasn't easy, and it wasn't out of some deep-rooted need to protect her either. Short of locking ourselves into Fort Knox, we weren't going to be any more protected than we already were. Besides, I could count the number of people who knew about my connection to this place on three fingers—two of them were in this bed and the other was buried in Rosehill Cemetery.

No, the real reason it was hard for me to power down was I didn't sleep with anyone.

Ever.

After I fucked, I left and no girl was ever invited back to my house. That was a complication I didn't need. So having another human beside me, conscious or otherwise, was making my skin feel too tight.

Such bullshit. If I could watch a man bleed out from a stab wound, I could lay beside a fucking human being and go to sleep. In the end, biology took over; my eyes unable to resist the long blinks I had going on. And whether or not I was *comfortable* with the situation, my body unplugged from my brain and went lights out.

••••

My phone buzzed, vibrating beside the bed demanding attention. Sofia stirred a little, but if she was awake she kept her eyes tightly shut as she rolled over onto her side. It was better to be honest; I wasn't the friendliest in the mornings, even less so if I had to deal with a face-to-face.

"Yeah." I lifted my ass off the mattress and walked toward the bathroom on the other side of the room.

It wasn't my concern about her getting enough sleep that ejected me out of the bed, whether she was *disturbed* by my voice or not didn't bother me. But I had no idea who was on the other end of the phone. Not that the walls between the two rooms were thick enough to block out my conversation, but it would afford me some sense of privacy.

"Michael, it's been too long, my man."

Yeah, not long enough.

Brendon Chambers was a special sort of crazy. He dealt heavily in H and Meth and liked to sample his product. Which meant he was unreliable, and high most of the time. And I was also fairly sure he'd fried whatever was left of that brain of his too, so talking to him was like conversing with a two-year-old.

"I've been busy." It was my generic response that translated loosely to, I-don't-give-a-fuck-so-cut-to-the-chase.

"Yeah? Anytin' interesting?" He coughed out a ridiculous laugh that sounded more like his lung was trying to eject via his throat.

"What do you want, Brendon?" I assumed I was going to have to be literal with this juiced-up motherfucker, because I had no interest in shooting the shit with him or anyone else this early in the morning. Scratch that, make that ever.

"I was just tryin' to make conversation, yo. Bein' polite. You lose your manners, dawg?"

Was it the drugs talking or was he really just trying to piss me off? Either way, I'd never been known for my patience, so high or not, this was coming to a very quick finale.

"You know I never had manners, and I'm allergic to conversation, so spare us both."

"You on your period, dude?" He had the fucking nerve to

sound surprised. "Okay, okay. So, I need a favor."

"I don't do favors, Brendon."

"Fine, fine. I have a job then."

Considering I was still ass deep in my last one, I wasn't exactly looking to extend my services elsewhere. Especially not to a junkie who last I heard had cash flow problems.

"I'm not currently in the market."

"Bullshit. You're always in the market." More maniacal laughter, the dipshit completely missing that the only joke here was him.

"Don't tell me what I am, asshole. I'm not in the mood."

"So the rumors be true den, huh? You holed up wit Jimmy's little girl? You fucked her yet? I heard she was a nice piece of ass." For someone who a few seconds ago was giggling his ass off for no reason, he sounded surprisingly lucid.

"You shouldn't believe everything you hear, Brendon," I deadpanned, sounding almost bored.

Sure I could have denied it, flat-out lied, but last thing I needed was more complications. And given that I wasn't in the habit of telling anyone my business at the best of times, the response he got was one hundred percent what he would have expected.

"Maybe I heard wrong then?" He tested the waters, seeing if I wouldn't give up a little more than the nothing I'd already given him.

"Maybe." He was getting jack shit.

"But the job part was legit, though. Like I have something for you."

"What is it and how much?"

While it seemed dumb to even entertain the idea, maybe this little side venture might actually help me out. See, the fucktard on the other side of the phone had a big-ass mouth.

Huge.

Couldn't keep it shut unless he was unconscious.

Which meant if I did this job for him, he would blab to anyone who would listen, which might inadvertently take some of the heat off my ass. After all, if I was guarding Jimmy Amaro's princess, I wouldn't leave her to do some tweeker's dirty work, now would I?

"Two K." He blew out a slow breath. "I need you to deliver somethin'."

"I'm not UPS. Stop wasting my time." My finger hovered over the end button on my phone, wondering if the moron had anything else to say. Because what he had said so far hadn't wowed me.

"I know that, M but this shit isn't the kind of stuff I can FedEx." His voice suddenly turned serious. "I got one hundred pills—Oxy—I need you to drop them off for me. That's it. Easy. And the two grand is yours."

Awesome.

Drugs.

No need to ask how he'd *acquired* them, the less I knew the better.

"It's a hundred pills; why not drop them off yourself?" I mean, really? He was going to pay me two grand to essentially be a runner? Not that I gave a shit either way how anyone spent their money, but surely getting off his ass would save him a hell of a lot of cash. And time. He could have already delivered them by now.

"Because it's my ex-wife, and she has a restraining order out on me. I'm not worried about the cops, they can suck my dick, but my old lady is packing. I go anywhere near her place and she is going to shoot me. She's done it before, she'll do it again."

I literally shook my head. What the fuck was I listening to? It was like a bad ghetto drama.

"Why the fuck do you want me to deliver Oxy to your ex-wife?"

Not sure why I asked, call me curious.

"Alimony. She doesn't get those pills and all hell will break loose. Come on, dawg. Do me a solid, will you?"

Alimony? I guess paying someone a monthly check for food and rent was a little outdated these days.

"Fine. I want the cash up front." Seriously, I needed my head examined. "No fucking surprises, Brendon."

"No surprises. All good. She'll probably give you a blowjob for free."

"I'm not interested in your ex-wife blowing me."

"Your loss, man, she has skills. One thing I miss about the fucking bitch." He almost sounded sentimental.

"Whatever. See you in two hours."

It had been a tough call. Take the job, leaving Sofia on her own and possibly walk into a trap, or refuse and have the dip shit confirm what he suspected—that I had her. It was a gamble either way, but I wasn't going to sit on my hands. Hopefully getting back on the streets would give me a better feel for the situation, maybe even yield some intel. As long as I kept my eyes open and my senses sharp, the outcome would be favorable.

Considering I was already in the bathroom, I figured I'd jump in the shower. My fingers cranked the faucets, the cold water hitting my skin as I entered the stall. I never really bothered waiting for the water to heat up—just get in, get clean and get out. Besides, I still had the *other* problem to deal with.

The one that was still in my bed.

She wasn't the kind of girl to sit still and wait, which meant that me leaving brought up a whole new set of problems. Tying her up could always works as a solution, but the warehouse didn't have a basement like the Brownstone did.

Shutting off the faucet, I toweled off and slung the towel around my waist. My clothes were in the other room, which meant the redress was going to have to happen with an audience. And it wouldn't be the first time.

Sofia was sitting up in bed when I walked in, her hair mussed from sleep while her knees were up tight against her chest. From the look on her face, I was confident she'd heard part of my conversation, which is why she probably looked like she wanted to run. Smart girl. And me leaving meant . . .

"I have a job to take care of today." I grabbed my jeans from the floor and pulled them on, not bothering with boxers or to look at her. The towel fell from my waist as I yanked them up. I didn't bother flashing my cock this time. There wasn't time to play games, and to be honest; I was short on the motivation. "Not sure how long I'll be gone. You're staying here obviously."

"Are you going to lock me up?" To her credit her voice didn't wobble, just asking me the question we'd both been considering.

"Nope." My fingers zipped up my fly. I didn't bother with a shirt, knowing I could grab one on the way out.

"Nope?" she echoed, no doubt not what she'd expected to hear.

"The way I figure it, you have had enough opportunities to run and you've been smart." I turned to look at her. "If you do decide to go, know that I won't try to follow you. We both know you probably won't make it twenty-four hours on your own, so your best chance is to stay with me. Now, if I leave and you decide that plan doesn't sit right with you, then that will be on you. But I won't lock you up."

It was another gamble, but I was giving her the choice. If she ran, then that was on her but I wasn't going to tie her up. Maybe some sick part of me was curious, wanting to see if she'd prefer to be with me than an unknown alternative. Can't say if I were her that I wouldn't take my chances. But we weren't the same type of person. And maybe it was a good time to remember that.

"Thank you." I watched as her body relaxed, her eyes filled with what looked to me like gratitude. Not what I wanted from her.

"Don't thank me, Sofia. I'm not your fucking savior."

I didn't give her a chance to answer, the gratitude making me uncomfortable as I stalked from the bedroom to where I dumped our bags near the computers. Then it was a quick pull on of a shirt, check my weapons and out the door. The sooner I met with Mr. and Mrs. *white trash* the better.

There was no way I was taking the car we boosted last night out in the daylight. I had meant to dump it and wipe it down when we got home, but it became less of a priority. Information and sleep took precedence.

Instead, I walked around to the back of the warehouse where I had a beat up Chevy Cavalier parked. The car was at least twenty years old and had come with the building, but the POS still ran, so I kept it serviced and made sure there was gas in the tank. It served its purpose on occasions just like this, and having it on the lot added to the rouse. Also it helped that it looked like a million other cars on the road, so cruising the I-90 meant I wouldn't even get a second look. Perfect.

The keys were kept in a meter box not far from the car, then it was simply get in, hit the ignition and hope the thing turned over. It had been a while since I'd last driven it.

It spluttered and protested, needing more gas, but eventually it got where it needed to be and didn't stall out. And once it got started, it ran like a charm. Things were definitely looking up.

Brendon lived in South Shore. He rented a room from

another drug dealer, Ramón, who actually was doing pretty well for himself. R-man kept his inventory purely to prescription pharmaceuticals, dolling out Xanax and Vicodin like it was candy. And unlike his buddy Brendon, *his* clientele was more refined.

The Chevy didn't have a working stereo, which meant the drive was done without a soundtrack. It was what I usually preferred and also gave me the opportunity to listen to my handheld police scanner and see if there was anything of interest.

The Camaro had been discovered. Prints came back to a Sofia Concetta Amaro and Clive Maxwell—a person unknown to police. There was a BOLO out on both of them, Mr. Maxwell being five eleven, blue eyes, grey hair and seventy-five from the information they'd pulled from his driver's license. And if they dug deep enough they'd find that it was the same Clive Maxwell who died five years ago. I even sent flowers to his widow the day I stole his social security number. Who said I didn't have a heart?

"Hey, homie!" Brendon was sitting on the front stoop, his ball cap angled to the side like a bad version of Vanilla Ice.

"Not your homie, asswipe." I yanked open the car door and stepped out onto the curb. "Give me the cash, the package and address." I may have agreed to do the job, but I still wasn't convinced this wasn't a set up, so sitting around waiting for the cavalry wasn't happening.

"Whoa, my brother." Brendon climbed to his feet, holding his hands up defensively. "We can't do this shit out in the open. You gone cray-cray. You is wacked."

Brendon was white. I'm talking milky white skin, blond hair and blue eyes. Any whiter and the dude would glow in the dark. But for some reason every time the dumbass got high, his heritage got a little messed up, crossed somewhere between

African American and Puerto Rican. He liked to mix things up and be an equal-opportunity stereotype.

"Have you checked out these streets? No one is looking, and anyone who is gets a nice fat paycheck from Ramón. So, let's get moving, shall we?"

Ordinarily there was no way I'd do business on the street. I liked any exchanges to be done with as few eyes on me as possible, but here, no one blinked an eye. Everyone was either on the take or under Ramón's protection. No one was calling the cops, and they gave even less of a fuck about the village idiot with whom I was currently engaged.

"You best watch yo' mouth when you're talking about the boss man. Sh-it, he'll pop a cap in your ass." Arms flailed in front of him for added theatrics.

"Can we do this now before I put a *cap* in your *ass*?" I lifted the front of my shirt to show him I wasn't kidding. This job was far exceeding the time I wanted to be spending out on the street and the two grand I was going to be paid.

"Relax M-man, we're doin' it." He nodded, climbing to his feet and going back into the house he'd been sitting in front. "Here." He tossed me a colorful backpack, something like you'd see a kid wear on their first day of school. "Money and address are in the in front pocket."

My fingers pulled across the zip from the front pocket and sure enough there was a white note with an address and twenty hundred dollar bills.

"You gonna count them right in front of me, dawg?" Brendon laughed, his eyes so bloodshot I was surprised he could even see what the hell I was doing. "Like you don't trust me?"

"I don't trust you." I slipped the hundreds into my back pocket and turned to get back into the car. "Give Ramón my best." I gave a half-hearted wave as I started the Chevy.

Jury was still out if the pick-up had been half of the rouse and the real work would happen at the drop off point. Of course, there was no way to know, but so far nothing had flagged as suspect. All good things.

Brendon's ex-wife lived in Hyde Park, right next to Lake Michigan, so I didn't need to spend too long in the car. The drive ended when I pulled up on a set of row houses with a neatly manicured lawn out front.

Not what I was expecting.

Ejecting from the car, I grabbed the kid's backpack and climbed the two stairs to the front door. I was already pissed off I'd agreed to do this job in the first place, but *keeping up appearances* could only help my cause. After all, someone had to know I was involved; the Audi wasn't a coincidence. So eyes were on me whether I wanted them or not, and how I used those eyes is what was important moving forward.

"Hello?" A thin brunette answered the door, her face made up like she was about to head out to a fancy dinner. "Can I help you?"

"Are you Kerry?" I looked down at the note dumbass had stuffed into the backpack with the address.

"Sure am." Her red painted lips spread into a smile. "Brendon send you?" Her eyes dropped down to the bag in my hand.

"Yep, sure did. I believe this is yours." My hand lifted, passing her the bag.

"Our son must have left it behind when he was with his dad." She winked as she accepted the backpack. "Danny is always forgetting things."

On cue, a kid who looked around three years old came running to the door. "Mommy! Is it Daddy?"

His eyes were almost too big for his face, but they were the same shade of blue as the lowlife I'd just left.

And that right there was proof you didn't have to be smart to be someone's parent. I honestly felt sorry for the kid, because with the kind of parents he had, he probably wouldn't stand a chance. That was assuming he didn't find either mommy's or daddy's drugs beforehand and end up a statistic. Or a corpse. I'd seen it happen before, and not as rare as people thought.

"Yeah, well enjoy." I waved goodbye as I turned to leave.

If I were halfway decent, I might have gotten involved. Said something and tried to give the kid a fighting chance. But I doubted there had ever been any decency in me to start with. I guess that I was even thinking about it meant I wasn't totally heartless, and wasn't that a fucking revelation. But that mess wasn't my problem, which is why I was fucking walking away.

"Wait," Kerry AKA Mother of the Year called after me. "You could come inside if you want. Danny is due for a nap." Her hands moved suggestively up my arms and I knew exactly what was on her mind.

I hadn't had sex in a week, so the idea of relieving some of that pressure sounded appealing. But I'd rather stick my dick into a garbage compactor than stick it in her.

"Why don't you go back inside and take care of your boy," I hissed out through my clenched teeth. "I've got shit to do and none of it involves you."

"Asshole." Her hand flew at my face, but I grabbed it before it could make contact.

"Yes, yes I am," I sneered at her, my voice barely a growl. "And you were about to let this asshole around your kid. Not very smart. There are lots of assholes out there just like *me* waiting for bitches like *you* to let us into their homes. Get close to their kids. And newsflash, they aren't going to play nice."

My words were like a slap to the face she hadn't given me, her feet taking a step back into her doorway. I wasn't sure if it was for her own self-preservation or that of her kid, but something must have kicked in as she braced herself against the doorjamb.

"Yeah. That's what I thought." I laughed as I turned my back for a second time and walked away from her.

Too bad her change of heart would only be temporary and probably by dinnertime she would be so high she'd forget to feed her kid. Still, saying anything at all was more than I usually did, but it was as involved as I was going to allow myself.

Shit. Even just thinking about it was weird, like I had developed a case of reverse Stockholm syndrome. Nope, not a good thing and I didn't like where it could lead.

Life was all about survival of the fittest and I had my own ass to worry about. And yet . . . something deep inside of me really hoped that kid made it out of here alive.

TWELVE

SOFIA

After he'd left, I got up and located my things. I hadn't explored the bathroom when I came into the room last night. The door on the far side of the room could have been anything, but I was relieved to hear water running when Michael had been in there. The idea of a shower washing away yesterday almost made me want to cry with relief.

I didn't waste any time, cranking the hot water till I was almost positive it was going to peel the first layer of epidermis from my shoulders. And it felt so good, the steam surrounding me with the only sound being that of the thunderous spray hitting the tile.

It was heaven, and I could have stayed inside the stall forever, but I didn't. I used whatever products Michael had—shampoo, but no conditioner—and went through the process—at least physically—of getting clean. My mind however was still the same muddy mess it had been last night.

He had walked in and unapologetically climbed into bed with me. I had wanted to squeeze my eyes shut and hopefully pretend that the nightmare wasn't real, something that was going to be hard to do when one of the main cast members was lying beside you. But to my amazement, it hadn't been as bad as I'd expected. Not that I would admit it to anyone—I was barely able to admit it to myself—but having him there actually calmed me. By his own admission he wasn't a nice person; no doubt he'd done a lot of terrible things, but as he laid beside me, inches away, I felt safe. Instinctively I knew he wouldn't hurt me.

Once I was dried and dressed, my survival instincts flared up. I needed to get a feel for my surroundings. Know where I was, and at the very least the layout of the building I was hiding inside. Something told me we'd be here awhile.

The inside was huge. Not just big, but when I said someone could park a commercial jet inside, I hadn't been exaggerating.

Despite the amount of space available, the living quarters were relatively small. Beside the bedroom and bathroom, there was a thin closet that housed a couple T-shirts, a pair of jeans, coveralls and a pair of work boots. Nothing else remarkable.

The bathroom had been simple. A shower—no bath—with a vanity/sink combo, and a toilet. There was a narrow linen closet in a corner that stored towels, extra toiletries and toilet paper. Once again, nothing out of the ordinary, and it was easy to forget the makeshift apartment was actually inside a garage on steroids.

Just outside the living quarters was an office space. Two trestle tables formed an L-shaped desk with two monitors and a large CPU sitting on the floor underneath. There were leads that attached everything and a modem that flashed continuously, but there wasn't so much as a paperclip sitting out of place.

Ironic that his inner sanctum seemed so structured and yet he lived his life in chaos. Coping mechanism or something else? I wasn't sure I'd ever find out.

Along the wall directly adjacent to what I was now referring to as *the office*, were two locked filing cabinets. Standard issue, four drawers—similar to what you'd find in almost any workspace in America. And I knew they were locked after trying each of the drawers with a healthy yank.

Fruitless.

Not that I expected someone like Michael to be careless and leave anything unlocked. Even in a fortress like this, the man had some very serious trust issues.

Further along the eastern wall was what I decided to call the kitchen. It had another trestle table with two fold-up chairs pushed up against the wall. It was missing the nice appliances of the house but it was functional. An old refrigerator that looked like it might have been an original part of the layout was sandwiched between the sink and the countertop.

Seeing the kitchen made my stomach rumble. The provisions I'd packed in the cooler had been abandoned last night, and I had no idea how long Michael would be gone. It's not like I could text him and ask him to go through a McDonald's drive-thru on his way back.

So, I decided to hunt for some food. Surely someone this organized would have some sort of staples around here somewhere. Tinned vegetables, non-perishables, crackers— that sort of thing. In case the end of the world came or whatever else men like him were afraid of.

The vast wide-open space worked in my favor, revealing another cornered off space similar to the living quarters along the opposite wall. It had also been sectioned with drywall, its door surprisingly unlocked as I twisted the handle.

Inside was his stash. Shelves of bottled water, MREs and assortment first aid items. It seemed that maybe he was actually ready for the end of the world, or at the very least a civil uprising.

I tore into one of the MREs, so hungry I didn't care what I was eating and devoured the spaghetti without heating it. It wasn't great, and I had never eaten pasta for breakfast, but my stomach and I weren't fussy.

Following my entrée was water, the Aquafina bottle crushed in my hand as I gulped the liquid. Well, at least I knew I wouldn't starve or die of thirst while I was here. I took what was left in the MRE—what looked to be Cheez-its crackers and Skittles—and continued to eat while I walked.

The rest of the warehouse was relatively benign. There was a workbench with one of those fancy red toolboxes mechanics had, but nothing else remarkable. Except for an old wooden sailboat mounted on a trailer. While it seemed completely out of place like the fridge I'd seen in the kitchen, it looked like it had come with the space and been kept. Michael didn't seem like the type of guy who liked to spend weekends fishing, so I imagined it hadn't seen the water in a long time.

It was when I reached the very front—or perhaps it was the back, it was hard to tell in the dark last night which way we'd entered—that I discovered a big black fuse box. I had seen a few of them around, positioned in different parts of the warehouse. I assumed they connected the sophisticated security system Michael had wired throughout the place.

The sensors were discreet but I'd noticed them, as were the thin black wires running along the grey exposed-brick walls. This one seemed more important that the others, larger and more industrial looking, almost like a small locker.

Getting up onto my tiptoes so I was able to reach the latch and open the front. The door swung open and revealed three analogue meters running slowly, similar to a regular electrical meter, as well as a numerical touchpad. Nothing out of the ordinary except there wasn't any way a representative from the power company would have internal access.

So what the hell was it?

I finished off my Skittles and went to grab one of the fold-up chairs, using it as a stepladder to get a better look.

With my fingertips, I traced along the thin bead of caulking sealing the border where the dials were held. It didn't look right, the revolutions running twice as fast as the display below it indicated. So whatever I was looking at was a rouse, a fake and some kind of decoy. But for what, I hadn't worked out.

My fingernails picked at the white caulking, the silicone protesting against my nails as I pried it from the wall.

Once I'd freed up most of it, I was able to pull out what essentially was a front panel, opening up to reveal the back. The other side proved that those meters were nothing but fancy props, their mechanical workings not hooked up to anything other than a power source. The touchpad, however, was authentic. The sheathed red, blue, green and yellow wires were connected in a complex configuration, and fed into the wall with the rest of the wiring.

So why have the fake meters and a larger than average box to house them in? None of it made sense until I pulled the panel out a little more and found a large envelope. The edges had yellowed either from time or moisture in the wall and judging from its tattered appearance it had been awhile since it had seen the light of day.

The skin on the back of my neck tingled in warning. Deep down I knew I had no business looking into whatever was contained in that envelope. But I couldn't help myself, my curiosity getting the better of me as to why Michael had gone to such great lengths to hide this folder.

The minute I pulled out its contents I knew exactly why.

Inside were a birth certificate, notepaper, paper clippings, file pages and old photos—pieces of a puzzle that was obviously Michael's life. I was caught feeling like an intruder while the investigator in me needed to know more.

Shoving the envelope under my arm, I did my best to right the meter box to the way I'd found it. Of course, it wouldn't stand up under close inspection. The caulking was missing from most of the edges of the panel but if no one paid too much attention, it would look as ordinary as I'd found it.

I folded the chair and carried it back to the kitchen along with the envelope. I had no idea how much time I had before Michael got back, but I assumed when he said he didn't know how long he was going to be, it was probably going to be a while.

Please, Lord, let him stay out a little longer, I silently whispered as I emptied the contents onto the table, the papers and photos scattering across the white plastic surface.

The police officer in me took over; examining each note, photo or shred of paper like it was important evidence in a murder trial. Slowly the man who had come to my door a few nights ago was starting to take shape.

He was abandoned at birth and left on the steps of Saint Margaret's, barely clinging to life. Hospital reports—which he'd either stolen or hacked into the system to get—suggested he hadn't been expected to make it through the night. Two nuns whose names were Sister Catherine and Sister Mary had apparently found him and rushed him to the hospital. And judging by the notations in the file, they had sat in at the hospital for days until he finally pulled through. No parents were listed on the birth certificate issued by the state, the name Michael Gabriel had been given to him by either one or both of the sisters.

The story then continues with documents from child welfare—once again probably illegally obtained—each page bringing with it one tragic heartbreak after another.

Michael was fostered a number of times. His first foster parents returned him to the state because he was inconsolable and cried too much after only three months. And then he was removed from the second family when he was three after he was found to be living in unimaginable filth and neglect.

It went on and on, the child being passed around like an unwanted toy until he reached the age of ten when he apparently found a stable home.

Social worker notes labeled him a "problem child, with an inability to show empathy or love." Another caseworker went so far as to call him a "psychopath with criminal tendencies." Page after page of psychological notes on how damaged he'd become and not a single mention of a prescribed treatment plan, therapy or a family who had loved him through his trauma.

Nothing.

They'd given up on him. Condemned him to the man he'd become.

The last of the notes said he'd run away as a teen. A police report was filed three days after he had apparently gone missing, but there were no notations on what investigations had been done. It seemed with his disappearance and his past problematic behavior, everyone just gave up on him all together. His file closed.

There were a few photos. Most likely taken by caseworkers on visits at different times. Each photo was a headshot, Michael staring directly into the lens of the camera. It was eerie taking that step back in time. His hair the same shade of brown but his skin was a shade paler. He looked thinner too, almost smaller and younger than the ages noted on the back. His face however hadn't changed. It was completely empty of emotion, like he had known they had given up on him too. The little boy who stared back at me had the eyes of a lost soul, those deep pits—desolate.

There were no further notes or files as to what happened to

him after he left his last foster home. No school records continuing after that date, no records for the DMV, registration to vote or service records of any kind. There weren't even medical records; and as far as the state of Illinois was concerned Michael Gabriel was still listed as a missing person.

That's what he had meant last night, when he'd said they wouldn't be able to place him in the car with me.

He was a ghost.

There were so many missing pieces. Like, how a man who, according to records, barely attended high school seemed smarter than some college students. Or how he'd managed to buy property, register a car, get a license and at the very least *exist,* when on paper he didn't.

I reexamined the envelope wondering if there was something I'd missed, or if there was a hint as to where more might be found. And there, stuck in the crease at the bottom, I found a tiny holy picture.

The small card was typical of what you'd get in a church, maybe on a saint's feast day or another type of religious occasion.

On the front was an artist's impression of Saint Michael the Archangel. His wings outstretched and his sword drawn with his foot stamping on the head of Satan. His body powerful and strong—that of a soldier, while his face remained beautiful and fearless. It was an image I'd seen repeated hundreds if not thousands of times through art and the history of the church. He was seen as the protector, the leader of God's army against evil. So significant and fierce was his legend, that he is mentioned in other ancient religions such as Judaism and Islam. Evil, by whatever name it was known, was trampled under his feet just as he had done with Satan.

On the backside of the picture, the plain white card had a notation so faint I had to bring it right to my eyes to see. And there, in faded pencil, was the word "rose."

Nothing else. No indication if it was the flower, a name, or even a street. The word was written without a capital letter or anything else after it, and seemed so insignificant. Yet instinct told me it was important.

"What the fuck are you doing?"

He came at me like a freight train, his arm pushing me back against the exposed brick as he held a knife at my throat. The blade just piercing my skin enough for me to feel a tiny drop of blood ease out.

I had been so engrossed in what I was doing I hadn't heard a thing.

Hadn't heard a car approach.

Hadn't heard a door open.

Hadn't heard the echo of boots on the floor.

And like the ghost he was on paper, he appeared before me, his teeth bared like a rapid dog, his eyes—terrifying.

"I-I." Words refused to come out as my heart beat wildly in my chest and I struggled to breathe. I never thought he would hurt me, but looking at him now, I didn't know anymore.

"I'll ask you again." His arm pushed harder against my chest, my lungs struggling to expand under his weight. "What. The. Fuck. Are. You. Doing?"

Each word was like a punch to my gut, as the fear bubbled up inside of me, another drop of my blood spilled onto my shirt.

"I'm sorry for what they did to you."

It had leaped out of my mouth before I had a proper chance to consider what I was saying. What I should have said was I was sorry for invading his privacy, for breaking into his special meter box and for reading his file. But I couldn't make myself say things I didn't mean. Even when I knew my life depended on it, I couldn't say I regretted what I did.

He knew almost everything about me, and I knew nothing about him. It hadn't been fair that he had held all the cards, that I didn't know who the man was that laid beside me last night. I deserved to know, so for that, I wasn't and would never be sorry. But even though he loomed before me, literally a hair between his knife and my jugular, my heart hurt for the little boy inside of him. The one who had never been shown love or compassion. For that, for *that* I was genuinely sorry.

"What did you say to me?" His brows bunched in confusion obviously not expecting the words as much as I hadn't.

"You were just a baby, the way they treated you—you aren't what they said, I know you aren't."

I had no proof of it, but it was something inside of me I just knew. Gut instinct told me that underneath all of this, he wasn't rotten.

He wasn't evil.

He wasn't broken.

"You think I give a shit about my past?" he sneered, like the words disgusted him. "That it means anything to me now?"

"I think you like to pretend it doesn't, but I don't see how anyone could survive all of that and not be changed. I read what they said about you." I figured I'd come this far, I might as well finish the job and jump off the cliff. "You weren't just abandoned, you were deserted by everyone who was supposed to care for you. You aren't the monster they expected you to become."

"You don't know me." His eyes bored into mine, reinforcing the anger that was spilling from his lips.

"No, I don't."

Essentially he was right. I didn't *know* him. Not in the way I knew my neighbors, friends or family, and yet, I saw him more clearly than he probably saw himself. "But you still have that knife at my throat and haven't killed me yet. Deep down, there is humanity."

"I haven't killed you because you are my pay check." His words dripped with venom and I knew he'd said them to hurt me. But I refused to believe them. Maybe I was the biggest idiot of all mankind or maybe, I still saw that little boy in those photos.

"The Michael on those pages," my eyes flicked across to the table where my evidence had been strewn, "would have chosen himself over the money."

Slowly the knife's edge moved from my throat, the sting immediate as the air hit the scratch it had left as his hand lowered.

"Careful, Sofia. This isn't some game you want to play with me." His face moved closer, his hot breath taunting me while he continued to hold me still.

"I'm not trying to play a game." My hand rubbed against my neck. "But I know what I know."

"You know nothing." His voice barely a whisper, and in some way it was more terrifying than if he had screamed it at me.

He didn't say anything else but I felt the pressure on my chest ease as his arm lifted. One foot and then the other stepped away from me, my body sagging against the wall as he walked to the table.

Following the timeline I'd compiled of file notes and photos, his eyes moved restlessly over each one. Scrutinizing each piece before he moved on. I could barely breathe, my body paralyzed as I watched his brow crease. His gaze dropped to the floor suddenly, at his feet the holy picture. Saint Michael the Archangel with his sword. He glanced at me, watching me cautiously before kneeling to pick up the tiny card off the floor.

My heartbeat quickened as his legs brought him back to full height, ignoring me while he gave his attention to the picture, almost as if he was studying it before turning it over.

Rose.

That one word.

When his eyes looked back at me, I could tell he knew I'd seen it. It was like the air chilled around him even though I knew that wasn't possible.

And suddenly I was terrified again.

THIRTEEN

MICHAEL

I hadn't expected her to sit in a corner and think about the good old days while I was gone.

It wasn't her style to be compliant.

I had no doubt that she would have gone through the warehouse and examined every doorway and window like it held some radical fucking clue. She would have wanted to be familiar with her surroundings. To know as much as she could about where she was and how to get out if she needed to.

It's exactly what I would have done.

What I hadn't counted on was her pulling a fucking Sherlock Holmes and finding that shit. How the hell did she even know where to look? Did she have freaking X-ray vision and a divining rod? That stuff was hidden in a meter box and buried in the wall. Chances of finding it were so remote, Sofia Amaro either had the instincts of a bloodhound or was the luckiest person I knew.

And I didn't believe in luck.

Seeing it laid out of the table, my past exposed, wound me up so tight I had my knife at her throat before I even knew what I was doing.

I hated that anyone knew anything about me. And that she had the grand motherfucking tour of my childhood pissed me off even more.

Heat jacked up my spine as I looked at the piece of shit card. The fact that I hated it more than anything in that file should have been enough of a tip off I wasn't sane. And yet there she was, looking at me like I needed a fucking hug.

I hated it.

That fucking look.

The pity.

And everything else that file induced.

I should have torched it years ago instead of holding onto it like a pussy. It was ironic that she found it. Shined a big ass light that at some point when I was compiling that boo-fucking-hoo bedtime story, I'd misplaced my freaking balls.

I tossed it down on the table with the rest of the shit and looked back at her.

She was shaking.

Her one hand was still tight against her throat where I'd held my knife while the other was wrapped around her midsection, like the arm would somehow keep her standing.

And the other thing—she looked terrified.

This whole time we'd dodged bullets, had fuck knows what on our ass, and now she had chosen to fall apart. Part of me was disappointed. That it hadn't taken more to get her looking like she wanted to run. While the other half of me was glad that even though she talked shit, she still had some self-preservation in her to know when her number was up.

"You still so sure I'm not going to kill you?" I eased back on the heels of my boots as a twisted sense of relief flowed through me. That even through this, I still had managed to maintain the upper hand.

"You won't." Her head moved from side to side like she was trying to convince herself as well as me. "You said to me once when I was thinking of running. If I was going to do it, I would have done it by now." She took a breath before meeting my eyes. "I think the same could be said for you."

Even with her back against the wall—both literally and figuratively, she was still trying.

"The difference is *you* have a conscience, and *I* don't."

"That's their words, not yours." Her finger shook as she pointed to the table. The *they* she was referring to not needing to be clarified.

"So, what do you want to do now?" I laughed tossing my knife on the table. "You want me to lay down and tell you about my feelings? Cry a little?"

Newsflash, neither of those things were fucking happening.

"Who or what is Rose?" Her back found its spine as she straightened, prepared for whatever shit storm she opened up with the mention of that word.

Rose.

It was barely legible anymore; I was surprised she'd even seen it. Of course given her fucking track record of uncovering shit I didn't think could be found, I really shouldn't be surprised.

I had seen it in her eyes when I'd walked in. And worse still that she understood it was significant.

"None of your business." I waved my hand casually, ignoring the blood in my veins simmering out of control.

"I don't believe you."

"Maybe it's the name of the whore I stuck my dick in last or maybe it's the name of the bitch I killed three weeks ago. Take your pick, because I don't give a shit what you believe."

"No, that stuff has been hidden back there for at least twelve months, maybe even years. And you wouldn't keep something like that if it was just the name of some whore."

I didn't know whether to clap or fucking shoot her. Did she really think I was playing? Because last time I checked, if you found yourself inside a room with a venomous snake you didn't fucking poke a stick at it.

"Do you want to die, Sofia?" I leveled her with my stare. "Because right now you are speaking like a woman who doesn't value her life."

"Who was she?" she asked again, completely disregarding anything I just said.

"Enough!" I screamed, my fingers grasping the top of the table and flipping it onto its side so that everything spilled onto the floor. "Get the fuck out of my sight."

She didn't need to be asked a second time, running to where the bedroom was, the loud slam of the door confirming that's where she'd gone.

"FUCK," I yelled, kicking the table with the front of my boot.

Inside I was raging, pissed off and wanting to put someone's head through a wall. Her fucking father would be my first choice given it was his doing I was even dealing with this shit.

I was so fucking mad, my skin feeling too tight against my bones as I paced around the room looking for something to destroy. And what pissed me off the most? That she had gotten under my skin.

Not Sofia, it was a different *her*.

And I couldn't believe that *any* of it still affected me like it did.

It was too late now; I'd tipped my hand. And it was fucking obvious that even I had something to hide.

Motherfucking Rose.

That one word—a name—is what undid me.

Not the years of being tossed from family to family. Not being beaten within an inch of my life on the street. Not the fucktards who had tried to ease themselves by concocting lies about who or what I was.

No, none of that mattered.

What threw me into a tailspin was the fucking whore who brought me into this world when I hadn't fucking asked.

My mother.

Oh yeah, Jimmy had tried to play that card when I first met him. But if he thought I hadn't already looked her up, then he was even dumber than I thought. I'd done some digging when I was in my early twenties. The nuns at the church where I'd been dumped all had wild cases of amnesia. Some not even remembering the night at all, others not having been there. They took that vow of silence shit to heart and gave me absolutely nothing.

Of course, me being me, figured there were other people who knew things who didn't suffer from the same devotion to keeping their mouth shut. It was on one of my visits that I met Walter, a groundskeeper for the church and surrounding convent. Old Walter had been there for over forty years and would probably die tending to those fucking topiary rose bushes that lined the front path.

It took some convincing on my part. Walter didn't have a wife or kids I could use as leverage. Poor old dude didn't even have a dog, so going in hard with a gun against his head wasn't going to get me anything other than his brains on my shoes. And I really fucking hated cleaning my shoes.

Nope, Walter needed persuading of a different kind. And I was more than happy to give him enough of the poor orphan routine; it played right into his bleeding heart. I think I even cried. Whatever it took to get that man to open up his trap and tell me what I needed.

And what do you know, a nun by the name of Rose showed up one day about seven months before my arrival. She was quiet and surprisingly beautiful—his words—and rarely spoke. She liked to spend most of her day in the privacy of the back courtyard in the garden, which is where he first saw her.

While the other nuns would chat with Walter, Rose would hide in the shadows. But even under that ridiculous black muumuu she and the other indoctrinated religious freaks wore, there was no hiding that there was one vow she hadn't taken entirely to heart.

Guess she had some serious explaining to do when she said her confession. "Forgive me Father, for I have sinned. I forgot my Bible, sung out of tune during evening mass annnnnnd fucked some dude and got myself knocked up. A few Hail Mary's ought to cover it, right? Awesome. Thanks."

Even as the months passed and she got more obviously in the family way, the pregnancy was ignored. And no one said shit according to Walter. Until one night when there been a bad storm. He'd been convinced that when he'd get to work the next day there'd be no yard to even tend. He showed up bright and early, ready to see the worst. And along with the destroyed azaleas, he'd found a fresh and poorly dug grave out the back.

I bet you can guess who was missing from the morning prayer meeting that day.

Yep.

Rose.

Same night I was born too. Quite a coincidence I'd say? Yeah, so the mystery of my maternity wasn't so mysterious after all. My father? Well who the fuck knew? Could have been a traveling Bible salesman.

Not that it mattered, because he either left the whore and I to face the music on our own, or the bastard didn't even know.

I hadn't asked to be born, fuck knows I'd had more than my share of misery. But to know this bitch had cared more about her reputation and her precious fucking church pissed me off beyond measure.

Of course, the story Jimmy probably had in his folder was

that *mother dearest* was a wayward teen from Wisconsin, which was the lie I had believed initially. Apparently that little fabrication was planted by one of the nuns, she even went so far to leave little trail of bread crumbs as evidence so if anyone looked, there was enough there for it to be plausible.

Unless you took a really serious look.

Which is exactly what I did.

Those nuns sure don't take the Ten Commandments seriously if they are fucking and lying. *Here, have a side of hypocrisy with your holy wine.*

That shit had gotten enough of my mental space. So I left the upturned table, and the Reader's Digest version of my childhood history on the floor, and stalked out of the room.

It had taken me two hours longer than I wanted to get back, needing to make sure I wasn't tailed after my visit with Brendon's drugged-up ex-wife. The last thing I needed was to draw the asshole who was looking for Sofia a map and lead them to my doorstep. Not to mention I hated entertaining.

So, with my mood fluctuating somewhere between gonna-kick-someone's-ass and punch-my-fist-through-a-wall, I sat my ass down at my computer and looked to see if my band of hacker brothers had turned up anything new.

The minute I logged on, my screen lit up like a Christmas tree. Ten or so messages pinged, urgently vying for my attention worse than a hooker in Streeterville.

Fuck.

Me.

Bounty had gone up.

Sofia's head on a platter was worth a cool one point five million dollars. And an extra five hundred thousand would be kicked in for any evidence recovered that tied anyone to anything.

The instructions were clear. No capture. Shoot to kill and

get it done ASAP. Any other subtext wasn't necessary; she was a dead woman walking.

And in addition to that wonderful piece of information, there was a message in my inbox, which in itself was a surprise.

The people who usually employed my services didn't like trails, especially one that could be tracked by the FBI. But there it was, sitting in my inbox just the same.

No name identifying the sender.

My firewall and three virus scans protected me against most garden-variety hackers, so it was either a professional or government. My finger hovered over the enter key, wondering if reading it was going to open up the apocalypse on my CPU. Curiosity was what made my finger actually hit the key.

The message had one line.

Meet me on the steps of Alder Planetarium. Five p.m.

There were very few men who had the resources—and the money—to encrypt a message like that and guts to meet at a public place. One of them was Sofia's father, and the other was Franco Santini.

And while it was it was still unclear as to who was bankrolling the bounty, he was most likely.

Franco was Jimmy's biggest rival, with an ego the size of Canada and balls to match. He loved baseball, sex and violence. Not necessarily in that order, but none of them held a candle to how much he loved money.

He was old school, a numbers man—extortion, embezzlement, bearer bonds—you know, the classics. And I was almost positive there were things on Sofia's little USB drive that would see the IRS so far up that dipshit's ass he would start shitting out suits. And those kinds of consecutive sentences— on federal offenses—would make a murder charge seem like a holiday.

So he'd either heard whispers about what I'd been doing to pass the time the last few days, or he was going to hire me to track her down. Sure, I could ignore the email, pretend I didn't get it. I mean, there was no way to know exactly which cocksucker had sent it, so pleading ignorance was also on the table. But that wasn't going to happen. For the same reason I'd gone to see that piece of shit Brendon and delivered his *alimony*.

Appearances.

And assuming I was correct and it was Franco, refusing to meet him would send up a red flag. Men like him didn't like the word no, so I guess I had a date at five.

"Sofia," I called out, hoping like hell she hadn't locked herself in the bathroom. "Get out here now."

Nothing.

Silence.

I swear if she'd slit her wrists in the fucking shower or something, I was going to save her life just so I could kill her again myself.

My ass flew out of my seat as I moved to the door where the bedroom was. My hand twisted the handle and threw open the door.

She didn't move, her eyes stayed shut as she sat on the floor completely still, with her legs crossed and her back against the wall.

"What the fuck are you doing?" I watched as she slowly opened her eyes. They hadn't been red like I'd expected but her chest was moving fast like she was trying to rein it in.

"Does it matter?" Her feet moved from under her as she stood, her hands brushing the dust from her ass. "I still have free will over my body and mind, and what I do with it."

On second thought, I didn't want to know. Because if she mentioned fucking meditation or praying there was a strong possibility of me doing to the bed what I'd done before to the table.

"We need to talk." I moved closer, my feet lining up right in front of her, and to her credit she didn't cower.

Her shoulders straightened as she took a breath. "Are you here to apologize?"

"Did you hit your head between now and the last time I saw you?" What the fuck did I have to be sorry for? "I don't apologize to anyone, especially not someone who went through my shit."

"But it's okay for you to do it to other people?" she baited, like I was bound to a same set of standards these other morons were.

"I never said I was ethical. And I'm not here to argue."

"So what are you here for?"

"I'm leaving again and I might be gone awhile, so I need you not to get any ideas and do more exploring."

She didn't respond, her arms folding across her chest with the nerve to glare at me.

"I am fucking serious and don't get any ideas about going outside. You stay in here, I don't care if I'm gone a month, you do not leave. You understand?"

I had no idea what was gonna happen at the meet, but if Franco even suspected I was involved, he'd put a bullet between my eyes and then come for her. And given I had no idea if it was a test or a job interview, I was going to play it on the fly, which meant I might not be back tonight. Or tomorrow.

"Something happened." It wasn't a question; we both knew she was smarter than that.

"Your bounty just went up."

"How much?"

"One point five."

"Million?"

"Million."

There was no benefit to me telling her. In fact, it would probably make my job harder if she became emotional. But I was hoping that her knowing might help her see how serious it was. So that she didn't get the urge to continue to be Dora the fucking Explorer.

"Do you know who?" she asked calmly, like it made a difference who was holding the purse strings.

"I have my suspicions."

"Are you going to share them?" Once again, she kept her voice controlled, non-emotional.

"Franco Santini, you know that name?"

"Of course I do." She nodded. "His family and mine came over on the boat together. He owns a bakery on Michigan Avenue, but his fortune hasn't come from selling cannoli."

"You were investigating him?" It might have been a question, but I was fairly sure I knew the answer.

"Of course I was, he's been indicted three times and nothing has ever stuck."

"Then I would suggest making your peace with *that* and get ready to move to Canada." And even that wouldn't be far enough. "He has operatives in Mexico, so your dad won't send you there."

"I can't run." She shook her head slowly, like she'd come to that realization while sitting like Gandhi on the floor.

"Then you are fucking stupid."

"My dad paid you to protect me, right?" She shrugged like I needed to be reminded of what the hell I was doing here. "So I wait it out here for a while."

"Get your head out of the clouds. Waiting it out?" We didn't have years, and even then I doubted it would be long enough. "You know these people, you think they are going to forget about you next week? I'm not babysitting you indefinitely; I have business to take care of. Besides, I don't need the heat landing on my fucking doorstep."

"So kill me then, collect the bounty, but I'm not leaving." She planted her hands on her hips, tilting her chin in defiance.

"Don't tempt me, Sofia. I'm not a reasonable man." And considering I'd held a knife at her throat maybe twenty minutes ago, not the kind of request you think she'd be making.

"Why? What have I got to lose? I'm dead anyway, right?"

Maybe she was right. I should save us both the time and effort and end it all now.

"I don't have time for this shit," I snapped, needing to get out before I changed my mind. "Stay inside and out of trouble."

I didn't bother with a goodbye. I was still fired up from her sticking her nose into my past and now dealing with Franco. The sooner I was gone, the better for everyone.

"What if you don't come back?" she called after me, her voice missing the panic most people would have saying those words.

"Go to the supply closet and look in the first aid kits. There's a cell phone in one of them. It has only one number on it. Mine. Call me, let it ring three times and then hang up. If I haven't answered, grab some supplies and ammunition and head north."

I tossed the words over my shoulder as I went to leave. "And if I were you, I'd trust no one."

FOURTEEN

MICHAEL

No matter how hot it was in the city, the wind that blew over Lake Michigan was always unforgiving. And today was far from warm.

It had been smarter to boost a car and dump it rather than take the beat-up Chevy, which was exactly what I'd done. Because there wasn't a chance I was giving Franco or his crew a chance to ID anything that could be traced back to the warehouse.

I popped the collar of my leather jacket as I stood on the steps in front of the planetarium, my watch showing four fifty-nine.

"You're early." A voice came from behind me, the owner of it no surprise—Franco Santini.

He was dressed like a stockbroker in a thick winter coat with his trademark fedora, and I assumed his three-piece Brioni suit underneath. He was in better shape than Jimmy, his body and face not looking anywhere close to fifty-five, which is how he got so much pussy. His wife turned a blind eye to Franco's indiscretions, but everyone else knew.

"I didn't take you for the museum type of man." I turned and saw he was alone. Also not a surprise.

Where Jimmy liked to have an army surrounding him,

Franco believed he was God and walked around like he was untouchable. I had no doubt he had men covering us from different angles, probably one with a long range shotgun trained right on my chest. But you'd never know. Like I said— big balls.

"My daughter loves it, about the only thing we have in common. Our love of the universe." He whirled his fingers in the air as he grinned. Although I was sure that his and his daughter's idea of the universe were vastly different.

"Is that what you wanted to talk about?" I smirked, the kid he was referring to absent. "What a wonderful father you are?"

"It seems the theme lately for you, huh?" He laughed, his chin tipping to the pavement indicating we should walk.

Franco didn't like to stand still, and judging by that little quip he assumed I was involved with Jimmy. "Daughters— daughters are trouble. My advice to you if you have kids, have only sons."

Yeah, because having kids of any kind were on my to do list.

"Franco, what is it you want?" I looked him dead in the eye, something I knew men like him responded to.

"I like you, Michael." He continued walking, ignoring the question. "You work hard, stay out of everyone's business. Self-made man."

"And you want something, which is why I'm here." I stopped midstride, at my limit with condescending bullshit as the wind cut through me like a knife. "What is it?"

"Sofia Amaro." He smirked, facing me. "I know you spoke to Jimmy."

"I talk to a lot of people, but like you said . . . I stay out of everyone's business."

"Not what I wanted to hear." The smile curled at the side of his mouth as he moved closer. "You either know where she is or how to find her." His hand clasped down heavily on my shoulder. "You have twenty-four hours to bring her to me, or it will be your head there is a price on."

"I don't have her." I didn't even blink as I lied to his face. "And I don't respond well to threats."

"Oh, no, no, Michael." Franco laughed, his hand digging into his thick woolen coat. "I never threaten. I'm a man of action."

For an older guy, he sure moved quick. Our guns were pointed at one another at the same time. We kept them close to our bodies, the people milling around oblivious they were seconds away from seeing one or two dead bodies.

"Like I said, I don't respond well to threats." I nodded down to the gun in my hand. "So, how about we go our separate ways."

"No." Franco smiled. "Not an option."

"You shoot me and I shoot you, kind of counterproductive, don't you think?" My grip tightened on my weapon as my eyes swept along the people not far from us.

"That we can agree on." Franco smirked. "I have a better idea."

I hadn't seen it coming. Which is why when the hit came to the back of my head, I went down like a sack of shit. I'd been careful, trying to keep my eyes moving, but there was only one of me, and clearly more of them.

My finger squeezed on instinct, a round shooting out of my forty-five before I dropped. Hopefully it caught Santini, but I couldn't be sure; the screams from the crowd were the last thing I heard.

They didn't waste time either, a second blow knocking me to my knees before I'd had time to move or recover.

And just before I blacked out, I remembered staring down at the concrete and Franco's shiny black shoes. Firstly hating it was probably the last thing I was going to see, and secondly knowing that I probably wasn't getting out of this alive.

• • • •

Very slowly my body came back online.

Everything felt wrong.

My eyes were barely able to crack open, the pain of the light so intense I had to shut them and reopen them again so they had time to adjust.

My head tried to toggle from side to side in the hopes of gauging where I was, but no dice, my body protesting at every step with zero cooperation.

My arms and legs had been forced apart but my brain was unable to compute why I was spread eagle and why I couldn't control my limbs.

Underneath me was soft—a mattress of some kind—while the only other thing I could make out was a ceiling fan whirling slowly above me. Its blades moving slower than they seemed they should.

Everything was foggy, like my eyes and brain couldn't focus right, my head felt like it was full of cotton and yet I couldn't lift it from the mattress.

"I've given him the maximum dose." A voice in the distance spoke, "He hasn't cracked. I think we have to accept the possibility he might have been telling the truth."

It sounded so far away, like I was in some kind of tunnel. The noises distorted so I had no idea which direction they were coming from.

"No, he knows where she is, and she needs to be taken care of," Franco's voice countered. "Give him another shot. If he won't talk, I want his mind so fried he doesn't remember this."

"Another shot could kill him."

"Worth the risk."

Intellectually—even without the preamble—I knew I'd been drugged. But my brain was misfiring so much that all

153

intelligent thought went out the window. I tried to will my body to move, but it was like swimming against the tide— nothing. I assumed my arms and legs had been tied but who knew, I could have very easily been tripping out with my incarceration being mental rather than physical.

My skin was hyper sensitive, like it had a million ants goose-stepping up and down my arms and legs, and then I felt a pinch in my forearm.

"No, no, no." I thrashed around as an uncontainable panic overtook me demanding I get my ass off this bed and to safety. "Noooooooooooo."

It didn't even sound like my own voice, the noise ripping apart like it had left my body and was floating above me.

My chest constricted, the expanding of my lungs such an effort that I wasn't sure I could continue the in and out they needed. And even though my eyes were open, I couldn't see a thing.

"He's going to stroke out; you've given him too much."

"He's still breathing."

"Holy shit, his eyes. He's freaking me out."

"Leave him. Get your things and leave."

There was a noise.

Loud.

Like a train thundering down tracks at full speed, but I had no idea where the train was coming from. Desperately, I tried to move but I wasn't sure if the effort I was expending was actually moving my fucking body or I was dreaming it. I was powerless, my heartbeat loud in my ears as I struggled against my body and my mind to get up.

And then it happened.

Everything got quiet.

Still.

And I had a minute of clarity.

This was the fall.

There was a tipping point. A pivotal moment where your body stops pumping blood to where it should and your brain stops firing synapses. And you know you're going to die.

And then you fall into the abyss of the end—the final breath, the final thought—all of it coming at you in a rush of darkness.

Freedom.

I'd imagined this moment a million times over, and in all those scenarios, it had never been this beautiful. My mouth opened, straining as I pushed out my last breath, and I welcomed the blackness.

FIFTEEN

SOFIA

I was never good at doing what I was told.
It was one of the reasons I fought with my father when I was growing up. That I wouldn't sit, be quiet and look pretty like a good little girl.

He hated it.

And I hated being told what to do.

Which is why the minute Michael left the warehouse, I dug out the cell phone. For days I'd had no communication with the outside world and then suddenly, there it was. A connection, something that I could control. But the minute I had the phone in my hands I realized I had no one to call.

No one.

So instead I turned my attention to the computer that was still logged on. The evidence was still on the screen—unlike him to be sloppy—but I guess he'd been in a rush. Either me finding out about his past or my new expensive price tag was probably to blame.

No password was required as I clicked on the computer and I found out more than I'd dreamt possible. He'd been dealing with hackers, using them to procure his information. And then finally I realized what I needed to do.

For reasons unknown—and a huge win for me—he'd left a car behind. An old Chevy was parked out back, the keys still in the ignition. Then it was just a matter of getting his shady contacts to trace his cell and text me the location.

I knew it was dangerous.

That I could potentially be handing myself over on a silver platter, but I couldn't sit still. And more importantly, I wouldn't.

It had been hours since I'd last heard from him. And I knew he would be furious, but something in my gut was telling me I needed to move. And years on the force had taught me never to ignore my gut.

His phone was active, on and sitting in an old rundown motel surprisingly not far from the warehouse. The kind of place that had matted shag carpet on the floor and charged by the hour. There was no clue as to whether he would even be with his phone, or if this was an elaborate decoy, but I needed to find it just to be sure. It was just a matter of narrowing it down to the right room.

I knocked at each door pretending to be a jealous wife, room to room with my Smith and Wesson palmed tightly in my other hand just in case. For the most part I got shouts of "fuck off" till I came to the final door. Corner room, floor level, with its dirty drapes tightly closed even though there was a light on. And when my fist banged at the wood, I received no answer.

The skin on my arms goose bumped as I jiggled the doorknob, hoping I could use my weight to leverage it open, but even with some shoulder action, it stayed firmly shut.

The only option was the window. It was open, just a fraction. Which was just enough for me to get my fingers into it and push it open.

It wasn't easy, the paint around the window frame slowing the slide of the glass, but eventually it gave, allowing me to curve my hand inside and unlock the door.

What I saw when I finally got in would haunt me forever.

Michael was on the bed, tied by his arms and legs, his face angled away from the door. And I had no idea if I had been too late.

"Michael," I whispered, my arms locked as I pointed my weapon into the corners, systematically clearing the room. "Michael." No response.

He was gray, the color bleeding out of him as his eyes rolled back into his head, but he was breathing. Not that he would be for long unless I got him out of there fast and got him some kind of help.

With a utility knife I'd found in the supply closet, I cut the ropes that bound his arms and legs. It was while I was freeing his wrists that I noticed the puncture marks on the inside of his elbow.

"Michael, you need to wake up." My arms wrapped around his torso as I tried to lift him from the mattress. It was like lifting dead weight, his body collapsing against me and pulling him down with me.

I tried again, shoving my nine into the back of my jeans to get a better grip, this time successfully moving him from the bed to the floor but with still no idea how I was going to get him to the car.

"What's going on here?" A large older guy with the shoulder width of a linebacker, a stained shirt and bad attitude poked his head into the room. "We've had complaints about you disturbing our guests."

"My boyfriend just partied too much." I hoped the panic didn't show in my eyes as my hand patted at my waistband at the gun concealed there. "If you can help me get him to the car, we'll be on our way." I had no idea if he was staff or one of the men who had done this to him, but I was willing to take a chance.

He looked us over, his eyes lingering over the rope still

fixed to the bed frame. "He O.D?"

"No, no. He's fine. He just needs to sleep it off." I nodded, going against the screaming instinct inside of me to ask him to call an ambulance and the police. "Please just help me get him into the car."

"You people want to kill yourselves with your drugs and kinky shit, do it in your own place." He sneered as he walked around and helped me lift Michael. "I don't need CSI sniffing around my business. You hear me?"

"I promise we'll leave." I grabbed Michael's legs and helped carry him out.

He didn't talk, just tossed Michael into the backseat of the Chevy and held out his hand expectantly.

"All I have is a twenty." I pulled out a crumpled bill from my jeans, my purse left back at the warehouse.

"Goddamn it." He snatched the money from my hand and slammed the car door. "Get the hell out of here."

I didn't need to be told twice, my ass hitting the worn cloth seat and starting the ignition so fast, I was sure the whole neighborhood heard me leave. So much for being discreet.

"Don't die, Michael," I begged, trying to keep my eyes on the road while glancing at his lifeless body on the backseat. "Please. Just don't die."

I'd been alone for so long, I wasn't afraid of that. But there was something deep inside; I just didn't want him to leave me. I'd finally begun to understand him, work out why he was so cold—the trauma he'd suffered indescribable. And in spite of that, he'd kept me safe.

There was a moan, which was enough for me to know he was still breathing so I kept driving, looking for signs that someone was following us.

Everyone was a suspect, my eyes moving constantly on the road as I did my best to do the speed limit and act normal. And while I was trying to be calm, my heart was beating so hard in my chest it felt like any minute it was going to explode.

Getting him into the warehouse proved to be a challenge. Parking the car around the back, I left him on the backseat while I darted inside to look for anything that could help me transport him. I settled on a wooden pallet with a jack, rolling him out of the car onto the pallet and then transporting him inside.

It had been hours, and still he hadn't opened his eyes.

He mumbled in his sleep but didn't say anything I could understand, his body continuing to move on the mattress restlessly.

Clueless as to what they'd done to him, if he would ever wake up and what they'd pumped into his veins. I worried that whatever had been done, there would be no undoing.

I had no idea what to do. With basic first aid training, this was out of my depth, but calling someone was out of the question. He said trust no one and I didn't. Using my limited resources and knowledge to keep his body going.

His breathing was so shallow I wasn't sure he'd make it back, but thankfully his lungs didn't stop. His pulse while weak also kept thumping, giving me some hope that he was going to pull through.

I spoke to him the whole time, not sure if he could hear me. Praying that my voice would give him an anchor, something to hold onto and pull him back into consciousness. Just words; half the time I wasn't even sure what I was saying, my throat hoarse from hours of unreturned conversation.

"Please, God. Save him." My head fell against my clasped hands, mentally and physically exhausted while I sat beside him. The whole time wondering if he was going to die.

There were no visible signs of trauma and that made it worse, not knowing if there was potential internal bleeding I was missing. All the good intentions would basically amount to naught if that were the case. Hospital was out of the question. So, I kept his body temperature regulated, monitored his pulse and hoped his breathing continued. And prayed that whatever it was they'd given him would eventually work its way out of his system.

It had to.

He looked so vulnerable. His big muscular body prone as it lay on the bed, his face lax with the front of his hair sweeping across his forehead. And while I knew there was man hardened by the life he'd led underneath those closed eyelids, all I could see was that little boy in those photos. His thin face, messy brown hair, and that empty defeated stare.

"Sofia." His voice was so weak I'd almost not heard it.

"Michael?" I sat up, my hand grabbing his, so relieved he was awake I almost cried. "It's me, Sofia."

"I'm alive?" His voice cracked like he was surprised, his eyelid slowly rising as he tried to focus on me.

"Yes, you are. You're safe." I clutched his hand tighter, squeezing it to reassure him. It should have felt weird—holding his hand—but I couldn't make myself let go, like if I did, he would slip away.

"How." He swallowed, clearing his throat before he could continue. "How did you find me?"

"You left in such a hurry, you left your computer logged on." The words tumbled out of my mouth as I watched some focus returning to his eyes. "So I got one of your nice hacker buddies to trace your cell."

I didn't bother telling him that I'd also searched his computer for the files he'd stolen from me while I waited for the trace. Or looked to download any other information that could help me. "I found the old car around the back with the keys still in the ignition. Then it was just a matter of driving to the location they texted me."

Of course, it was a little more involved than that. There had been a lot of curse words, and I'm positive the guy who had helped me get him into the car would talk to anyone who handed over anything higher than a twenty. So how safe we were at the present time I wasn't exactly sure. But I'd save the more detailed version for when he was looking less like a corpse.

"Why?" His brow scrunched in confusion.

It had been the only time I had seen him not look sure, the wall around him cracking a little and letting me in.

"What do you mean *why*? Because you were going to die."

His hand squeezed mine, his strength a fraction of what it had been. "You should have saved yourself and let me die."

"I couldn't do that." I moved in closer, not wanting to stop holding him.

Both his eyes opened, connecting with mine.

"I would have left you."

"I don't believe that." I lied, not knowing if he would have or not. "You're an asshole sometimes, and incredibly rude, but you wouldn't have left me."

His eyelids slowly opened and closed before he refocused on me, his mouth parting like he was going to speak but then he stopped.

For the first time since he'd shown up on my doorstep, it was like he didn't know what his response would have been. He coughed, his voice still hoarse. "I am an asshole and clearly a hard one to kill."

"Agreed." I nodded, not sure how many others would have survived what he just had.

His lips curled into a smile as his eyes closed again. "Tired."

He wasn't out of the woods yet, but I was confident it would be better for him to try to sleep off the rest of the drug, and hopefully I could get some sleep too.

I didn't ask his permission, sliding onto the other side of the bed and laying beside him.

The lamp on the nightstand stayed on, darkness was just something I didn't think either of us could cope with tonight as I pulled the comforter up. I didn't bother changing, staying in my clothes but kicking off my shoes as I settled under the blanket.

My eyes stayed fixed on the ceiling, unable to close. Not that it stopped the flashbacks of the last few days rolling around my brain on a loop. That slideshow was happening whether I wanted it to or not.

This was so not what I envisioned my life to be. Running from everyone, laying beside someone who a week ago I would have been desperate to arrest. There had always been a line. Black. White. Good. Bad. And now those lines were blurred, never to be the same again.

Even though I wasn't looking at him, I could hear his breathing. It was more labored than it probably should be, but steady. And the whole thing made me feel weird. Not in that it felt uncomfortable, but it actually was the opposite. A calm washed over me with each one of those breaths he took, and while it made no sense that it felt good to lay beside him, at that moment there was nowhere else I wanted to be. It wasn't just about keeping myself safe either. It was about him.

Keeping him safe.

And that was something I just didn't understand.

"I can hear you thinking from here, Sofia." Michael's voice was like gravel, the words catching in his throat.

"I don't know who the bad guys are anymore," I whispered back, hating how vulnerable my voice sounded. But I didn't try and hide it, not having the energy to process all of it and pretend I was okay.

"Maybe it's time to stop trying to find them and take care of yourself."

It was words I'd heard from him before but without the usual venom, like there might be some sincerity behind them.

"Aren't you tired of being a part of all of this?" I turned to face him, needing to see him. "Just for a second be real with me, okay? No one will ever know."

"This is who I am, this is as real as I can be." His eyes fixed on me, his gaze sending a shiver down my spine.

That look.

That vacant look of resignation chilled me like my blood was made of ice. Exactly the same look he'd had in those photos when he was a boy, too young to have given up.

"Who is Rose?" It had come out of my mouth before I had a chance to stop it, the words louder than I'd intended them to be.

"My mother." The two words hissed out of his mouth slowly, his eyes closing.

I'd had my suspicions about the word on the back of the holy picture I'd found. Deep down I knew it had been a name. A name I had asked him about and he'd refused to answer.

"Did you find her?" I held my breath, knowing it probably wouldn't have been a happy reunion.

"She's dead." He shook his head, meeting my gaze. "When I was born. I've literally been killing people since the day I entered this world."

I fought the urge to tell him he was wrong, that he had no part in his mother's death, but I didn't. Partly because I knew that no matter what I said, it wouldn't change what he thought, and because I felt like that was a scab I wasn't ready to lift.

"Do you know who she was?"

"I know enough."

And just like that he shut down, the conversation about his

mother finishing before it even really began.

Small steps but progress nonetheless.

His eyes stayed on me, waiting for me to say something else. Like he knew I wasn't done. But I surprised us both by not pushing it further.

"Well, goodnight." I rolled onto my side, my words so benign they were almost ridiculous.

"Goodnight." I felt his body shift on the mattress but he didn't move closer. "It's going to be okay," his voice rasped, softer than it ever had been. "I'll make sure of it."

Something had changed that night. Whether he chose to admit it or not. When this all ended—and it would eventually end—both of us would be walking away different people.

Both better and worse.

SIXTEEN

MICHAEL

I wasn't sure what was more surprising.
That she'd found me or that she'd dragged my ass back here. We both knew that if the roles had been reversed, I would have been long gone. Taken my chances and tried to make it to the border. I still wasn't entirely sure I knew why she hadn't. The cross around her neck probably was a clue. Like maybe saving me would give her extra credit for an afterlife that didn't exist.

She didn't move, her body coiled on its side facing away from me, but I could tell she wasn't asleep. She was analyzing the situation just as I was; knowing that sooner or later our lucky number was going to be up.

Franco wasn't the kind of man who just left unfinished business. And if he hadn't been watching the whole thing unfold from a distance, I'd be very surprised. Which meant he probably knew exactly where we were.

She should have left me.

Whatever had been pumped into me was slowly wearing off, my head starting to gain the clarity it missed after the many hours I'd been out. Unfortunately, my recollection of those hours was still sketchy.

I remembered getting hit; the goose egg at the back of my head was a nice souvenir. But after that it was a bunch of not-really-sure, the mental piece-by-piece probably not going to happen either.

No bones felt broken, so I assumed it had just been drugs. Smart really. I'd taken beat downs in the past and they'd achieved jack shit. It would take more than a ball peen hammer crushing my hand to make me sing. Been there, done that and my left hand still had the kink at the top where the bones hadn't mended right.

Nope, Franco and his crew were more efficient than that, and probably figured they'd save themselves the time and energy. Just shoot me up with what felt like enough sedatives to tranquilize a horse, and *hope* I hallucinated into opening my mouth.

Desperation will make you do stupid things.

And Franco didn't like losing.

I didn't want to sleep, needing to keep alert in case shit went down, but biology took over and the next thing I remembered was waking up alone.

Sofia was gone, the bed beside me empty as I sat up and looked around. The dull thumping at the back of my head reminding me it hadn't all been a dream.

"Hey, I thought you might be able to eat." She waltzed in, her hair wet from a shower I hadn't heard her take. "This stuff is pretty nasty, but if you are hungry enough it will suffice." She held out a steaming brown bag of Beef Stroganoff. "If you eat all of that I'll let you have the M&Ms as well." She grinned, shaking a smaller bag in her other hand.

"I must have hit my head a little harder than I recall, because last I remembered, *I* was telling *you* what to do." I took the MRE and started to chow down. "And if you are going to stand between me and M&Ms, I hope you have more than just a smile to back you up."

"Oh good, you're back to being an ass again." She sat down

beside me, her smile widening. "Looks like you are going to live after all."

"Looks like it," I mumbled between bites. "But all jokes aside, Sofia, this isn't a game."

She might have woken up with a positive disposition, but absolutely zero had changed between last night and this morning. The hailstorm of shit was still going to rain down on us; it was just a matter of when.

"I know." She nodded, her smile fading a little. "And I was thinking about that." She took a deep breath. "I know you aren't going to like it, but I need to go public. The things on that drive, they would assist federal prosecutions. It would lock lots of men away."

Clearly, we both had varying ideas about what keeping alive would actually entail i.e. getting the fuck out of Dodge and keeping her mouth shut.

"Firstly, I've never been a rat and I sure as shit ain't starting now. So, if your plan is to go live on CNN, forget it." I turned and faced her. "And secondly, I may not have a fancy education like you do, but I am assuming the reason you hadn't gone *public* yet is because you didn't have enough shit for an actual conviction." Her face paled as I spoke. "Close enough only counts in teenage sex, and DAs aren't going to waste their time or reputations on it *sorta* looks bad. Don't kid yourself, sweetheart. Those men you are so keen on locking up have deep enough pockets to bury all of that and you unless your evidence is rock solid."

The look on her face told me everything I needed to know. She had a little bit of this and a little bit of that which amounted to *"Hearsay, Your Honor, we would like to petition the court for a shut-the-fuck-up motion."*

"I know I can access what I need if you let me use your computer." Her sideway glance hinted that she was pretty sure that answer would be n-oh. "Those friends of yours, I'm sure they could fill the holes that I have."

I stopped eating, the plastic fork frozen between my lunch-in-a-bag and my mouth. She was actually fucking serious.

"They aren't my fucking friends. I don't have any *friends*." I laughed, her idea so freaking crazy she might as well have suggested infiltrating the Pentagon. "They do work for me, I pay them. It's a transaction."

"If it's money you are after, I can get it for you." She held up her hands defensively. "I have a trust fund I haven't touched. I have money."

"Sofia, if you have a fucking trust fund, why the hell were you renting that shithole you were calling a home?"

"Because it's *his* money." She didn't need to clarify who the *he* was in that statement. "I didn't want it. He signed over control to me before I entered the police academy. I haven't touched a dime of it because I know how he earned it, and there is no way I could sleep at night taking anything from him."

"But you're happy to crack it open for illegal hacking activity." I looked her in the eyes to see if she was serious. What do you know, she didn't blink. "Seems like your upstanding morality has conditions."

Amazing how shit could change once you took the rose-colored glasses off and actually saw the world for what it was. It was a huge contrast to her earlier views and how she'd never be one of *us*. Not that I was bound by the same fucking set of ethics, but she'd been pretty clear on which side of the line she stood.

"It's different." She shook her head, ready to plead her case. "In this instance the money would be used for good. I couldn't think of a better purpose for it."

"And you're totally cool with breaking the law, right?" I

169

pointed out the fucking obvious. "Those guys don't get their information via Google."

"Do you know what this whole thing has taught me?" She waited like I had any idea on what her journey into self-discovery had produced. "That there is a very thin line between good and bad. And maybe sometimes you do something that isn't exactly good, but you need to do it for the right reasons."

"I can't believe you are still hung up on this whole good and evil shit." I couldn't help but laugh. "Do you understand what's at stake? There is only one person concerned about doing the right thing here, and it's not them."

"I know." She nodded, her hand playing with that cross around her neck. "But I need to do this."

Wow, had she not heard a word I said? "My answer is still no, Sofia. I'm not going to help you be a rat. Besides, we have bigger issues right now." I didn't give her a chance to ask; we both knew it was coming so I saved us both the time. "I'm sure me not ending up a corpse was a huge disappointment for Franco; he's doesn't usually leave his toys unattended, so I would imagine he probably followed you."

"No, I was careful." She straightened her back and her head did the tell-me-it's-not-so. "No one followed me, I checked."

I pointed to the back of my head where there was still a decent size reminder on how even I wasn't careful enough. "Do you think they got the jump on me because I had my head up my ass?"

There wasn't a chance to elaborate, my cell phone vibrating, demanding attention.

"Yeah." I gave my standard greeting, the caller ID tipping me off it was Jimmy on the other end of the phone. He sure seemed to find out about shit super quick these days. And I was really getting tired of the micromanagement.

"You're alive." There was a distinct note of dissatisfaction in his voice.

"Awww, Jimmy, and here I thought you cared." The mention of her father's name made Sofia still, her eyes boring into the phone like the connection might give her ears more than what they were getting.

"I need you to meet me."

Words I'd been hearing all too frequently lately.

"Yeah, well I'm not taking any *meetings* right now, so whatever you need to say will have to be over the phone."

"You know that can't happen."

"Need I remind you, Jimmy, that you're the reason that we are where we are?"

Franco knew more than he should which meant someone was talking. Chances are that leak was coming from Jimmy's house, because it sure as shit wasn't mine.

He took a pause, the breath he sucked in causing him to cough. "Where is she?" It sounded like he was trying to kick gravel up his throat. "You need to bring her to me."

"Yeah, because *that* is gonna happen. Think of a different plan." Not a request.

Sofia was getting antsy, one-sided conversations would do that to most people, especially when they knew *they* were the topic of conversation.

"I need a secure line," Jimmy coughed out. "Five minutes, send me a suitable number."

"Will do."

Goodbyes weren't exchanged, both lines going dead simultaneously as I lifted my ass off the bed.

Hmm.

Getting vertical so fast wasn't such a great idea. My arm extended and caught the wall as my feet stayed in the same spot even though I swayed like a tree in the breeze.

"Fuck." I tried again, hoping this time my legs might decide to actually operate.

"Let me help you." Sofia's shoulder shifted under my arm, not waiting for me to accept her offer. "And before you say anything, I know you don't need it, but it will make this go quicker so just let me do it."

I had to hand it to her, she had a point. And I wasn't really in a position to argue. "My desk." The only direction I gave her as we made our way out of the bedroom and into the space next door.

It was interesting I still had my phone, I would have assumed when Franco took my guns he would have taken it too so either he had been sloppy—not likely—or it was part of a grander plan. Either way, the thing was history, the SIM card snapped into two a second after I'd messaged Jimmy some new contact details.

"There's a furnace all the way toward the back, it's in the boiler room. I need you to toss this in and burn it." I handed her the broken SIM and the phone.

"You don't want me around when you talk to him." She took the pieces but stayed where she was standing.

"No, I don't and I also should have gotten rid of this last night, but I had an issue with consciousness so need it taken care of now. You still so sure you weren't followed and everything is fine?"

"Fine." She turned, her dark hair flicking over her shoulder as she moved toward the direction of the boiler room. I had maybe five minutes—ten if she stayed and watched the fucking thing burn.

While my head wasn't pleased with being upright, my body was happier with the change in position. It was also good to have access to a gun again, the forty I had in the top drawer of my desk finding its way into my hand before I had even pulled in my chair. You never knew when the next threat was going to come and that steel against my skin was going to make me feel better than anything else.

As far as secure lines went, my computer was as locked down as I could make it. I was running two fifty-six bit encryption with routers bouncing my IP address every thirty seconds. And one of my newer toys was a program which had end to end encryption on voice and data calls.

I'd barely rebooted when I was alerted of an incoming call, my finger accepting it a second later.

"So talk. And no more surprises."

"He offer you money? Santini?" Even though the call was secure, Jimmy was being cautious. His emphysemic spluttering, the punctuation mark.

"What does it fucking matter?" I couldn't believe he was wasting time with this shit. "I would say what's more important is that everyone seems to know where she is, considering what you hired me to do, that doesn't speak wonders for your housekeeping."

"I'm surprised you didn't take the deal."

"I didn't say there was one."

"You didn't say there wasn't."

"How did he know?" I was done playing this bullshit back and forth, and Jimmy knew a lot more than he was telling. I didn't like surprises and I especially didn't like being blindsided.

"You need to bring her to me, Michael." He took a long raspy breath. "Things have gone further than they should have."

"No offense, asshole but how did you *not* see it going this way? Someone in your camp has been talking out of school." Oh, and he was still avoiding which was starting to piss me off.

"We'll rectify that. Bring me the girl."

The plan had always been to keep Sofia safe until he made

173

other arrangements. Whatever those arrangements would be weren't my concern, that's not what I was hired to do. So bringing her back to her father seemed logical, sensible even, but the timing was off. He'd had days to call me in, and his insistence to have his daughter back seemed too desperate. It didn't sit well in my gut and that had nothing to do with the beef stroganoff I'd eaten for breakfast.

"What did you do?" I asked slowly, the leather of my office chair creaking under curled fists.

"It wasn't supposed to be like this." He sighed, regret not something he was known for.

"Like what?"

"Why did you think I hired you in the first place?" he shot out, impatient I hadn't put together whatever fucking puzzle he'd supposedly given me.

"Jimmy, enough with the fucking riddles." It was my turn to be impatient. "Either say what you fucking mean or get off the phone."

"This was supposed to be done already. The incentive was there. I gave you ample opportunity."

"Sofia?"

"Yes, the bounty on her head? That was my doing," he cursed out with so much annoyance, I could almost feel him in the room with me.

"What. The. Fuck." The headache I had was nothing on what was taking up in my frontal lobe right now. "Why the hell would you hire me—" There was no reason to finish the sentence, I knew why.

It all made sense.

The reason why it was me and not one of his own men who had been tasked with the job. He wasn't worried about loyalty; he was worried about saving face.

Asshole couldn't take care of his own problems so he

needed a fall guy, someone not connected to any family. That kind of thing would have the capacity to make World War III play out on the streets of Chicago. Avenging the death of a child isn't something you can just forgive, not in the eyes of your enemies. It was all about keeping up appearances.

"There was no leak of information, all the players knew the plan except me." I fought the urge to put my fist through a wall.

"I honestly thought the money was going to be enough." His death rattle caused him to pause more than usual. "You had an opportunity for more money than you've ever earned. And I handed her to you on a silver platter. I'd never guess you'd act honorably."

"You motherfucker." I hated to be played, and I was beyond pissed I hadn't fucking seen it. "I've met a lot of pieces of shit in my time, but you take the fucking cake."

"Don't pretend to be offended." Jimmy laughed, like the cocksucker was fucking amused. "This was business. There was no way for me to sanction a hit on my only daughter. Not publically. You honestly think I didn't have the means to protect her if I needed to? It had to be you."

"So Franco was what?" The last time those two assholes were in the same room, three people died. Their vendettas ran deep. "A motherfucking charade? You two hate each other."

"The enemy of my enemy is my friend," Jimmy rasped, his voice getting hoarse from the conversation. "You ever hear that saying? In this instance we needed to work together. Like I said, it was business. But he was getting impatient and thought you needed more persuasion. He was never going to kill you."

Oh, good to know. Because being fucking double-crossed is totally cool as long as the asshole doesn't kill me.

"Go fuck yourself, Jimmy. This isn't how I operate."

"You're right, and maybe I should have been more upfront."

T. GEPHART

He had the nerve to sound apologetic. "Saved the time, but it is what is and I couldn't risk her mother finding out. The shock .. . well, it would kill her and I would already be mourning my daughter."

There weren't a lot of times I'd been speechless, but this was one of those times. Not because of what he was asking me to do. I'd killed for a lot less money and even less motivation. But I was no one's fucking puppet and I refused to have my strings pulled so some asshole sleeps better at night.

"Finish the job, deliver her body and you'll get the money." Jimmy filled the silence when I didn't speak. "It's time this ends."

"And what if I don't?"

"Don't pretend you grew a conscience." His words were slow, breaths jagged as he tried to form the sentences. "We both know you have no soul, why do you think I picked you in the first place? You have a gift, son. You can do what other men are afraid to do. Don't fight your nature and kill her, take the money."

I didn't bother with a response, ending the call with a click of my finger. There was no need to turn around and see Sofia; I'd felt her eyes on me while I was talking. Part of me had wanted her to hear it, wanting her to know that her father thought her life was worth nothing more than a bundle of cash.

"You won't kill me." She came up behind me and rested her hand on the back of my chair. "I know you won't do it."

"You should have run."

The gun in my hand was pointed at her before I'd even realized what I was doing, the barrel pressed up against her stomach. All I had to do was pull the trigger. Just one squeeze, and like Jimmy said, end it.

"You have a soul, Michael." She kept her eyes locked on mine, refusing to acknowledge the gun at point blank range.

"I've seen it. There's good in you. Don't do this."

"If it's not me, it will be someone else. I'll make sure it's quick."

I stood slowly, rising to full height as she stayed in place in front of me. She had to be afraid but she wasn't showing it, her hands idle by each side as I watched.

Never had I seen anyone confronting their death with not even a twitch. And yet, for whatever reason she didn't move a muscle. Like she'd become a statue in front of my very eyes.

Fuck, she was beautiful.

I'd seen it before—the superficial stuff at least, the pretty face, hot body—but it was her fucking courage that was currently giving me a hard-on. In all these years I'd never met anyone so fearless.

"I know you are capable of doing this. Maybe you even want to, but don't." She raised her hand slowly, showing me her open palm before she rested it on my heart. "You have a soul, I promise you."

And fuck me if I didn't want to believe her.

Women had touched me before, but only while I was fucking them and only with my permission. But her hand on my chest didn't feel like that, the connection not sexual. It made my skin heat, and I had no idea if I liked it.

"I don't want to kill you." I meant it too. "But this is who I am."

"No, it's not."

I wanted her to beg for her life. I wanted her to cry and get down on her knees and pray. I wanted to see fear in her eyes. It was what I was used to; it's what was safe. But she wouldn't give me any of those things. And it was scrambling my head so bad I almost wanted to turn the gun on myself.

"How do you know, Sofia?" I grabbed her arm, her skin probably bruising under my fingers. "How do you fucking know?"

"Because you are standing here considering an alternative." She didn't pull away even though I was sure I was hurting her. "Let me be the alternative."

SEVENTEEN

SOFIA

It wasn't easy to hear your own father say he wanted you dead.

I'd always suspected he'd do whatever it took to further his own interests, even if it meant getting rid of me. I just never thought he had the guts to actually do it. Turns out, I was right on that part. He wanted me gone, but he didn't want to get his hands dirty.

But Michael was conflicted. His instincts were telling him one thing while the humanity he'd tried to deny was telling him something else.

And I knew.

In order to save myself, I was going to have to save him first.

I had to believe both of us would make it.

Slowly the gun moved away from my body, his hand still gripping my arm.

"Fuck." He shook his head, and pushed me away. "FUCK!" The chair he'd been sitting in flew across the room in a fit of rage. "Fuck, fuck, fuck." He backed further away, widening the distance between us.

If he was trying to scare me, he was doing an awesome job of it, but my feet refused to move. Watching him freak out in front of me as his body flexed in agitation. His eyes darkened as his hand raked through his hair.

"So, what's the alternative then, Sofia?" He stalked closer, the light catching on the rise and fall of his bare chest. "Because I've got nothing right now."

"My father will assume you'll kill me." I forced my eyes up to his. "So they won't be able to predict what we'll do next."

"We?" He said the word like it didn't quite fit in his mouth, his brows knitting in confusion.

"Yes, we." My eyes connected with his as my hand slowly reached out to his fingers. "Give me the gun, Michael."

"I won't kill you, Sofia, but you aren't getting my gun." He looked down at the forty he was still palming and lowered it onto the desk. "I've not totally lost my mind."

"Well that's a start." I tried to smile, which was ironic seeing as there was little about this situation that was actually funny.

"So, what's the plan?" He folded his arms across his chest and waited for me to respond.

It had been the first time he'd ever asked me for my input, and I had a hunch he didn't make a habit of asking people their opinions.

"Leverage." I pointed to the desk and to the computer sitting on it. "Give me a few days, let me get some evidence together."

"I told you, I won't be a rat." His jaw tensed.

"You won't be, I will." I took a breath. "Not that anyone will actually know it's me, the information will be sent to various sources anonymously. And then I'll disappear. At least then, it will be worth it."

There was no way I could go public, and it had nothing to do with being afraid for my life. Well, not totally for that reason, anyway.

"The information is going to be illegally obtained, which means that unless it's discovered by someone not connected with the investigation, it won't be admissible in court. I'll take myself out of the equation. They may have suspicions, but they won't be able to prove it's me, and by that time I'll be gone anyway so it won't matter."

My father had shown me how to play the system before I'd even learned to drive, but there were two sides to that coin. How we played it now only I would decide. And there would be so much evidence there was no way all of it could be suppressed. Not without a huge public outcry and backlash from constituents.

"And *how* will you disappear?" He smirked, not offering any other commentary.

"That's the *we* part. I'm going to need your help." I bit my lip, knowing there was no way I could do this successfully without his assistance. "I know you hate that I looked at your files." I lifted my hands defensively as I started talking faster. "But you have been living without an identity since you were fourteen. Nothing exists that ties you to the person you once were. Help me do the same."

"You want to disappear?" He stalked closer, watching me intently. "Then you will have to be willing to do things on the other side of the law. You think you can do that? That your God will forgive you?"

"Yes. Whatever it takes." I didn't hesitate.

Whatever I did or had to do would hopefully be justified in the end. It was the only thing that mattered. That one way or another, my life would have meant something. Something good. Something positive. It had to.

"You have no idea what this is going to involve." He shook his head and for a second I was convinced he was about to say no. "But fine, I'll help you."

I could have cried with relief, my body sagging as the tension eased out of it.

"What are we going to do about my father?" The call had been pretty clear and while there hadn't been an agreement reached one way or another, he wasn't the kind of man who liked waiting.

"You better start working your magic; you think you can get what you need in a couple of days?" Michael tipped his head toward the computer. "This isn't going to be cheap either."

"I have my trust fund, I can wire—"

"Paper trail." He shook his head. "You want to disappear, you can't leave one of those. I'll take care of it."

He sat back down in front of the computer, his fingers busy until there was a voice coming through the speakers.

"I take it you've calmed down." My father's voice coughed. "I hope you have good things to tell me."

"Firstly, go fuck yourself, Jimmy," Michael spat back. "You'll hear from me when I want you to. I want access to her trust fund. All of it, and that one point five mil, that's mine too."

"I don't have access to her money—"

"Not my problem," Michael snapped, not giving him a chance to finish. "If you want this done, you'll find a way. My usual account."

"It will take a few days." My father breathed heavily. "And this is already taking longer than I would have liked."

"Then tick-tock motherfucker."

Michael ended the call and then turned to look at me. "Your dad is a cocksucker."

"You'll get no arguments from me."

• • • •

Waiting for the money gave us a small reprieve. Until the sum had been paid, I could legitimately stay breathing. Not the best of circumstances, but you had to find positives where you could.

Initially, I'd been worried my dad would renege on the deal and possibly come up with another solution. It's not like he was honorable or anything. But the one thing my father hated more than losing money was losing face. He'd come up with the idea of neutralizing me, it had been his plan to involve Michael, and if now he had somehow lost control of that—well, there was no telling what the trickle down would do. No. He would play this out—he had to—at least until it became obvious there was no other choice.

Getting the information I needed was like looking for a needle in a haystack. Combing through pages and pages of accounts, transcripts and surveillance footage. Literally piecing together criminal activity in a timeline with a trail of proof. It would take weeks—weeks I didn't have.

Michael didn't say much. I mean he interacted normally, asked me how things were going, but for the most part he let me be. His file had been packed away, or destroyed—he didn't tell me which—but I knew it still bothered him that a part of him had been exposed.

"How long you think we have?" I whispered in the dark.

It was either late at night or early in the morning, I couldn't tell which when he finally walked into the bedroom. He'd usually come in and not say a word, just lie beside me and sleep. But tonight, with the lights off, I didn't feel the barriers there usually were.

"Not long, a day. Maybe two." He blew out a long breath. "I expect he'll send the money soon. After that he's going to want a return on his investment."

I nodded even though he couldn't see me.

"Are you scared?" he asked, his voice turning toward me.

"No." My hand absently went to the cross around my neck.

"Liar." He laughed. "You should be scared. Any sane person

would."

"Are you?"

"No."

"You just said any sane person would."

"I think you answered your own question."

Even though my eyes had adjusted to the blackness, all I could see was his silhouette, the strong lines of his body. His face was hidden in the shadows and somehow that made it easier to talk.

"Do you think you are insane?"

"I've always known I was different. My mind works differently."

"How?"

I didn't expect an answer, but I couldn't help asking.

"When I was fourteen I left the foster family I'd been assigned to. I was done being with people who didn't want me and being around a piece of shit who thought hurting little kids was entertainment. There was a local library that didn't have surveillance cameras. It was warm inside and I didn't have to worry about some pervert trying to rape me in my sleep or stealing whatever I had. First time ever that I could remember feeling safe. I read a lot—newspapers, books, magazines— reading until I couldn't keep my eyes open any longer. Figured if knowledge was power then I wanted as much of it as I could gather."

I stayed silent, pushing aside the questions that were burning through my mind hoping he would keep going.

"Learning wasn't hard for me for some reason. I guess I wasn't as dumb as people had assumed, I used what I'd learned and applied it to the street. I slept in that library for four years before they finally upgraded their security system. By then, I had gotten what I needed and made enough money to get my own place."

"Is that when you went looking for your mother?"

"No, I went looking for her after I killed my last foster father. I wanted to kill her too," he responded with zero emotion.

I gasped. I couldn't help it.

"Yeah, that part didn't make it into the file." He turned, the smile in his voice. "They never connected it to me. He'd deserved it. They had another foster kid living with them at the time—a girl this time—and I'd heard he liked to touch her while she slept. Liked to brag about it when he was drinking at the bar and there weren't many places the asshole liked to drink. I'd been biding my time. As for my mother—the whore who'd brought me into this word—well, she was guilty by default."

"Do you know who your father is?" I winced, wondering if I'd pushed it too far.

"Nope." He answered easily, missing the explosive none-of-your-business I expected. "Some asshole who liked to fuck nuns at Saint Margaret's would be my guess."

"Huh?" My head snapped in his direction. "What?" My mouth was polite enough to leave off "*the fuck?*" that my mind was thinking.

Michael laughed. "Yeah, didn't see that one coming either."

I held my breath as he told me what he knew, honestly expecting at any moment to open my eyes and have dreamt the whole thing. But it wasn't an illusion, his voice steady. How he'd learned years ago the church had hidden her existence, and if not for a well-meaning maintenance man, he would probably have never learned the truth.

It was hard not to feel a connection, knowing that he probably hadn't shared the information with anyone, and yet he was telling me.

He continued to talk, like a seal had been lifted as he purged parts of his past. It was safe in the dark for both of us. Suspended in a state of semi reality, like we were isolated by the moment.

My heart ached as he recounted stories of abuse, his foster father burning his skin with cigarettes. How he'd been beaten and robbed on the streets until he'd found the sanctuary of the library. Never once had he been loved or protected, and I doubt very much he'd even been hugged.

I wanted to put my arms around him, to hold him. To show him what it could feel like, but instead I wrapped my arms around myself, tears prickling my eyes.

When he was done, he asked me about my childhood and I wanted to throw up. How could I tell him I'd lived in a house so big I could ride a bicycle in its interior and not hit furniture? Or that I had been sent to the best private schools money could buy? Or that despite my father being a cold-hearted killer and my mother being a submissive enabler, I'd never been treated badly?

"I'm sorry." It was all I could say, the tears I'd been trying to keep at bay spilling over my cheeks. Ah, crap. I didn't want him to see me cry.

"For what?" he asked, sounding genuinely surprised. "Are you crying?"

"Yes," I choked back, unable to say more. My will to stop wasn't working so there was no point hiding it.

It was so subtle I almost hadn't felt it.

His fingers reached and lightly touched my hand. It felt so unnatural; his body rigid beside me while his fingers gently swept the length of my hand. In his own way, he was trying to comfort me.

That's right, *him* trying to comfort *me*.

And my heart broke all over again.

"I'm not worth your tears, Sofia," he said softly as his hand tightened around my hand. "Don't cry for me."

I didn't ask, probably because I knew he would say no, but I reached out into the darkness and curled as much of my body as I could around his. He stiffened, his breathing becoming more rapid as I moved closer, but he didn't pull away.

"You don't have to hug me back, okay." I sobbed into his chest, the fabric of his T-shirt underneath my cheeks getting wet. "But please don't tell me what you're worth. I still get a say on what I get to cry over."

His hands awkwardly closed around me, absorbing my weight. I knew this was strange for him, he was not used to being held—feeling affection even less—but he didn't turn me away.

My feelings were a mess; my head completely scrambled but there was something there. And as ridiculous as it sounded I cared for him, and for maybe the first time in his life, I wanted him to feel that.

It was insanity.

We were in the eye of the storm, neither of us knowing where or when this was going to end but I needed to hold him, and I needed for him to hold me back.

His breathing deepened, his hand moving slowly against my back. "I thought I'd seen it all," he chuckled, trying to lighten the mood. "But if some asshole told me two weeks ago I'd be lying in bed with Jimmy Amaro's daughter and she'd be crying over me, I'd have told them to lay off the crack."

"Yeah, I'd have probably said the same thing." My head rested against his chest. "That first night, in my head I'd shot you at least three times. Not killed you, somewhere less fatal like your knee caps."

"Well that's disappointing." His fingers continued to trace circles along my back. "When shooting someone, it should always be fatal."

187

"We should sleep." I yawned, unsure of whether or not I should let go.

I didn't want to, needing all the comfort I could get.

"So sleep," he said, his hand staying where it was.

I forced my eyes shut and concentrated on my breathing. Morning would come soon enough and bring with it reality. I wasn't sure if we'd ever have this moment again, or if I wasn't dreaming it in the first place but for now we were both alive and safe.

"If you need to leave, please wake me," I mumbled, wondering if the minute I fell asleep he would disappear.

"Haven't got anywhere to be until tomorrow night. Go to sleep."

"Where are you going tomorrow night?" I fought against fatigue, my eyelids falling shut while I tried to stay awake and listen.

"Something I need to do, it will help with your dad."

"How?"

"Trust me, it's one of those things you aren't going to like."

My mind was too foggy to process what that meant. It didn't sound good and I probably shouldn't have asked. But I couldn't make my mouth say the words, so instead I let it go.

All of those concerns would be there consuming my tomorrow; I wasn't going to give them tonight as well.

EIGHTEEN

MICHAEL

"**Hey baby, you looking for a good time?**" Cecile leaned in on the open window of the car. "Oh hey, sugar. You looking for a repeat?"

I had never fucked Cecile. I preferred my hookers less diseased and not resembling a corpse with fake tits, but hey, not everyone is as picky about what the hole looks like when they stick it in.

I'd procured her services a few weeks ago, a classic sex in exchange for information. She was too high to remember it hadn't been my dick buried in her. Worked out well actually.

"Yep, you want to take a ride?" I flashed the small cellophane bag of coke between my fingers, giving her a smile. "I brought party favors."

"Ohhhh yeah." She opened the door and threw herself into the passenger seat. "Whatever you want." She snatched the cellophane bag before I'd even eased away from the curb.

Sadly for Cecile, this wasn't going to end well. She was about the same height as Sofia, and if she hadn't been a crack whore, she might have even had similar features. She was also about two hits away from finding her own way into her coffin, so really helping her along was just a public service.

Her arms and legs were covered in scratches and puncture marks, most of which had scabbed over while still leeching blood at the edges. She also had a solid case of the shakes, so it had been a while since her last hit, something she was in the process of fixing as she took large inhales of the fine white powder.

"Wow, I needed that." Her hand brushed against my thigh as her head fell against the headrest. "I'll do whatever you want me to do."

"We're just going to drive for a bit."

She shrugged, her finger digging into the little baggie a few more times as I drove toward the airport. Not once did she ask where we were going or what we were doing, and to be honest, I doubted she cared.

"Hey do you have anything to drink?" Her head lolled to the side, her pupils dilated.

"No, but we can get something later."

We pulled into an industrial estate, not far from the warehouse, the road too well lit for what we needed. I eased the car up behind a dumpster, putting it in park and engaging the emergency brake.

"Okay." Cecile looked around and nodded, the surroundings not unlike other places she'd probably been asked to perform. "This is fine."

"Give me your arm, Cecile."

She didn't hesitate, outstretching her arm as she leaned back into her seat, her eyes in a dead stare.

"Just going to give you a little sweetener." I pulled out the syringe from the glove compartment; her head nodding like an excited puppy.

It was hard to find a vein, most of hers blown out and collapsing as the needle hit them, blood trickling out of the tiny pricks I'd made from unsuccessful attempts.

"My toes." She slid out of her worn patent leather stilettos and shifted in her seat. Her foot landed in my lap as her head rested on the passenger side window. "I think there's a good one near my little toe." She wiggled her pink stubby digits, the red nail polish covering them cracked, hiding the dirt that was living underneath.

She was right, there between her last two toes was a viable vein, or at least one I hoped would hold up so I could pump in the drug. After that—well, after that, she wasn't going to have much use for any of them.

My thumb compressed against the plunger. The dirty liquid filled her, the mix of Heroin and Fentanyl lethal enough to kill someone twice her size. Her coke appetizer would hopefully speed things along but then you could never tell with junkies. Their meth-filled bodies outliving cockroaches.

It didn't take long, her arms twitching a little as her eyes glassed over and then finally her eyelids started to droop, her breathing starting to slow down.

"Won't be long now, Cecile." I moved her foot out of my lap and recapped the syringe, carefully wiping any fingerprints off.

A used needle wasn't going to raise any alarm bells on this side of town, but I didn't need anything tying me to it.

"Thank you," she whispered, her face losing muscle control. "T-th-annn-k yyy-ouuu."

Maybe she knew I was ending the cycle, that this was going to be the last time she was going to have to get into a car with a stranger because of her habit. Before meeting Sofia, I wouldn't have cared. But watching her die, I felt like in a way I was setting her free. And as fucked up as that sounded, I felt a weird sense of calm in that.

Her eyes closed as her body twitched in the seat, but it wasn't long before that stopped too.

And then nothing.

Her lungs and heart stopped fighting as whatever little color she'd had drained from her pasty skin.

It was over, just as quick and easy as I'd hoped.

I rearranged her back into her seat and fastened her seatbelt. For anyone who happened to glance our way she looked like she was sleeping. Then I started the ignition and drove back to the warehouse.

The roller door rose with a hit of the button, the car moving quickly inside before I let it slide back down behind me. The next part of this operation needed to be done in private.

"Hey, honey, I'm home." I slammed the door of the car, leaving Cecile in her seat. Rude of me, I know, but she was too dead to complain.

When we woke up this morning, we didn't really talk about what happened last night. Hell, I wasn't even sure what happened last night. I had gone into the bedroom with no intentions other than to go to sleep. It had been a long ass day and the last thing I wanted was conversation. So why the fuck it ended up like an episode of *Dr. Phil* was a complete mystery. Still don't know why, because me talking about my past has happened exactly zero times before. But fuck me it felt good. Almost too good, which is why this morning we went about our business like I hadn't held her all night.

Sofia had probably been at the computer most of the day, not having a problem dealing with my online *helpers* even though it was clearly crossing the line of legality.

"You're back." She looked up and smiled, her hair curled into a bun at the back of her neck as she tapped away at the computer. "You do whatever it was you needed to do?"

"Yeah, I did." I took a seat on the fold-up chair beside her, wanting to get a little closer. "It's gonna take some extra work to prepare, but I think we can make it convincing. I'm going to need some hair, maybe a little blood from you though. And a shirt you don't mind losing."

"What for?" She stopped typing, her eyes narrowing.

"Michael, what did you do?"

I figured the way the color was draining from her face she already knew.

"I told you there would be hard choices, Sofia. Your father wants a body; I'm giving him one."

Her hand went to the cross that hung around her neck, her eyes closing. "No. Not like this. I don't want to be like *him*."

She was always going to struggle; she was deluding herself if she thought any different, but the only way out was to get dirty.

"You aren't like *him*. Your father—that cocksucker wouldn't have cared. So, even though this isn't who you are, know it's what you needed to do."

Circumstance was the biggest motivator I knew. It had shaped outcomes almost every day of my life. And I wasn't going to feel bad about it. It showed me exactly what I was capable of; hopefully it would do the same for her.

"Where did you get a body?" She hesitated through the words like she was forcing herself to say them.

"Really?" I cocked my head to the side wondering if she was honestly asking *that* question.

"Please tell me you didn't kill anyone." She looked down at her hands and held her breath.

"I did, but trust me I was doing her a favor." I had no inclination to lie to her, and not because I was trying to be an asshole either. It was different, like she deserved the truth from me. She'd earned that. "She was going to die anyway, but my way made it peaceful for her. She was thankful; I know you can't understand that, but she was. I gave her the out she needed, and she gave it to you."

"I-I." She stopped, taking a mouthful of air before continuing. "I hate that you killed for me. I hate . . . I hate so much." Her head fell forward, resting against her chest. "I hate all of this."

"Hate is powerful, Sofia, but it's more reliable than any other emotion you're going feel." I'm not sure why but my hand reached for hers, my fingers squeezing tight. "Don't fight it; accept it. Let it carry you, because I guarantee, it will get worse before it gets better. I told you this wasn't going to be pretty."

She wouldn't look at me, her eyes scrunched as I tightened my grip on her hand. "Remember *why*, Sofia. Remember why this is happening and what your alternative is."

She'd proven she was tough, and she had earned a truckload of respect from me by the way she'd handled herself. But I didn't know how much more of it she was really going to be able to take. She had broken down last night—no judgment because most people would have cracked days ago—but seeing her like that stirred something inside me. Not sure if I liked it and I sure as fuck didn't understand it.

I could see the war being waged in her head. Her muscles clenched as whatever argument took place continued. If she wanted to live, she was going to have to fight. And there was only one person who could convince her of that, and it couldn't be me.

"I can do this. I can do this," she whispered, blowing out a long breath like that decision had been made, her eyes meeting mine. "I want to see her."

Instinct told me that was a bad idea, but I saw no point in hiding. Maybe it's because of the way she looked at me, like I wasn't a monster. And the unexplained need I had to prove that I was.

"She's in the car."

Sofia pushed herself out the office chair and waited for me to take the lead. She followed me close behind to where the car was parked, her feet keeping up and showing no hesitation.

The bright overhead halogen reflected off the windshield making it difficult to see her face. From the angle we were standing it looked like she was just sitting there, waiting for her door to be opened, her thin, wasted body fixed in the seat by the seatbelt across it.

"You knew her?" she asked, moving to the passenger side door. "Or was she just some random girl?"

"I knew her; she didn't know me." I wasn't trying to be cryptic, but it's not like we had been BFF's or anything. "She is about your height and age. Chances are no one is going to look closely enough, but if they do we want them to think it is you. I figure if we mix her bone fragments with your DNA it will be convincing enough. Your dad isn't going to be able to submit samples to a government lab, so we don't have to worry about it too much."

Hell, he'd be pissed as fuck that I destroyed her body but that would be easily explained. He hadn't specified how he wanted the body, just that Sofia's remains had to be returned. Maybe she struggled, gun went off and she was shot in the face. Or maybe his fucking don't-kill-her-no-I-mean-kill-her routine pissed me off enough that this was what he got. It didn't matter to me, there wasn't going to be any customer satisfaction survey at the end of it.

"You're going to burn her." It wasn't a question; she continued to look through the closed side window.

"He wants something to bury; I'm going to give him that."

Her eyes got glassy as her lips pressed into a thin white line.

There was no need for words, her body told me everything she needed to say. She hated what I was about to do, her arms were folded across her chest so tight I was sure I could hear her bones protest.

"I never really cared about what happened," I said,

watching her body tense as I spoke. "To the bodies. But trust me, this is far better than what she would have gotten, and her end was coming fast."

"You don't know that, you can't have known that." She didn't move, her feet stuck on the floor beside the car.

"Yes, I do. Life is predictable for people like her. Hell, even for people like me. She was hooked on drugs, selling her body, and not because it was her choice. It was here or a dumpster. A few months difference, but the result would have been the same."

She sighed, taking a deep breath while her hands dropped in front of her and knotted at the fingers. "Do you need help? I mean, you're doing this for me. I should. I mean, I don't know—"

"No, I'll do this alone." Her eyes clocked mine and the relief was immediate.

She might have been offering help, but neither of us wanted her hands on this. Her, because she was worried about sleeping at night knowing what she did, and me because I preferred to work alone. Or at least, that is what I told myself.

It was getting harder not to care about Sofia, harder to keep the distance between her being a reason for a payout and because I didn't want her to end up like Cecile. It felt like putting on a suit jacket—the thing fit weird and was tight in all the wrong places. The suit and the feeling weren't good for men like me. It could only mean bad things.

"Turn around, Sofia, go back to the computer."

She waited, tossing up whether or not to argue because I'd told her what to do or stay to prove a point. "Okay, I'll be around if you need me."

It was a throwaway line, something people said to each other. Like housewives who saw each other in grocery stores and "promise to catch up" with no intention of ever doing so.

But I hadn't *needed* anyone in a very long time, and that wasn't going to change tonight.

"Mmhmm." I didn't bother to correct her, watching her turn around and leave. The soles of her sneakers barely made a sound as she about faced and headed back to where'd she came.

"Alrighty, Cecile. Time to get this show started." I yanked open the door and looked at what we had to work with.

An open fire wouldn't get near hot enough to do the kind of damage I needed. And given I didn't have a crematorium stashed out the back, I'd have to make do with the next best thing.

There was maybe an hour or two before shit got critical. There was no hard and fast rule for rigor mortis, and the last thing I needed was to have to hack up the body because I had pissed away time getting philosophical about what the fuck I was doing.

I snapped off her restraint and lifted her out of the seat, carrying her through to the back door. Right to where a rusted-out fifty-five gallon drum was sitting on two cinder blocks.

Burn barrels weren't a big deal, especially in an industrial part of town and as long as you didn't have it going when business hours were on, most people in the vicinity turned a blind eye. Last thing those bastards wanted was the EPA poking its nose into their business, my redneck incinerator, small fry.

Nothing destroys evidence like a fire— not burying it, not tossing it in Lake Michigan, and not hiding that shit in the woods. Eventually, it all came back to bite you in the ass, which is why that rusted out piece of metal was more reliable than the new school methods. Just had to have some holes in the bottom, a generous amount of accelerant and a slight downwind to keep the smoke moving.

She folded easily inside, her body collapsing on itself like a broken rag doll as her weight hit the bottom of the barrel.

It was the first time I ever really looked at her face, knowing I was going to be the last person to see her. I'd never thought about that before, or more importantly cared. But this time was different, her death different than the others. It shouldn't matter; the end came for all of us. But this was the first time the fall would be painless, and I wasn't sure if that said more about her or about me.

I shook off the feeling and continued with the process. Next was the kerosene. While most people went ahead and used gasoline, dumbasses didn't realize they could easily head to a camping store in the winter, pick up a reasonable amount of kerosene and not attract so much as a sideways glance. Shit is also more stable laying around, provided it didn't get too close to a match, which was where it was heading today.

Her skin was shiny with sweat with her hair pasted against her face. The moonlight made the parts of her that were exposed shimmer like an oil slick. Which was sort of the point I guess, the match tossed in as I gave her one last look.

She burned.

Her skin tightened against her skeleton as it crackled and then dissolved, the fire consuming her from the outside in. I sat and watched the entire time, listening to the hiss of burning flesh, as the hours passed and she was reduced to bones.

Sofia didn't come out. Whether she'd given up and gone to bed or stayed by the computer, I'd have to wait another few hours to find out. And part of me was annoyed that I'd even bother to care.

Problem was, it wasn't just thinking that had been my problem the last day or so. It was a gnawing feeling deep inside of me which was giving me the scratch. Which is why I was forcing myself to sit outside until the end. Gather what was left and let that toxic smell of burn get so far up my nasal passage, hopefully my brain would kick in.

This was who I was.

This is what I knew.

Not soft and fucking compassionate.

And I needed to remind myself.

Even if a part of me was fucking twisted in wanting what I couldn't have.

•••

She was asleep when I came into the room. The lamp on the nightstand was still on, the pale yellow glow throwing shadows across the drywall as I moved. Even the sound of my boots dropping on the floor didn't get so much as a twitch in my direction.

I'd had to wait until the barrel had cooled a little and with some help from some heavy-duty gloves, I retrieved enough of Cecile to pack into an old coffee can to repurpose as Sofia. I'd add some necessary DNA in the morning—make that later in the morning—so if old man Jimmy swabbed it with a who's-your-daddy-DNA kit, it would show enough markers to convince him it was his dearly deceased kid.

I'd hit the shower, the stench so deeply ingrained I'd have to gargle a gallon of bleach just so I wouldn't smell it anymore.

I didn't bother with the redress, slipping into the sheets in my boxers. Sofia hadn't moved, her body curled up on itself as she laid on her side facing the opposite direction.

Fuck, it was next level fatigue washing through my body. Like I hadn't slept in a week and it wasn't just physically. The fucking gray matter up in my cranium was in a serious need of a reboot too.

Too wired to sleep, my head hit the pillow but my eyes stayed open. While I had been doing my burn-baby-burn outside, Jimmy had managed to funnel Sofia's trust fund into my offshore account. Either that or he gave up totally and coughed up the total himself. Paying the grand sum of three point seven million dollars, which was exactly the amount Sofia had told me was in her account. Interest had been favorable which had inflated the initial figure, not that it mattered now. The money would cover her extensive hacker habit as well as get her a new identity, the falsified documents coming her way would stand up to even an FBI analysis.

"Is it done?" Her voice croaked, her body remaining in the same position.

"I thought you were sleeping?" My fingers linked behind my head, anchoring at the base of my skull.

"Off and on." She flipped over, her bloodshot eyes needing a good dose of Visine. I doubted much sleep had happened. "Is she . . . all gone?"

"Yes."

There was no point elaborating, and for reasons that bewildered the shit out of me, I didn't want to. All part of that see-saw mind fuck I had going on which seemed to get foggier the more time I spent with her.

She closed her eyes, absorbing the word as her face tightened under the tension. My head turned, studying the lines in her forehead as she lay there silently.

"Your dad came through on the cash too, so it looks like tomorrow will be show time. We can stall for maybe another day but that's as far as we can push it."

"Whatever we need to do." Her lids slid open and she looked at me, those fucking eyes nailing me from across the other side of the mattress. "If I'm dead, who will I be?"

"Sarah Lopez. Always good to go for a first name that is sort of similar so you maintain some recognition but not so similar people make a connection. And you also got a new nationality. Congratulations, your family is from Juarez, Mexico, but you're moving to Toronto because you can't stand the heat."

"Wow, that's pretty detailed." Her eyes widened, clearly surprised the details had been fleshed out already. "I figured I'd have a say. I'm not trying to sound ungrateful, but I have to be this person for the rest of my life."

Ordinarily I wouldn't have bothered with the conversation. She didn't have the luxury of choice. What she had was one fucking lifeline, and if she didn't like it, there was the door. But instead of telling her all of that, I shocked us both when my mouth opened and started talking. "Sofia, you'll still be you inside. Does it really matter what your driver's license says?"

"No, I guess not," she sighed, my point made without the preamble. "How am I going to get new ID, a trip to the DMV is going to be out."

"There's a Polack out in New York. He's not cheap but he can provide full documents. He's good. *Really* good, and he knows it which is why he charges premium. Not the kind of guy you go to if you want to go out underage drinking, but if you need to skip the country or—" I tipped my head toward her, "become someone else, he's your man."

"He can make me disappear?" A mixture of pain and hope flooded her eyes.

"Yes, he can."

"What about you? What will you do?"

"I disappeared a long time ago."

I hadn't meant to do it. My brain tried to tell my body to stay on my side of the bed and mind its own fucking business, but my arms pulled her in anyway. She came willingly, her warm body up against mine before I could stop it. Not that I wanted it to stop, even though I knew that I fucking well should.

She didn't hesitate, laying her head against my bare chest as my fingers found their way into her hair. "If I could change this, I would," I whispered against her forehead.

The gasp could have been from either of us, my behavior so far from the norm I wasn't sure I knew myself anymore. But more than just those words, I actually meant them as well. And as much as I wanted to front, shit had most definitely fucking changed. And I actually gave a shit about what happened to her.

It wasn't about getting laid either. While Sofia had a body that made the front of my jeans tight, I could go work out that urge with anyone else in a heartbeat. Fuck, I could have done it tonight easily. But Sofia stirred something inside me that couldn't be eased by a blowjob.

"Michael." Her head tilted back as her lips parted, a rush of air pushing past.

"Shhhh, Sofia." I brushed my fingers over her lips, unable to stop what was about to happen. "It's too late now."

NINETEEN

SOFIA

His mouth was on mine before I knew what was happening. His lips taking what they wanted as his tongue explored my mouth. He wasn't gentle, his hands moving against my body as he pulled me closer possessively. It was raw and hurried, a need burning inside us both as my body responded to him.

I didn't think, rocking against him, unable to get close enough. My head was telling me this was all wrong, but I had no interest in listening—I couldn't listen—the fear, the anger, the emotions of the past week ripped through me demanding some relief.

The kiss sent us spiraling out of control, our hands clawing at each other like savages as the insanity of our situation boiled over. I wanted him, and I wanted him to take me. We needed this, to feel alive even though it would solve nothing.

He wasn't the kind of man I'd ever entertain giving myself to. Hell, if anyone else had pulled that shit they would have met the business end of my Smith and Wesson and given a lead last meal. But with him, I felt powerful. There were no victims in this bed; we were equals.

My fingers dug into his skin but he didn't flinch, instead he held my head as his lips were hungrily seeking mine like no one else existed.

In truth, no one else did—not even us.

He wasn't gentle, clawing at the T-shirt I'd worn to bed and ripped it off, tossing it to the ground. His hands returned to my naked skin as I desperately sought the closeness. Needing his touch, needing to feel a connection and to feel something tangible right now.

My back arched off the mattress, pulling my mouth away from his, the intensity lighting my skin on fire.

"You want this?" His lips moved down my neck. "And I'll know if you're lying, so don't bother."

He didn't stop but he was giving me an out, a chance to say no even though I could tell he wanted this as much as I did.

"Yes," I moaned, the one word the permission he needed.

He rolled me onto my back and pressed his weight onto me, his arousal hard against my stomach as my legs scissored apart trying to seek the friction I needed.

"You're fucking beautiful," he growled, his fingers wrapping themselves around the sleep shorts I was wearing. "This isn't going to be gentle."

"I know."

He wasn't kidding, taking my shorts and panties off roughly at the same time and tossing them onto the floor. He didn't bother to slow down, his hand going straight to the juncture between my legs and pushing a finger inside.

"This is how it is with me." He looked me dead in the eye as his thumb rubbed against my clit. "And I've wanted to fuck you for awhile."

His boxer shorts were the next thing to go, one hand whipping them off while his other stayed busy against my core.

He was heavy on me but I didn't ask him to move, his legs pinning my thighs open as he took his hard cock and guided it into me.

It was fast; pushing himself deep before I was fully ready, filling me completely as my body shook underneath.

I cried out, my body struggling to accommodate him as he thrust again, his powerful muscular arms punching either side of me as I writhed underneath.

He bowed his neck down and caught my mouth with his, kissing me as his hips swung again, my hand wrapped around his torso as my body responded to his.

There was nothing romantic about it; he was raw power as the muscles in his abs flexed as he moved against me. Surging faster and faster as if he was in a race against himself.

I was hot, slick and needy for release as my hips bucked against his, the touch of his skin on me making me feel more alive than I'd ever been.

It was too much, the desperation building inside me quickly until in a blind rush it exploded, every cell in my body tingling as the waves rushed through me.

A second later he'd found his own release, his body shaking as the tension in his face bled out. His eyes softened as they looked down at me, his skin glistening with a thin veil of sweat.

We didn't talk, our chests heaving in and out as we tried to rein in our breathing.

I couldn't look away; he was beautiful in this light. The soft glow of the lamp beside us danced against his slick skin, the scars and marks reduced to shadows, and without his usual scowl, he looked almost kind.

The heaviness had disappeared, the lines from his forehead relaxed. Like at that moment, he wasn't fighting whatever war he usually was and he was still with me.

Before I could stop myself, I raised my hand to his face, my palm flattened against his cheek. He hadn't shaven in over a day, the hair prickling my skin as I slowly moved against him, his eyes widening as I continued to study him.

"Why are you looking at me like that?" His brow creased as he shifted.

"Your face . . . it just looks different." I swallowed the rest of the sentence, not sure exactly how the words would be received. I assumed telling him I thought he looked beautiful wouldn't be seen as a compliment.

"Yeah, well. It's the same face it was last week." He pushed off me in a hurry and landed flat on his back.

"I know, I just meant . . . you looked happy?" I hadn't meant it as a question, but once again words were not my friends. I felt like if I said anything too observant he would spook.

"Don't." His face hardened as the darkness returned.

"Don't what?" I asked, turning onto my side to face him.

"Whatever you are thinking right now, just don't."

It was like whatever door had opened, slammed shut and took with it everything that felt good.

"I wasn't thinking anything," I lied, trying to smile. "But it's okay to admit you enjoyed the sex. I did too."

His body visibly tensed, like he wasn't sure if I was feeding him a line or baiting him for a response. In truth, I wasn't trying to do either. I craved the closeness, needed the connection even though I knew it wouldn't lead anywhere. I wanted to have the night, to feel good again. And as dumb as it sounded, I wanted the same for him. To connect with him in the only way he'd let me.

"Is that so?" His brow rose, while his mouth twitched at the edges, hinting at a smile underneath.

"Yes, I would have thought the orgasm was enough of a clue." I smirked back.

Okay, so I wasn't entirely honest, but if I told him exactly how I felt, he would read it completely the wrong way.

I didn't have my head in the clouds, planning the seating arrangement of our fictional wedding, but I wasn't the type of girl who slept with a man she didn't care about either. And I cared for him. As much as I didn't understand why, I really, *really* cared for him.

"You going to freak out if we do that again?" His hand stretched out, his knuckle grazing my belly.

"The sex, or talk?" I cocked my head off the pillow, interested in where this was going.

"You know I hate to talk."

"I'm not a china doll, Michael. You won't break me."

"Good, because I don't want to."

Was he still talking about the sex, or was he saying something else? Short of driving myself insane dissecting the sentence, I decided he meant the sex. He wasn't gentle and I could tell part of him was still holding back. But his darkness didn't scare me.

"You won't."

With a nod he shifted closer, and I was surprised at how much I wanted this. No victims, remember? And I wasn't going to start acting like one now.

••••

I lost count of the times we reached for each other—three, maybe four—but the last time it had been different. Maybe it was fatigue, both of us worn out, but he was slower, more deliberate than he'd been before.

He wasn't holding back either. He was still just as raw as the first time, but different. Like he was giving me more of himself, and whatever mask he'd been wearing was well and truly off.

When I looked into his eyes, I saw him. I saw who he was, not who he thought he'd become, and I saw kindness. There was humanity in him, there was good in him, and he had to have felt it too. The layers slowly stripped away from both of us.

I don't remember deciding to fall asleep, I don't remember wrapping myself around him, but I do remember feeling calm and safe as my eyes slowly began to close. We were naked together—it had nothing to do with our state of undress—and no matter what the consequences were tomorrow, I wouldn't regret it.

TWENTY

MICHAEL

Consciousness came at me in a rush.

Like I'd been kicked in the ass, my eyes flew open while my spine felt like some asshole had it hooked up to a car battery.

I was holding her.

Not just holding her, but our bodies were so intertwined in a twist of limbs that I wasn't sure where mine ended and hers started.

Her hand was resting on my chest, and I could feel her hot breath blow out of those puffy pink lips as she slept soundly.

This shit was out of control.

It wasn't the sex. Hell, if all that had happened was fucking, I could have lived with it. Two consenting adults, and even though circumstances weren't great—no harm, no foul.

But we hadn't been just fucking.

Nope.

Fuck knows what the hell I'd been thinking, but my last few interactions with Sofia had been far too close. And the sex— that just sealed the deal and put me into a sea of what-the-hell- was-I-doing that spelled a world of trouble.

Edging her off me, I moved off that bed so fucking fast, the indent of my body was still left on the mattress. I needed away from it, away from her, as my throat constricted and I felt like I was going to be physically sick.

The same hands that had been minutes ago palming her tits, slammed the bathroom door and locked it as my vision started to go. My chest expanded and contracted like it was supposed to, but the amount of air I was getting not enough to keep me conscious. What the fuck was going on? My fucking body swayed like a big ass tree about to go over until my hands hit the wall to stop it.

Not good.

My legs couldn't be trusted to keep me upright so my ass hit the toilet just in case. Splitting my head open on the sink because I'd fainted like a pussy wasn't happening. It was bad enough I felt like I was having a heart attack, I didn't need a concussion as well.

"Michael, are you okay?" She knocked at the door, her voice faint against the wood.

I had no idea if she was whispering or something had fucked up my hearing, but none of it was registering.

"Go back to bed, Sofia." My head fell against my open palms as the useless airbags in my chest did the best they could to keep me breathing. "Just . . . go to sleep or something."

"If you're sick, I can help you." She stayed at the door, not listening to a word I'd said about leaving me the hell alone.

"I don't need help, go back to bed," I shot out, hoping that this time she'd take the hint and go back to sleep. It was bad enough this shit was going down in the first place, I didn't need an audience.

"O-kay," she agreed reluctantly. Either that or she was saying whatever she thought I wanted to hear and was camping outside the door. Now that I thought about it, the second option was probably the most accurate one.

What the hell was I doing? And why the hell did I care so much? My head had gotten so fucking messed up lately, I was forgetting that guys like me didn't get to be with women like her. Not because she was too good for me, because I didn't subscribe to that bullshit stereotype. But because guys like me had no fucking future. Not one we could offer anyone.

And not that it fucking mattered because in a day or two, she was going to be history and then what was I going to do? Cry into my fucking Wheaties like a fucking five-year-old? Please.

"You're breathing too fast, you're going to hyperventilate." Her voice came from beyond the door.

See, option number two. I knew she hadn't left.

"I'm fine, Sofia." I gritted out through my clenched teeth.

"No, you aren't. You are having a panic attack," she responded, like she was the all-seeing oracle and knew what the hell she was talking about.

"I don't get panic attacks, so stop trying to WebMD me."

Panic attack? If anything I was having a heart attack, which was completely inconvenient and needed to rectify itself pronto.

"Open the door, Michael," She called out, not willing to let me die in fucking peace.

"Jesus Christ, woman. Can't you just let it go?" My hands fumbled with the lock and tossed open the door. It was either that or listen to her bitch through wood, and I knew she wasn't giving up.

"You don't believe in Jesus Christ." She folded her arms across her chest. The chest that had previously been naked was now wearing one of my T-shirts. "Now put your head between your knees and slow down your breathing." She took a step forward, crossing the threshold into the bathroom while keeping her eyes pinned on me.

"No offense, but I'm not in the mood to attempt to give myself a blowjob." I nodded toward my dick. I hadn't bothered with pants, being too caught up with getting the hell off the bed and into the bathroom to worry whether my cock was covered.

"Then concentrate on your breathing. In for three, then out for three." She demonstrated, puffing out her chest as she took a mouthful of air and then slowly blew it out.

My breaths started to mimic hers, keeping time with the long ins and outs, and what do you know? The pain in my chest started to ease, with my heartbeat slowing down as well.

"It wasn't a panic attack." Three in . . . three out. "I must have inhaled too much smoke or something before I came to bed."

"Right, because smoke inhalation takes hours to show up." She rolled her eyes, not buying what I was selling.

"Fine." The word fired out of my mouth. "I woke up with you all up on me and I didn't like it. Whatever is happening between us can't happen."

"It's too late for that," she hissed, not backing down.

And fuck me, she was right. Damage had already been done. Exhibit A was that I was in the fucking bathroom having the conversation in the first place with exhibit B being I'd not only agreed to spare her life—going against everything I'd ever done—but was helping her do the *right* thing.

"Tomorrow I'm delivering the bones to your father. What happens after that I have no fucking idea, but I know that you can't be part of that equation." She lifted her hand as if to protest but I cut her off. "Don't get defensive; the only way I can do this is alone. I know you don't understand that, but it's not because I don't care, Sofia. You were right, it's too late. But I know that if you are with me, you are constantly going to be looking over your shoulder. Only one of us died tonight, don't toss away your free pass to be with me."

She opened and shut her mouth a few times before she

finally settled on what she was going to say. "Whatever I decide, it should be my choice."

"Not if it involves me."

Her face pinked like she'd been slapped, her feet taking her back out the doorway.

"I'm not asking you for anything." She wrapped her arms around her chest, her body dwarfed by my shirt. "I'm not expecting you to change."

"Yes, yes you are." My eyes nailed hers as I stepped closer. "You think this is something you can fix and I can't be repaired. It's enough that I don't want to kill you, don't ask me for things I can't give you."

It was as honest as I was going to get. She'd cracked me open, and I'd told her things that no one else could know and still be breathing. She had been the first person I'd ever wanted to keep safe, and while those emotions made no sense to me, I indulged them anyway. Probably because I had no idea what the fucking alternative was.

"I need to go out." I didn't wait for a response, grabbing my duffle and pulling out some clean clothes.

"You're running away." She moved slowly to the bed, her ass lowered onto the mattress as she watched me pull on a pair of boxer shorts.

"No, I'm not." I shook my head still wondering if my bright fucking idea wasn't going to explode in my face. Hell, this had bad news written all over it and the fact I was still considering it was boggling.

"That's bullshit, I never run." I snapped a little more than I would have liked. "I want nothing more than to climb in that bed with you, get inside you some more and forget what we are dealing with," I said slowly, deliberately meeting her eyes so she knew I was on the level. "But the reason I'm walking is *because* I feel that way. I need to make sure you come out of this whole."

"That doesn't make sense." Her brows scrunched up in confusion, not having the benefit of my plan to help her connect the dots. It was better if she didn't know. There were still no guarantees any of it would come together anyway.

"Then just trust that I gave you my word." I pulled on a pair of jeans and zipped up the fly. "It's all I've ever had and I don't throw it around lightly."

She nodded slowly, hopefully understanding what those words meant but continued to watch as I got dressed.

"Try and get some sleep."

I walked over to where she was sitting on the edge of the bed, tipping her face in my hands. Her eyes were glassy, and she was blinking fast but no tears fell.

She wouldn't cry in front of me right now; I knew she wouldn't. She wanted me to know she was strong, that she could do whatever it would take and she figured not crying would send me that memo. What she didn't know is that I already knew she was a gladiator; I'd seen her strength time and time again. But I didn't tell her that, probably because if I did then she'd give herself permission for those tears to fall. And I just couldn't see that now.

"One way or another, Sofia, this will all end soon."

I grabbed the rest of my stuff and walked out of the room.

••••

It was still dark when my boots bounded up the stairs of the old church. The heavy doors slammed behind me, the sound ricocheting off the walls loud enough to wake the dead while the moonlight filtered through the big stained glass.

I hated this place.

I'd fantasized about torching it and watching it burn so

many times I'd been almost surprised to see it still standing. But there it was, still rock solid on its foundation. The huge ass crucifix mounted on the back wall glaring accusingly at any of the sheeple gullible enough to swallow the lie, and in my pyro daydreams, it was the first thing I'd set alight.

It never closed, a twenty-four hour minimart dealing out redemption to those who believed their slate could be wiped clean. Except it couldn't, but the lie they told themselves helped them sleep at night, and it was cheaper than Ambien.

"My son." The collared asshole who seemed to be in charge walked toward me, rubbing his eyes like he'd just woken up.

His kindhearted smile faltered when he saw my heated glare. I didn't exactly have a good track record with parental units in the past and I sure as shit wasn't looking to expand now.

"I'm not your son." I squared my shoulders as my skin prickled, warning me killing this dumbass wasn't a good idea. Even though it would give me an insane amount of pleasure, I would let this useless meat suit keep living. For now.

He stuttered, the usual response when someone looked at me for the first time. "We are all God's children."

"Save it for the ones who toss coins into your collection plate." I barked out a laugh. Seriously? He was going to get all Colossians 1:16 on me? I'd read the Bible, which is how I knew it was all a bunch of fairytales designed to make people conform. "I'm not here looking for salvation."

To my step forward, he stepped back, his hands adjusting the collar around his neck like it was a noose tightening. "What is it that you want?" His Adam's apple bobbed like he couldn't quite swallow what he had in his mouth. "We don't have any money here. No drugs."

Another laugh, this time a little louder than the last. Of course this asshole would see a guy like me and assume he knew the score. So much for not judging and *we are all God's children* blah, blah, blah. I didn't even bother setting him straight, not worth wasting the breath correcting him because I really didn't give a shit.

"I want to speak to Sister Catherine." I casually moved to one of the pews and sat down making it clear that I wasn't going anywhere.

"Sister Catherine?" He looked at me like I'd suddenly grown another head. "What is this about? And it's the middle of the night."

"So, wake her up. Or would you prefer me to do it?" My sick smile curled at the edges and I watched him visibly shrink into his skin.

"Is it that important?" He shifted on his feet uncomfortably possibly trying to play the hero and save his flock from the likes of me.

"Trust me, she'll want to see me; we go way back."

"S-surely this can wait until later in the morning." His hands shook as he wrung them nervously in front of him. "Perhaps there is something I can help you with."

"No, it can't and no you can't. So get *her*."

There was no room for debate. He was going to turn his happy collared ass around and get me the fucking nun I wanted to see or I was going to go through the nunnery myself. It would be easier for all involved if he did it.

And I guess he had half a brain and decided to see it my way, taking a few backward steps before heading out a side wooden brown door.

He could be calling the cops, in which case I was going to be SOL. But I hadn't laid a finger on him or made a threat. So telling 9-1-1 there was a scary dude in a church late at night wouldn't be a top priority for the Chicago PD. And hopefully that urge to *save me* might translate into getting what I needed. And what I needed was to talk to the person who apparently saved my life. I wasn't here to thank her either. I hated her just a tiny bit less than the whore who had birthed me.

"You asked for me?" She didn't bother with the child or son, walking slowly out the side door. If she was scared, she wasn't showing it, her face impassive as she took even strides toward me.

This wasn't the first time she had made my acquaintance. We'd met once before when I'd come looking for answers. She'd tried to pull that shit then and it didn't go so well for her. Especially when I threatened to hang her from that charming crucifix I loved so much using the thin red curtain ropes.

"You remember me?" I tilted my head, knowing the question was more rhetorical. She was older now. Her face was filled with deep set lines that cut into skin that might have once been pretty, but the years hadn't been kind.

The priest who'd gone to summon her was waiting quietly close by; he didn't have the same intel as his habit-wearing buddy, which was probably just as well. But to his credit, he didn't move, locking himself in place a few feet away.

"Yes, Michael. I remember you." Her wrinkled hand waved in the air to the asshole who'd been watching with hawk eyes. "You can leave us, Father Patrick. No harm will come to me."

"But, Sister, this is highly irregular." He cleared his throat, his feet doing the shuffle from underneath him. "I would feel a lot better staying."

"She's right." I nodded slowly, leveling him with a stare. "I won't touch her."

"You heard him. You can go." Another wave of the hand, this time she kept her eyes on me.

He hesitated a few seconds, probably fighting his own internal battle on what the right thing to do was, but eventually his feet got moving and took him back through the side door. I didn't doubt he'd be close by, but for now he was gone and that was all that mattered.

"He's well trained." I tipped my chin to the closed door. The two of us left alone. "Tell me do all priests lose their balls when they put on the collar, or just the ones who work in this church."

"What is it you want, Michael?" She sighed, closing her eyes slowly before opening them as she sat beside me. And while she didn't appear to be in the mood for my shit, she wasn't about to tell me that either.

"I need you to do something for me." I leaned back against the hard surface of the pew, the wood creaking in protest under my weight.

"I'm sorry, but this is one place you can't bully people into doing what you want." She shook her head slowly, her hands calmly folded on to her lap. "We won't be party to your criminal activity."

"You're assuming a lot." Rage crept up the back of my neck, needling me that this bitch thought she had me all worked out. "You're forgetting you don't know me."

"Why else would you be in a church in the dead of night?" She gave me a sideways glance. "I may have given my heart to God, but I still have my own mind. I'm sorry, but I can't help you." She lifted her ass off the seat, ready to leave.

"You owe me, and you owe my mother," I snarled, grabbing her arm, not willing to accept no for an answer. "You will do this for her."

Well that got her attention. She stopped dead in her tracks, her ass dropping back down as she turned around to face me. "We have no idea who your mother is, you were abandoned." Her voice lowered as did her head, and I knew right then and there that everything the maintenance man had told me was true. My mother had been one of them.

"Bullshit." I smirked knowing I had her on the hook. "Just because you've been saying the lie for thirty years doesn't make it any more true." I barked out a laugh. "You still saying Hail Mary's, or did you give up pretending you were a good person?"

"Such hardness of heart." Her eyes closed as her frail body trembled a little. It wasn't from fear, I could tell she wasn't afraid of me. No, that was the weight of the lie she'd been keeping. "I didn't want this for you. None of us did."

"Well tough shit, because when you dump a kid into the system it's not going to end up like it does in a Disney movie. So take a good look, because you're as much to blame as anyone else."

My past was my past and I didn't believe in looking back. It changed absolutely zero. And usually I was better at keeping a handle on my emotions. But as she sat there with that fucking look on her face, like she'd somehow had it worse than me, I wanted to snap her neck right off her spine.

"I'm sorry, we just wanted to protect you." She bowed her head, her voice almost a whisper.

"Protect me from what?" It didn't make sense. They had bundled me off to stop something bad from happening? Well bravo, bitches, because you'd put me straight from the frying pan into the fire. I couldn't believe this indignant cunt.

She brought her knees closer together, her feet shifting uneasily as she clamped her mouth shut. Yeah, she was done talking.

"It doesn't matter now does it?" I snapped, the stroll down memory fucking lane had been a real treat—not—but I was done jerking around. "Water under the bridge. But you still owe me and I'm here to collect."

"I'm not sure there is anything I can do for you," she

whispered softly, her fingers locked so tightly in her lap her knuckles had turned white.

"It's not for me, it's for a . . . friend." I coughed out the word, not sure it felt right given the situation. Not that I had a better substitute, so it would have to do. "And she is the one who is going to need protecting. Hopefully this time you won't screw it up."

They'd done such a stellar job with me I wasn't sure they were up to the task. But they'd managed to keep their mouths shut for a long time about me and the piece of shit who birthed me, so at least they had that going for them. This would be the last place Jimmy would look. Sofia would be safe until I could figure out a way to get her out of the country.

"She needs sanctuary? Is she in trouble? Who is this girl?" The questions came out in a rush, more flustered than she'd previously been.

She couldn't help herself, because as much as she probably hated me, she wouldn't turn her back on someone in need.

"Jimmy Amaro's daughter." I didn't bother elaborating, everyone in the city knew of him and his reputation.

There were even rumors that he had clergy on the payroll. He'd obviously bought into the lie, thinking he could cleanse his fucking soul by giving the church a new candelabra. "I need her out of sight and as far away from me as possible for the next few days. You can hide her in the back like you did my mother."

"How do you—"

"Know?" I finished the sentence for her, my smile creeping at the edges. "I have my sources. But more importantly is that you are no longer denying it, which is good. It will save us a lot of time."

The look on her face said it all. Defeat. Worn down by thirty years that she and the rest of her *sisters* hadn't been able to breathe a word about my existence, she was giving up.

"What has she done?" She spoke slowly, not knowing that Jimmy was capable of killing his own blood.

"She was born to the wrong man," I answered drily, wondering how different her life would have been if she'd been born to someone—anyone—else. "Now he wants her dead, so her only hope is to leave."

She winced, sitting up straighter in her seat. "You care for this girl?"

"Not your business."

She closed her eyes slowly, taking a deep breath before reopening them and focusing on me. "Bring her here; she will be safe." Another deep breath. "I promise you."

"I don't care for your promises." I waved my hand dismissively. "But you *will* keep her safe, or I'll come back and cut that lying tongue right out of your mouth." Her eyes widened as she trembled in her skin. It wasn't a threat, it was consequence and one I would have no problem carrying out if something happened to Sofia while she was with these assholes.

"We'll be back in a few hours, and it goes without saying that the fewer people that know the better." I rose off the pew, my legs coming to full height as I looked down at her. "I'd say keeping that number to single digits is in your best interest."

There wasn't anything left to say, and the sooner I left this place the better, so without bothering with a goodbye, I turned to leave.

"She loved you," she called from behind me. "She gave her life for you."

"Who?" I turned, wondering what the hell the old woman was going on about.

"Your mother." She rose slowly, her small feet padding across the floor to stand in front of me. Her eyes started to pool at the edges. "She loved you even before you were born, and when the time came she sacrificed herself so you would have a chance."

Lies.

All of it.

The only thing that bitch had cared about was protecting her own reputation. She'd spread her legs and let some asshole fill her with his seed and what a fucking surprise, she got knocked up. So she did what she needed to do to protect herself. Because if she'd given two shits about me, she would have given me a fucking last name so I wouldn't have spent the first fifteen years of my life wondering who the hell I was.

"Sucks to be her, because it looks like she wasted her life on me." My voice was more like a growl, not bothering to hide the fucking rage and agitation.

"She—" She tried to continue.

"Save it," I snapped, having heard enough bedtime stories to last me a lifetime. "It doesn't matter now." And more importantly it wouldn't change anything. "You will do this, and you will do it right this time. No one will know and then in a couple of days I will come get her and you will never see me again."

"Okay. I can do that." She nodded, wisely keeping all other details about my whore mother to herself.

"Glad you are so agreeable. I need to go."

TWENTY-ONE

SOFIA

The sun was just about to come up and Michael still hadn't returned. I had no idea where he'd gone or what he was doing, but his suggestion that I go to sleep wasn't a good one. I couldn't have even if I wanted to, my brain churned, processing information as I tried to put them into neat compartments inside my head.

It was one step forward, two steps back when it came to him. He had opened up to me and shown me kindness, but he refused to accept he was anything other than a monster. He'd been inside my body, it had eased us both, but more importantly, I'd let him inside my heart.

And yet, here I was, alone and confused and clueless if any of it had even made a difference.

The metal scraping of the roller door opening echoed through the warehouse. And it was strange at how surprised I was that he'd come back. Part of me had expected him to go, leave me and all of this behind and take what was left of my trust fund money. It would have been easier and something he might have even contemplated. It shouldn't have thrilled me so much that he came back, but it did.

"Did you sleep?" he asked, walking through the doorway and closing it softly behind him.

"Not really." I sat up in bed, clutching the covers around my chest. "Did you do what you had to do?"

He hated questions, but it never stopped me from asking.

"Yes, I did." He took a deep breath before continuing. "You're going to be staying at Saint Margaret's while I go meet with Jimmy." He raised his hand to stop me from opening my mouth, knowing I'd want to have a say in what happened to me. "This place is safe." His hand waved around the room. "But I can't risk you being here. Jimmy knows some of my aliases and he has people who can find out things. And I'm almost positive that while he hasn't shown up on my doorstep yet, he would have been stupid not to track my phone when Franco left me in that hotel room. If he didn't, then he was a fool and he won't be making the same mistake twice. Any place that can be tied to me is not safe for you. No one will look for you at Saint Margaret's."

It had been one of the first times ever he'd divulged information without me pulling it out of him one word at a time. I blinked back in surprise, my mouth opening and closing a few times before I finally found the words I wanted to say.

"How long will I be there? And what will happen after?"

"I will come for you." He moved to the edge of the bed and sat down. "As soon as I can, and I'll get you across the border. Those new documents should be ready by then. Once you're in Canada, you can jump on any plane you want and put as much distance as you can between here and you. You need to stay away for as long as you can, but if I were you, I'd stay gone."

He didn't need to tell me that I would probably never see him again. It was more than implied.

"And what will you do?" I stopped short of asking him to come with me again, knowing the answer was and always would be no.

"What I have always done." He shrugged. "Take another job and move on."

There was a beat of silence that passed between us, as if both of us had agreed that whatever those words were, they were better left unsaid. But deep down I knew I hadn't been just a job. Both of us had been affected. Both of us probably a little afraid to admit it, even if it was just to ourselves.

"Do you have everything you need? For the investigation?" His hand rubbed the back of his neck, no doubt uncomfortable in what I had planned to do. No matter how much it was justified, he hated what I was doing.

"Yes, it's enough." I nodded. The last few days had been spent creating a solid case for prosecution. Even if only a third of it were ruled admissible, it would be enough to put my father and his friends away for a very long time. "And I've left a trail for them to find everything else."

"Good, that's good." He nodded. "I'll let you get packed up." He stood, moving to the doorway and leaving the room.

My feet kicked the covers off my body, knowing that I wouldn't have a lot of time. My bags were in the corner of the room still mostly packed, but I shoved whatever else was left inside before getting out some clean clothes and checking my gun.

I quickly showered, brushing my skin pink as I toweled off and dressed all without him returning. My eyes floated around the small room. Even in the middle of the day, it was still pitch black. The windowless walls starving any light before it had a chance to enter. But it was in here that I'd felt safe, and I knew that I was saying goodbye—never to return. Not to this room or to anything familiar again.

Michael was in the kitchen area when I found him. He was checking his guns and ammunition while sitting at the table, beside him a large coffee tin. "I need some DNA, some hair, saliva and some fibers from your clothes." He tipped his chin in the direction of the can.

"Of course. I can do that." I dropped one of the duffels from off my shoulder and pulled out a hairbrush. My fingers massaged the bristles pulling out as much hair as I could. I made a neat pile on the tabletop before grabbing the nightshirt I'd been wearing for the last few nights. With the help of my army knife, I shredded the edges, taking pieces of the torn fabric and adding it to the pile.

"Here," he passed me an enamel camping cup, "Spit in this."

It was so clinical, but I did what he said, spitting into the cup as he took my hair and the shredded fibers and torching them lightly with a cigarette lighter before tossing them into the can.

I handed him the cup, and he added it to the mix. Giving everything a good shake after he reattached the lid.

"Do you think it will work?" I asked, taking a seat beside him.

"Who knows? It's worth a shot either way though, right?"

There was no way of knowing if my father would believe it, but at the very least it would stall him. Give me a day or two buffer to get away. And if a miracle happened and he believed it was me, then maybe it would give me a small window of opportunity to live a normal life.

"I'm ready." My back straightened, hefting the duffle on my shoulder, my overnight bag on the other.

"This is yours." He handed me the thumb drive he'd retrieved from my house before he blew it up. It was hard to believe that it hadn't been that long ago, it felt like more than a year had passed.

"Thank you." I shoved it in my pocket. The rest of the information on another drive sitting beside the computer. "I'll go get the rest of my things and meet you at the car.

I waited, hoping he would say something more, but he didn't, so I walked out of the room and made a beeline for the computer. It was still humming, not having been turned off in days as I quickly downloaded the last bit of information and sent it to an email address one of the hackers had set up for me.

It had a fail-safe, an insurance policy. Designed to send out the draft email and all the attachments within ten days unless I stopped it. So if anything happened to me, I would still be able to make sure the work I had done wasn't in vain.

My hand fumbled with the monitor, switching it off before carrying my bags to the Chevy that was parked on the inside of the roller door. It had been a far cry from the Camaro he had initially driven, but in the end, it had been more useful.

My body slid into the passenger seat and waited for Michael to join me. I tried not to focus that it was the same place a dead woman had sat not so long ago. The mental distance needed because I couldn't afford the physical one. Thankfully Michael appeared a few moments later with a green canvas messenger bag draped across his shoulder.

"You good?" he asked me, sinking into his seat and putting on his seatbelt. "No turning back."

"All good." I faked a smile and stared out the windshield, ignoring there was no view to concentrate on.

The roller door behind us rose; the sound of metal scraping bringing with it the bright sunlight. It was hard on the eyes, forcing them to close as the warmth hit my back.

Before I opened them, the car had started moving, reversing out of the warehouse and onto the road. The neighboring businesses had started their work day; the noise of trucks and workers spilling into the cabin of the car as we drove past them. No one so much as glanced in our direction.

There was no speeding, no erratic lane changes, no explosive road rage as we traveled to Saint Margaret's. On the outside it looked like two regular people in a car, little did anyone know there was nothing regular about the car or the people inside.

The trip continued in silence. Michael didn't even give me a sideways glance, his hands locked at ten and two on the steering wheel while his eyes roamed between the windshield and the rearview mirror. My fingers tightened around the seat belt, every mile we got closer to Saint Margaret's plunging my stomach into a sea of knots.

It was a quiet neighborhood, but he drove around the back, parking in a side alley. He exited the car, carefully closing the driver's side door and waiting for me to do the same from my side. He removed my duffel and my bag from the trunk, carrying both in one hand and didn't bother locking the car. Instead he made his way along the back alley, giving a quick look over his shoulder checking to see I was following.

I hated the silence.

Hated it.

But there was nothing to be said.

There was a large hedge, thick and lush, that barely hid a chain link fence that was approximately eight feet tall. Between the hedge and the fence it seemed there was no way in from this side. It wasn't until we got up close that I noticed a small gap in the brush, just wide enough for a person to push through, and just beyond that, a door. Michael stepped through first, his hands making quick work of the lock, swinging the door open and stepping through. He held it open for me as I followed, closing it and reaffixing the lock as soon as I'd cleared the threshold.

The garden was extremely well-maintained. The grass felt soft and spongy under my feet and all the garden beds had been neatly tended, with not so much as a weed out of place.

The church stood in front of us, its stained glass windows catching the morning sunlight while its large wooden door remained tightly shut. There was a stone path leading to the concrete steps, but we didn't walk in that direction.

The property was bigger than it looked from the outside. The yard extended wide on the left hand side, distorting the symmetry of the block.

And almost hidden beyond the tree line was a medium-sized dwelling with a small graveyard edged up between the house-looking building and the property boundary.

"This way." Michael tilted his head toward the house. "There is someone waiting for us."

That person either heard us or had been watching as we crossed the yard because the door to the house opened before he even had a chance to knock.

Michael's feet continued uninterrupted, taking a step though the doorway with me taking a second or two until I joined him the dimly lit entrance.

Standing calmly to greet us was a small woman in traditional nun attire. The habit she wore seemed heavy; the shapeless cloth unable to hide how incredibly thin she was underneath. And as she waited her hands were clasped in front of her, patiently. Her deeply lined face was impassive as she focused on me.

"You must be Sofia Amaro." She spoke softly, her lips curving into a cautious smile. "I am Sister Catherine. You will be safe here."

She had amazingly clear blue eyes, with a porcelain pale diminutive face. And while I knew nothing about her, when she spoke it was like a calming wave of warm water washing over me.

"Thank you." I nodded, returning her smile. "It's very kind of you to take me in."

Her eyes shifted to Michael, who didn't acknowledge her at all, instead looking beyond her into the hallway and asking,

"Where's her room?"

"Let me show you." Sister Catherine nodded, her light feet barely making a sound on the tiled floor as she led the way.

There was obviously a connection between them, the air almost crackling with tension as we walked silently along the corridor passing rows of closed doors.

Sister Catherine took an old brass key from inside her pocket, slipping it into the keyhole and turning. The old lock popped as it opened, her hand pushing the door open via the handle.

"This can be locked via the inside too." She smiled, stretching out her hand in my direction. "And this is the only key." She dropped it into my open palm.

"What about the skeleton?" Michael barked, walking inside and surveying the room. "Or a master key?"

"The master key went missing a long time ago." Her voice trailed off like she had meant to add more to the sentence. "It was never recovered. Other than that key, the only way to get inside this room is removing the lock."

"Good. That's good." Michael nodded, staring at her intently. "I'll get her settled."

Sister Catherine nodded, understanding she'd been given her cue to leave us alone. She was just as quiet as when she walked in, her feet barely making a sound as she turned and closed the door behind her.

"So, she's a friend of yours?" I couldn't stop the nervous laugh escaping my lips as he dropped both my bags on the floor in front of an old wooden wardrobe.

"I don't have any friends," he answered drily, "but she owes me, so you will be safe here."

"This was where your mother lived, right? Where you were born?"

"You shouldn't need to be here for longer than a couple of

days; either way, no one will bother you." He avoided the questions entirely without breaking eye contact.

"I know." I walked around the small room and took in my new surroundings.

There was a metal-framed single bed pushed up against the wall with large gray woolen blankets tucked into tight hospital corners. The walls were off-white with a small window facing a courtyard; the coffee-colored drapes had been pulled to the side, letting in some natural light.

It was a stark contrast to where I'd been sleeping the last few nights. And even though the room felt warm and secure, I had felt safer with Michael.

"I've got to go." He cleared his throat. "Try and stay out of trouble."

He didn't bother with a goodbye, instead turning and taking a step toward the door.

"Michael."

He stopped midstride and looked over his shoulder.

"Thank you."

There was a slight nod of his head and then he was gone, leaving me in the empty room as I listened to his heavy boots echo down the hall.

My body slowly lowered onto the firm mattress, the room suddenly seeming larger now there was only me inside and I was left to my own thoughts. *It will be fine,* I told myself, *it's only for a few days.*

It was only a few moments after Michael's departure that Sister Catherine reappeared, materializing through the doorway without a sound.

"If there is anything we can do for you, please let me know." She took another tentative step waiting for a permissive nod before she came any further. "Our accommodations are very basic but what we have we are happy to share. There is plenty of food and drink in the kitchen and the bathroom is on the other side of the hall."

"Thank you, you're very kind." I tried to manage a smile, but I was almost positive I wasn't convincing. "Do you have a computer?"

"Yes, there is one in the living room. And yes it has internet." She smiled anticipating my next question.

"His mother lived here, didn't she?"

"Is that what he told you?" she answered cautiously, so rehearsed if not for the sadness in her eyes I would have assumed she didn't know what I was talking about.

I'd seen that look before, usually when answering the call of a domestic dispute and the woman refused to acknowledge there had been an altercation. The busted lip and blackened eyes explained away by a clumsy accident on their part while they insisted their husband loved them and would never raise a hand to them.

"Yes, he told me about her. That she lived here until she died giving birth to him." I watched as Sister Catherine's body swayed, her feet shifted softly to keep her upright. "He also told me she was buried outside."

She sighed, her chest expanding with a heavy breath as she walked to the small window. "This was her room. No one has been in here since she left us."

No matter how many years had passed, I could tell it was something that still weighed heavily on her. She continued to look outside, her face slowly falling into her hands as she took another deep breath.

"You don't have to talk about it." I hurried off the bed feeling like an asshole. She wasn't the enemy and I had no right to question her. "I just tend to talk a lot when I get edgy. I'm a police officer and investigating is something that is a hard habit to break. I'm sorry if I made you uncomfortable."

"It's been a long time." She swallowed, her hand rising up to her throat. "A very long time since I've spoken about her. But I think about her everyday."

"Were you close?" I gently touched her arm joining her at the window.

"Everyone loved her," her eyes filled with tears. "She was filled with such light, always put the needs of others before her own. Her heart was so pure . . ." She trailed off wiping away a fallen tear. "Anyway, you're here now and I know she would have wanted you to have her room. She said she'd always felt safe here and I hope you'll feel the same."

There was a lump in my throat, it shifted uncomfortably as I swallowed, not anticipating feeling so emotional being in the room I knew Michael's mother had lived.

"Well, if you need anything my room is the one right next door." She stepped away from the window and padded slowly toward the door. "Our next meal is at twelve if you would like to join us, or if it would make you more comfortable I could bring a tray to your room."

"Thank you, but that won't be necessary." I smiled. "I'll be happy to join you."

There were no more words, a curt nod her final goodbye as she disappeared just as silently as she'd appeared. And then I was alone again.

My eyes roamed once again to the tiny window, and I imagined Michael's mother standing in that spot rubbing her belly. There were many unanswered questions, like why Sister Catherine had mentioned that Rose had felt safe here? Safe from what? Persecution because she'd gone against her vows and fallen pregnant? Or was there more to it than that?

It was like an itch I couldn't quite reach and it bothered me. Why had she had to die in the first place? Why not take her to a hospital? Surely the church would have preferred to deal with

233

the scandal than to try and hide a body. And why had there been no investigation? There would have been some record of Rose being sent here from somewhere, how was her disappearance so easily explained to other church officials? How far did this cover up go? And why?

It was none of my business. I had so many problems, I didn't need to borrow extra trouble but the itch remained, begging to be scratched.

"Damn it." I blew out a breath, my hands bracing either side of the window as I cursed myself. "Damn it to fucking hell."

TWENTY-TWO

MICHAEL

It was later in the day when I finally met with Jimmy. I had called him after leaving Sofia, telling him that *it* was done. He assumed I meant I'd killed her, and I didn't clarify, instead telling him I was ready to collect what had been promised to me. He was pleased, the condescending bastard congratulating me on a job well done as I gave him instructions of how the rest of it would play out.

He'd been surprisingly accommodating, the asshole falling over himself to seal the deal as soon as possible. He even had the nerve to chuckle, saying while it had cost him more than he would have liked, he'd happily employ my services again. Like I was looking for the endorsement.

Our meeting point was a shipping yard just off I-90. The brokerage company had come into financial hardship recently and so was running on limited funds. Security had been the first to go, the company preferring to keep its workers who could bring money in on their payroll rather than fat mall cops who sat on their asses watching television all day.

So it was the perfect solution, secure and away from roving eyes. It also was neutral territory with the owner not being connected to Jimmy or Franco and the best we could do without crossing state lines.

"Michael," Jimmy rasped, his breath tearing at his throat as he coughed into his hands. "It's a good thing I like you, I'm not usually this patient."

He hadn't come alone. His number one, Tony, was a dumb fuck whose gut was so big he probably hadn't seen his dick in years. He also took the stereotype a little too far, looking more like a fucking parody of *Goodfellas* than an actual wise guy.

Sal, his personal bodyguard, was also in tow. And that guy was a straight up killer, so the only one I actually had to worry about.

There was also the possibility that the trio hadn't traveled light, a bigger entourage waiting in the wings because we all knew Jimmy didn't have the balls to face me alone.

"Cut the bullshit, Jimmy." I barked out a laugh. "You don't like anyone, and you waited because you knew I was the only one who could get it done without you looking weak to your enemies."

"You always were too cocky for your own good." His lips spread, giving me a look at his yellowed front grille. "But you better watch it, son, your good luck won't last forever."

"I'm not your son and considering the way you treat your kids, it's probably just as well." My arms folded in front of my chest as I leaned back on the heels of my boots. "And I don't believe in good luck."

Anyone who looked at me and thought any of this shit happened because of good luck was either stoned or had some serious psychological issues. No fucking leprechaun getting an ass fucking by a rainbow was responsible for my success. That shit had come hard fucking earned, I had the scars to prove it.

"You armed?" Sal asked, giving me a grin.

"Do you still have a small dick?" I smirked back, flashing the forty and nine I had on either side of my chest. "And you guys know I'm not good in social situations, so if you'd like to keep breathing I'd advise you to stay where you are. Since my run in with Franco, I'm having trust issues."

"We're not interested in taking you out of commission." Sal held up his palms, the eye roll unnecessary. "So maybe everyone can relax their trigger fingers."

"Where is she?" Jimmy asked, ignoring Sal and looking at the parked Chevy that I'd driven up in. "Her mother will insist we go through the motions. Our family will want to pay their respects."

"Right here." I tilted my head to the old Folgers Classic Roast tin sitting on the hood of my car. "Things got a little toasty."

"Fuck." Sal whistled through his teeth, his hand twitching by his side. Tony shook his head, stepping aside for Jimmy to move forward.

"This is not what we agreed." Jimmy's eyes narrowed. "What the hell happened?"

"Your daughter had a big mouth." I picked up the tin and handed it to him. "And I'm not known for my gentle touch, so you get what you get."

Jimmy snatched the tin from my hand and peeled open the lid as a film of ash rose into the night air. His hand gently tilting it to the glow of the overhead lights, examining the contents. Hell, not sure why I bothered putting in the effort. I could have torched a goat and fooled the dumbass, his head shaking from side to side as he investigated the cremated remains.

"How do we know it's her?" Tony spoke for the first time, Jimmy's right-hand man proving he didn't totally have shit for brains like his boss.

"Because who else would it be?" I didn't even blink as the lie passed through my lips. "I'm not in the habit of collecting pets. Take it, test the DNA, it's her."

"Damn you." Jimmy replaced the lid and gently lowered in

237

onto the hood of his car. "What the hell am I supposed to do with this?" His eyes wild as his gravelly voice got more animated. "This is not what we agreed."

"So register your dissatisfaction on fucking *Yelp*, mother-fucker," I spat out through clenched teeth, not needing to manufacture my anger. "You tried to play me, and I am not a fucking pawn in your chess game. You don't get to fuck me over and call the shots. In our world, all debts need to be paid and no one gets a pass, not even you. Consider this my fee."

"You." He took a step forward, only stopping when my hands disappeared beneath my shirt and went for my guns.

And all that did was set off a chain reaction, Sal and Tony going for theirs, all of us drawing at the same. My left and right both palmed bad news, one aimed at Jimmy, the other aimed at Tony.

"Steady." Sal tried to be the voice of reason. "Don't do anything stupid now, Michael."

"If you're gonna take your shot, Sal, take it." I nodded to the barrel pointed in my direction. "But you better drop me, because after I pierce both these two assholes' hearts, the next bullet will be for you."

Jimmy didn't have a gun; he was a delicate fucking snowflake who believed he'd done his time with steel in his hand and now wanted someone else to do his dirty work. And Tony hadn't been up close and personal with a kill in over a decade, feeling the same sense of entitlement that his boss was suffering. So there was just as much chance he would knock himself out on the recoil as he did of actually hitting me with a bullet. These guys were nothing more than dirty businessmen, douchebags who relived the glory days but hadn't been in fucking trenches for years.

Now, Sal, he was the only one of the three who would pull the trigger and would guarantee me a toe tag. But he also was smart, and knew I was just the right amount of crazy son-of-a-bitch to risk doing the damage I was threatening as I took my exit. It's amazing what can be achieved when you aren't afraid to die.

"No one is taking the fucking shot." He lowered his gun a hair. "Tony, put the gun away before you shoot yourself in the fucking foot."

"I can handle my business," Tony protested, his hand getting a case of the shakes, clearly not as tight as he thought he was.

"Are you done yet?" My arms stayed locked in position. "Because I feel like shooting him just for boring me."

"If he doesn't put the gun down, I'll shoot him myself." Sal lowered his gun and turned his attention to Tony. "Let me handle this, I'm not in the mood to clean up your mess."

"Everyone needs to stop." Jimmy raised his hands, the asshole still believing he had control over what was going down. "I can't fucking think."

"Take your daughter and fuck off." I nodded to the black on black Mercedes E class they'd arrived in. Hard to believe the cocksucker was her father. He sure as shit didn't act like it. "And I'll want the rest of my money."

"You want the rest of your money?" Jimmy's diaphragm went into convulsions. "Check you out, the balls on you."

"If you wanted a bargain, Jimmy, you should have gone to K-mart." I had yet to lower my weapons. "You *will* pay me the remaining amount."

"Or what? What are you going to do?" he spluttered, clearly believing his own press in thinking he was God. "You're nothing more than a street thug. You don't have any power."

"You're right. I'm nothing more than a street thug. But before I blew Sofia's brains all over my shoes, she had a lot to say about things you've done. Seems your little girl was willing to sing like a fucking canary in order to save her life. So I let her get as chatty as she wanted, and when she ran out of shit to talk about, I finished what I started. So I'd be careful about who you threaten."

Jimmy lunged for me, and if not for Sal wrapping his meat hooks around the dude's torso, he may have gotten a little further.

"You little cunt!" he yelled, fighting a losing battle against the extra eighty pounds Sal had on him. "All I have to do is let it be known what you did to my only daughter; you'll be dead within a day."

"Oh, like the bounty you had on Sofia?" I laughed. Couldn't help it. The idea that Jimmy thought he had one over on me freaking hilarious considering how deep he was in his own shit. "Yeah, 'cause that worked out so well for you. Not to mention that me taking her out just alleviated a lot of headaches for almost anyone willing to take the job. I'd say they'd be more inclined to shake my fucking hand rather than help you."

"Watch your back, boy!" Jimmy yelled, Sal pulling him back toward the Benz. "This is far from over."

Tony wisely didn't interfere, his hands instead got busy holstering his gun and helping Sal contain Jimmy.

"It really pisses me off when assholes like you call me boy." I eyeballed him as his entourage forced him to take a backward step. "And it's *you* who should watch *your* back."

There was some posturing on their part, mainly from Jimmy, but Sal managed to convince them that they didn't want to do it here. He took the ash can with him, his eyes trying to burn a hole in me as he got in the car and peeled out of the shipping yard.

His reaction had been predictable. I wasn't expecting him to high-five me after I'd supposedly S'mored his kid, but I'd played it straight down the line, and the sentiment was exactly my MO.

After giving a quick three-sixty of my surroundings, I slipped back into the Chevy and took the long way back to the warehouse. Not that it mattered now, even if they did follow me, they wouldn't find anything there. Still, it's not like I wanted to roll out the welcome mat for these dipshits either. And another thing, I needed another set of wheels. Losing the Camaro had happened days ago, and while there had been more pressing issues at the time, kicking it in the POS I had been currently driving was getting old. Not to mention when I finally went and picked up Sofia I needed something with a little more power under the hood. Something that could outrun their fleet of foreign douche mobiles if it came to it.

When I returned to the warehouse, it was empty. *No shit,* considering that was the way it was supposed to be. But I could still smell her in the air even hours after she'd been gone.

It was too soon.

We would both have to sit tight for a few days until I was positive I wasn't being followed. Only then could I risk heading back to the church. Then maybe I would indulge my fantasy and watch the fucker burn, either way I'd sooner stab myself right in the dick than ever set foot in that place again.

"Yeah." I answered my phone, the fucker buzzing beside me displaying no caller ID. Not that this was a surprise given the company I had been keeping the last few weeks.

"Your shit is ready. But you're paying double because I had to rush the order."

"Well hello to you too." I laughed into the speaker. "Is it still up to standard?"

"Suck my dick, Mike." It was his turn to laugh. "Everything I do is quality."

"Fine, double."

"Pleasure doing business with you."

The call ended without the need to confirm any more details. Leon AKA The Polack and I had done business before and we had a system. He'd have everything I needed personally delivered to a predesignated PO box, and I'd reciprocate with payment. There'd be no follow up, and we wouldn't speak to each other again till either of us needed something. It's the way shit worked with people like us.

Fuck, I was edgy.

I couldn't sit still, my ass out of my chair as I walked around the room with nowhere to go. My feet—like the rest of me— were restless which wasn't a good way to be. The job wasn't over—far from it—so taking a day or two and working on my suntan wasn't going to happen.

There was also the matter of keeping up appearances. Jimmy had told me to watch my back, which went without saying because I didn't trust the fucker as far as I could throw him. But the sooner they saw it was business as usual, the more convinced they would be that it was Sofia in that can. And while he would still be pissed about the lack of body, he would ultimately get over it.

So I needed a job. Something not too involved that took all my time, but that was public enough for it to be noticed.

I picked up my phone and dialed, waiting for the call to connect. It didn't take too long, Damon famous for his excellent customer service.

"Who's this?" he hissed into the phone, my new number not one he recognized.

"Your BFF." I smirked against the phone. "You want to get together, eat ice cream and talk about boys?"

"Mikey, where've you been, you crazy son of a bitch?" Damon's voice exploded into a laugh. "I've heard some interesting things about you. Very, *very* interesting."

I'm sure he had, although I didn't bother asking which version he had heard.

Damon was a bookie who had a side business as a loan shark. His one-stop-shop for gambling was also where a lot of his customers usually got into trouble. Between his willingness to open large lines of credit and his aggressive interest margins, he was responsible for a lot of men going AWOL. Either by their own means or being helped along by people like me.

And another thing, Damon liked to talk. Only thing the Irish fucker liked more was probably to drink, and usually after a pint or two the bastard had both of those things well combined. Which meant if I was doing something for him, almost everyone would hear about it, especially those who needed to.

"What can I say? Someone needs to be a rock star and you're too old and too fat."

"Very true." He chuckled. "So tell me. You want to do some freelancing for me? Or you still have a full dance card?"

"Nope, I'm a free agent."

"Excellent. I have a few customers that need a home visit, and it's been tough to find good help these days, Mikey."

I'm sure it was, and I was only too happy to give my five-star guarantee.

"How about we meet at our usual spot and discuss. Tomorrow afternoon? Pretty sure you owe me a beer."

Damon laughed. "You haven't paid for a beer in your life, you bastard. Sounds good." He took a breath. "And Mikey, it's good to have you back."

"Don't get sentimental on me, Damon. I like you better when you're an evil prick."

The call ended with neither of us wasting unnecessary

words. He would send me a message with his preferred time and I would either agree or give him one that worked better for me. Then he'd give me a list of people who I needed to visit and remind them of their financial obligations.

It would also take care of two of my problems. Stop me from sitting around an empty warehouse like a moody bastard and give me the visibility I needed. And as a bonus, Jimmy wouldn't want to interfere in Damon's business while I was earning for him. He and Damon shared a few mutual interests, and he wasn't man enough to kill the association when it had been so lucrative.

All I had to do now was hope like hell Sofia didn't do anything stupid while we waited it out. Yeah, and maybe Santa Claus would bring me a new ride too.

Fuck. It was going to be a long few days.

TWENTY-THREE

SOFIA

It hadn't been hard to find her grave. She was the only one missing a headstone; an otherwise unexplained gap right in the middle of the graveyard where the grass had grown over and a bush of pale pink roses had been planted.

Roses, for *Rose*.

It was a silent tribute, reinforcing that no one was to know where she'd been buried. The question as to why, was still a mystery.

It had been two days since Michael had left me here, and I was starting to feel the walls closing in. He promised he'd come back, help me get out. But as of yet I hadn't heard from him. I had no idea how to contact his *Polish guy* to get my new documents. And had he even seen my father yet?

The anticipation was killing me with constant incessant questions refusing to stop as they tumbled endlessly inside my mind. I hated being in the dark; the not knowing killing me.

Being outside in the back courtyard and the garden was about the only thing that kept me sane. With the high hedges and tall fences designed to keep nosey neighbors out, I felt safe enough to sit without risk of being discovered.

The once filled halls were now largely vacant with only four nuns living at Saint Margaret's convent but it was only Sister

Catherine who I spoke to.

The other three seemed kind, all of them politely acknowledging me whenever I happened to be in a room. But none of them asked questions. They kept their heads bowed at meal times; eating silently before leaving the table to continue whatever activity they had left. Maybe Sister Catherine had already filled them in, telling them why I was here, or maybe they just didn't want to be dragged into a mess that would soon be gone.

I felt insulated by an invisible bubble. Like if I opened up my mouth and screamed the sound would be absorbed by nothingness, like I was in danger of becoming.

"She liked being out here too." Catherine's kind face appeared beside me. "You are a lot like her, you know. Not in appearance, she was fairer than you, and shorter, but she was just as fierce as you are. One of the strongest women I ever knew."

"I don't feel very strong hiding out here while my fate is left undecided. It makes me feel pretty helpless if I'm honest."

My mouth involuntarily opened, spewing my emotions without thought. What did it matter at this point? She had more volatile ammunition to use against me if she wanted, like my location for instance. Exposing my vulnerability didn't seem so bad in the end.

"Be at ease, child." Her hand gently rose and brushed against my cheek. "He may act like his father, but deep down there is more of his mother in him. Even if he has tried to deny it, he is very much her son. He will be back for you."

It was like the wind had been knocked out of me as I literally struggled to breathe. And not because she was so certain of Michael's return.

"You knew his father?"

Usually when speaking about Michael, Catherine was

always tight lipped. Abstract almost, but she knew a hell of a lot more than she had said to either of us. The man who'd impregnated Rose mentioned for the very first time.

"Yes, I knew him." She nodded, her hand dropped from my cheek, gripping at the rosary beads she kept in her pocket. "Maybe we should go inside; there's a breeze out here and you aren't wearing a jacket." She rubbed her arms absently, giving me a tight smile. "The last thing you would need right now is to catch a cold."

"Who is Michael's father? Was he married? Is that why she was hidden away? Did he force himself on Rose? Did she consider leaving the church and he rejected her?"

The questions fired out one after the other with barely a breath in between, leaving no time for Catherine to answer as I continued my hard line. "Was he involved in the church too? Was she worried about the scandal?"

"What?" Catherine stepped back, her face whitewashed as her feet struggled to keep her upright. "I thought you said Michael told you about his mother?"

"He did, he told me she was a nun here." I took a step forward wondering if she was going to pass out. She sure didn't look steady, any remaining color draining out of her skin. "He spoke to an old groundskeeper, someone who had been around when Rose was here. He told Michael about his mother, how she'd obviously felt the disgrace, hiding herself away and giving birth in private. He never found out who his father was."

"Oh, God, forgive me." Her eyes looked up to the sky as her hands shook. "You must never speak of what I just told you. He can't know. Ever."

Terror. Absolute terror shook within her. And not the kind you could fake. This wasn't an oops-I-wasn't-supposed-to-say-anything slip; it was a deep secret she had promised never to reveal.

"He has every right to know." My blood turned cold as my voice rose. "You mean to tell me you knew who his father was this whole time and never told him? How dare you keep that from him. It doesn't matter what sins they may have committed, they were still his parents."

She would have undoubtedly been publically condemned by the Church. But I couldn't believe an institution that preached forgiveness would turn their back on one of their own, especially when an innocent child had been involved.

"She didn't commit any sins." She closed her eyes and whispered, her body swaying as her shoulders sagged. "She was married and a good wife. Devout, who loved her husband."

Her lids slid open as her hands wrung nervously in front of her. "But then he turned into a monster, beating her, forcing himself on her and no matter what she did, she couldn't bring him out of the darkness. He desperately wanted children, blamed her for her inability to provide him an heir. So when she finally fell pregnant, she knew it would be a son. She risked her life leaving him, under the cover of night she ran without even a change of clothes. She left everything in the hopes of saving her son. That he might have a better life and not be part of that world."

I felt sick. Unable to comprehend what she was saying even though deep down I had to have known the answer. My brain rationalizing that it could be anyone—that I couldn't be right.

"Who, who is his father?"

My own body had trouble fighting gravity, the blood leaving my head in a rush as I held my breath.

"Franco Santini." Her legs buckled from underneath her; her knees hitting the grass.

"What? How?" I joined her on the grass, my hand reached out to her torso, cradling her in my arms as I felt her entire body tremble.

She took a few minutes, using the time to try and compose herself as I held her. My fingers tightened around the heavy cloth that covered her slight body, willing her to keep talking. *Needing* her to keep talking.

"Rose was Franco's first wife." She took a breath, settling into the words. "When she left him, he looked for her, embarrassed that she had turned her back on the marriage. It made him look weak to his peers, that he couldn't control his own wife. She had nowhere to go." She nodded, affirming that there had been no other choice.

"Franco knew everyone and those he didn't know wanted the money. Even *your* father joined in the effort, every corner of the city turned upside down as they searched for her. Yet, no one came here. She was safe as long as she stayed within these walls. For her it was a small price she would willingly pay, if it meant her child were safe. We hoped that by the time the baby was ready to be born, Franco would have stopped looking."

"He hadn't."

Not a question. The look on her face said it all. Franco was exactly like my father, and he didn't give up easily. Nine months would have been a drop in the ocean when he had a vendetta to settle.

"No, he hadn't." She shook her head slowly. "He was enraged, assumed she had snuck off with another man. The vile lies he spread about her. Hateful, hateful things." She closed her eyes, shuddering at the memory.

"So when the time came she made us promise that no matter what happened at the birth, she wouldn't be taken to hospital. That she would rather die than go back to him. It was one in the same, in reality. Franco would have killed her just for leaving him. If he had know she had tried to keep away his child—a son—he would have killed not only her, but anyone who ever loved or helped her."

Sister Catherine pushed out a breath, her hands grasping at the cloth around her chest. "That night . . . that night will haunt me for the rest of my days and then an eternity after. It was one of the worst storms we'd ever seen. The wind so wild I was sure the church would lift right off its foundation. There was no power; the neighborhood had been plunged into darkness. We had moved her into the church where she could be surrounded by the candles, hoping that under the Father's watchful eye that both of them would be given a chance. But it wasn't to be, and she succumbed just as he entered the world. A chilling sliding door between death and life."

"Surely there was something you could have done?" The question was completely redundant, but my mind was unable to reconcile that Rose was willingly left to die. "Taken her to the hospital under a fake name?"

"The minute she would have left these walls, someone would have seen her. One of *his* spies would have reported back. No," her head shook in conviction, "it was the only way. He never knew she was with child, so Michael was safe as long as no one knew who his mother had been. We hoped a kind family would have adopted him, loved him in a way we knew Rose would have done had she survived. But our hands were tied." Her face fell in defeat.

"A year or so later, the church declared the marriage annulled. Giving him the freedom to re marry." Her eyes got wide as she continued. "There were rumors circulating that he'd killed her. That he'd found her with a man and he shot them both. We were positive he had concocted the story so he could save face, preferring to have people believe he was capable of killing her, rather than allowing her to leave him."

"He never knew he had a son," I whispered back.

"No, he had two other wives. The second, Ophelia, was also unable to get pregnant. She was found in her bathtub drowned with an empty bottle of pills lying beside her on the floor. It was ruled a suicide, but no one knows for sure and his current wife, Selena, finally gave him a daughter fourteen years ago."

"We can't keep this from him."

"I promised his mother." Sister Catherine shook her head, her hands trying to steady herself as she leveraged her weight off the lawn. "That woman suffered enough. There is no telling what will happen if he finds out and that is something I will refuse to be part of."

It took her a few tries, rolling to the side before her legs were able to find purchase. "Sofia, please. Let this go." Her hands gripped mine tightly.

"I can't make promises I can't keep." My eyes locked on hers. "I'm sorry."

She closed her eyes slowly before reopening them and adjusting her robing. "We really should be getting inside." Her back straightened as she tried to force a smile. "You're not wearing a jacket and this chill will cut right through you."

I blinked a few times wondering if I fell into a wormhole and imagined the whole conversation. And if not for the grass stains on Sister Catherine's habit, I'd been convinced it never took place.

"You're right." I smiled back, taking a tentative step back toward to door. "It is cold out here."

"I'll be in my room if you need me." Catherine waited until we were both safely inside. "I'm feeling a little light headed, so I'd like to lay down before dinner."

"Would you like me to bring you something?" I asked nervously, Sister Catherine's face still absent of any color. "Maybe a soda or a candy bar?"

"No, no, I'll be fine." She patted my hands gently and then

excused herself, her feet moving slowly toward her bedroom.

Great.

Sister Catherine was the only person in this place who spoke to me and I was almost positive that door had slammed shut. Because I didn't have enough people hating me, I had to alienate the one person who was literally risking their life for me. That's not even taking into consideration she was a woman of the church. That alone was enough to send me rocking manically in the corner in a guilt-induced stupor. But what was my option? I wasn't sure I could look into Michael's eyes and *not* tell him what I knew.

My head was going to explode with the information. This whole time, Franco Santini's son had been right under his nose and he'd never known. Hell, if he found out it would send a tidal wave of ramifications that I couldn't even begin to imagine.

Oh my God, poor Rose. She must have been terrified. She had lived in fear for months, hidden away here while she tried to bring her child into the world. She was right about one thing. If Franco had ever found out about Michael, he would have never let him go, pulling him so deep into his world there would be no humanity left.

It was such a cruel twist of fate that he ended up in that life anyway. It begged the question as to how hard can we really fight our DNA? Had the echoes in his blood of Franco's brutality drawn him to the underworld? There was no way we would ever know. The only saving grace was that he didn't have ties to anyone, no formal allegiances. All he had to do was leave and he would be free from it, from *them*, something that wouldn't have been possible if his last name was Santini.

Look at what happened to me. I was living proof that blood ties were almost impossible to break.

I understood why Sister Catherine fought so long and hard

to keep it buried. Even though deep down inside me I knew he deserved to know, once that lid was opened, nothing in his world would ever be the same.

Will you tell him? A voice whispered from deep inside of me.

"I don't know." I answered the empty room.

TWENTY-FOUR

SOFIA

There was a large field.
In it tall pale blue cornflowers grew, their petals curling up toward the sun's light. The thin green stems bent just slightly in the gentle breeze. It was beautiful, peaceful, and as I looked out into the horizon the endless landscape seemed to stretch eternally.

There was a woman, mid-twenties with long, wavy, dark hair walking through the cornflowers with slow steady steps. The white dress she wore was covered in a fine film of blue powder but she was laughing, clearly not minding the stain.

"Hello." I smiled as she came closer, her brown eyes so bright they almost didn't seem real. "I'm Sofia." I held out my hand, waiting for her to take it.

"I know." Her pale pink lips spread into a grin before she turned back to the horizon. "It's a beautiful day isn't it?"

I dropped my hand feeling a little stupid that I didn't know who she was. "Yes, it is."

She breathed in deep, her eyes closing as her chest expanded to maximum. "Such a beautiful day."

I watched her, mesmerized as she pushed out the breath and threw her head back in a throaty laugh before continuing to walk forward.

"Where are you going?" I called out, her body moving faster

through the sea of blue flowers taking her further and further away.

"Wherever I want to." She laughed, her hair flowing behind her as she continued to run until I couldn't see her anymore.

"Wait!" My body tried to surge forward, hoping I could catch her and at the very least ask her name. "Wait."

But I didn't move; my legs staying rooted in their spot despite me willing them to walk. It was then when I looked down hoping to see what was wrong with my feet that I saw that I was wearing the same white dress.

Except instead of the soft hew of blue smeared across the front, there was a deep shade of red.

And it was on my hands too.

"Quick, you must wake up!"

I wasn't sure if I'd dreamt it or someone was in the room speaking to me. The landscape faded taking with it the cornflowers, the field and the sun. I returned to black, my eyes slowly sliding open as the light beside my bed turned on.

"You have to hide or they will find you." This time the voice was more insistent, startling me awake.

"What?" My body shot up off the mattress as my brain suddenly kicked into gear. "What's happening?"

"There's no time." One of the nuns—I think her name was Rachel?—tossed my clothes at me. "They will be here soon."

"Who, who is coming?" I sat up, throwing jeans and a sweater over my pajamas. The urgency in her voice hinted that I didn't have time to properly dress.

"Sister Catherine is sick, we had to call an ambulance." She picked up my two bags I had purposely left packed and held them out toward me. "Please, you must go hide before they get here."

"I can help," I ignored the bags hurrying toward the doorway. "I've been trained in first aid."

"No, you can't." She cut off my exit, dropping my bags in front of me and bracing her arms either side of the door. "They will find you and then we'll all be in danger. Please, you can't be here when they come. You must hide."

I had no idea what was wrong with Sister Catherine but whatever it was I knew that every second counted. She needed me, and I owed her.

"Please, I'll be quick. Just let me see her and then I'll do whatever you want me to."

Sister Rachel hesitated, her fingers turning white as they squeezed against the doorframe. "One minute, and then you have to go."

She had barely moved to the side when I sped past her, my bare feet pounding against the floorboards as I raced into Sister Catherine's room.

I gasped when I saw her and not because it was the first time I'd seen her without her habit.

She was lying in her bed, a simple white cotton nightgown poking out of the top of the heavy woolen blanket. Her long gray hair had been coiled on top of her head while her slender arms rested on her stomach. Her usual pale skin so colorless she looked like she was made of wax. Her eyes stayed closed while her chest expanded just enough to show she was still breathing.

"Oh no." My knees fell beside her bed, my fingers reaching for her icy cold hands. "Please no."

"Save him."

"Please."

"Save him."

Wracked with guilt, my fingers gripped tighter, knowing I would do whatever it took to keep that promise as the life literally drained out of her in front of my very eyes.

"There is nothing you can do. Please." Sister Rachel tugged

at my arm. "She would want you to be safe."

I nodded, words getting stuck in my throat as I raced back into the room and collected my bags. My eyes did a quick sweep of the room to make sure there was no other evidence left as I followed her back into the hall.

It wasn't my own personal safety that I was worried about. Me, being here, was putting them all in danger.

"Quickly, this way." She darted down the narrow hallway to the far end of the house and out a side door. "The ambulance will be here any minute."

The cold wind slapped me in the face as we stepped outside. The crescent moon was hidden by heavy clouds and offered little light, the silvery glow making the yard ominous as we walked quickly across the grass.

"In here." Sister Rachel pulled open a large metal black door of a large brick building that bordered the property from the other side.

I had assumed the windowless building was an old factory or storage facility, long forgotten by an unfavorable economy. But the old rusted metal sign bolted into the brick told me otherwise.

Three yellow triangles, each meeting at their points surround by a circle.

It was an old bomb shelter, one of the thousands that had been built during the Cold War.

"It locks from the inside." Her fingers held the door, the wind trying to force it open. "Be safe."

Her eyes said it all. She was just as scared as I was, the heavy metal door shutting between us with a loud thud, taking with it any light.

I fumbled in the dark with my bags, dropping them onto the concrete floor as my hand searched inside one and then the other for the cell I had hidden inside.

It was one of Michael's burners, given to me under the strict instructions that I only use it in a case of life or death. My hand padded through the bag until I felt the hard surface, searching blindly for the on button, until the screen glowed.

The darkness ebbed just enough for me to see my surroundings, the phone carried in front of my face like a flashlight as I walked deeper into the building trying to find anything I could use.

There was nothing, the place had either been gutted or looted years ago without even a candlestick left. And with no idea of how long I would be in here, I slid the lock into place on the door and cut the power on the phone. As much as I hated being in the dark, I might need it again later.

The sirens came soon after. Their muted whine almost completely drowned out by the thick walls. I had no idea what was happening out there, but I was almost positive Sister Catherine wouldn't survive.

I was sure it would be chalked up to natural causes, her age a contributing factor, but I knew that it had been the stress that pushed her over. Years and years of protecting a secret had finally taken its toll. Me, discovering it—with no idea on what I would do with the information—had probably shot so much fear into her world that she wasn't able to recover from the tailspin.

My body shivered as it slowly sunk to the cold, hard floor, my cheeks getting wet. I hadn't meant to cry, my eyes leaking before I had a chance to stop them. Not that it mattered in here; there was no one to see. No one I needed to be strong for.

The tears didn't stop, streaming down my face as I sobbed silently. The weight of the responsibility was killing me. I wish I could end it, stop any more people getting hurt because of me.

And then I remembered the dream—the woman in the

white dress running in the field. It felt so real, the heat of the sun on my face, the gentle sway of the cornflowers. I wanted to run, run like she had and be free of all of it. Throw my head back and laugh with complete abandon. But it wasn't possible. That future had disappeared as quickly as the woman had. Or had I been the woman the whole time? It didn't matter anymore. Moving away, making my father accountable wasn't enough. I'd never be able to run far enough—never be free.

My stomach twisted as my head fell into my hands. There was only one way to guarantee the conclusion. To save us both.

My father and Michael's father needed to die.

It was hard to breathe, the idea of killing someone I'd once loved, horrifying. I had planned to bring him to justice, of doing it the *right* way. Never had I imagined the alternative. Never had I thought . . . Killing my father? Killing Franco? But too much damage had been done—to Catherine, to Rose, to Michael and to me.

It was the only way.

A tremble rose from inside of me, a vibration so strong that I had to check that the floor underneath me hadn't shifted. But there hadn't been an earthquake, and what I felt was my resilience to survive. Not only to survive, but thrive.

Maybe I had been fighting too long for something that had always been inside of me. Maybe I had always been capable and I just needed the right motivation. My father had killed for greed, for power, for—who knew what else. But for me it was different. It was personal. The things I'd seen in the last few days had changed me, and my world was never going to be the same.

I used to believe I was naïve as a child, ignorant to my father's life and what he did. But my real naivety was in my adult life. Things had *never* been black and white. And sometimes, murder was justified. Sometimes it was the only way out, and you just had to be strong.

I'd tried.

Believed there were other ways. But it all brought me back to here.

Here.

Where two men had ruined the lives of so many people, and I had the power to change that. To stop the cycle. To stop the pain.

I wouldn't enjoy it, and my heart would still pray for forgiveness, but their blood would cleanse ours.

And I would do it.

And then finally we'd all be able to rest.

•••

It was hours later.

I only knew because I occasionally checked the phone. With no reference of light, its bright digital display was my only connection to the outside world. Sleep impossible as I sat alone with my thoughts.

"Sofia?"

It was barely a whisper; the thump on the door confirming I hadn't imagined it had been wind.

My legs bolted upright, sending my body vertical in a rush as I wrestled with the lock in the dark.

The door swung open, the morning light blinding me as my eyes fought to adjust. Sister Rachel didn't speak, stepping inside the door and closing most of it so no one could see from the outside. She stood patiently as I fought against my falling eyelids.

"She's gone," she said when my vision finally returned.

"I know."

We both stood for a while, just looking at each other, neither of us really knowing what to say.

"You can't come back yet. There are too many people . . ." She took a breath. "It's too risky."

"I think it's better if I don't come back." I swallowed, not knowing if I could walk past Sister Catherine's room and not be eaten from the inside out by the guilt. "Do you think you can get me some supplies? Just a few things so I can stay out of sight for a couple of days. Once the attention dies down, I'll move on."

Mentally I'd been preparing the list for hours. Water. Candles or a flashlight. Some food. Just the basics. Ditching most of my clothes and moving to one bag was also the plan— the lighter, the easier it was going to be to move.

"Where will you go?" Her eyes widened as she reached for me. "Please just wait a little longer and then come back, she would have wanted you safe with us."

"None of you are safe if I come back." I shook my head. "I'll be fine, I know I will be."

"And what about Michael?" She tilted her head to the side. "What will we tell him when he comes looking for you?"

Other than last night, this was the first real conversation Sister Rachel and I had had since I'd arrived. I had no idea what she'd been told but obviously she knew the key players.

"Tell him that it was time for me to go and that I didn't need a hero." I sighed imagining how infuriated he would be when she told him. "And that I will be okay."

"Give me a list of what you need; I'll do my best to get it together, but I really wish you would reconsider."

"Thank you, Sister Rachel, but I've already made up my mind."

We made a plan for her to return in a few hours. She would bring food, water, a small kerosene lamp and notepad so I

261

could write down a list of things that I needed. I hated being shut in again, the dark enveloping me as the door closed but I knew it would only be for a little while longer.

There needed to be a plan, one that helped me move around undetected. I assumed by now news of my death had spread. If my father bought the lie then he would have been compelled to play it out.

A funeral, a period of mourning—a wake. All the pomp and circumstance that was required to prove what a loving father he'd been. An obituary would have also been mandatory which meant my face would have been widely circulated. The department might have made their own announcement, the Chicago Tribune possibly running a story on my mysterious disappearance and death. Of course my father would never allow an investigation, he would grease whatever palms he needed and have my death ruled accidental. Possibly a car crash, it would explain the ashes. Or some freak natural occurrence that could be signed off by a coroner—there was always someone willing to take a stack of cash.

My stomach growled in the dark. The loud noise sounded like some kind of beast was trying to jailbreak from my belly. It had been hours since I'd eaten something, skipping dinner after the incident in the garden. Not that there was anything I could do about it now. Food, like everything else, would have to wait, but it gave me something other than my situation to think about.

When was she coming back?

I tried not to check my phone again, the hours seeming to go slower when I did. It wasn't sure why I was struggling so much, I had been alone most of my life. But my thoughts had never been this dark. And I wondered if it was what was inside my head that was making me claustrophobic and not the room.

Finally there was a knock at the door. I pressed my ear

against the metal but didn't hear my name. It made me nervous but other than Sister Rachel, who else would know I was in here?

Just to be sure, I grabbed my gun, carefully sliding off the safety as I tentatively unlocked the door. There might not be a lot I could do if there was more than one person on the other side, but at least I could take one or two of them out before I went down.

"Couldn't keep yourself out of trouble, huh?"

Even with my eyes squinting trying to adjust to the light, I knew it was Michael. His voice low and he pushed his way inside and shut the door behind us.

"What are you doing here? Did anyone see you?" I asked, my heart racing, unable to decide if I was glad he was here or terrified of what his appearance meant.

There was small click, a flashlight illuminating the entire room as he looked me dead in the eyes.

"I told you, I was coming back."

TWENTY-FIVE

MICHAEL

Well shit had hit the fan, hadn't it?
The plan was I stayed busy doing the rounds for Damon. Sure the busting kneecaps with baseball bats was so fucking cliché it actually hurt, but it beat sitting around looking out of my window like a paranoid fucktard. Of course the *plan* got shot straight to hell when I heard over the police scanner that a meat wagon had called in a DOA from Saint Margaret's. Coincidence? Please. There was no such thing.

It took the better part of the morning to get some answers. Knocking on the wooden doors and asking questions wasn't an option and neither was heading to the morgue and getting an eyeball at the corpse. But a few well place phone calls got me the information I needed.

Sister Catherine had decided to take a dirt nap. And fuck me if that wasn't inconvenient. This bitch has literally been fucking up shit since the day I was born, and I hated her more now than ever.

"So, you want to tell me what happened?" I reaffixed the lock even though the chances of anyone coming through the door were slim. "Last time I left here she was a pain in the ass, but still alive."

"I'm not sure." Sofia shook her head nervously, her backward step hindered by a bunch of shit on the floor. "I left before the ambulance got there, but when I saw her she didn't look good. Probably a heart attack."

Sofia's usual confidence was missing. She was rattled, her eyes wide and hands fidgety, unable to stand still on her feet as she looked at me.

Of course, being stuck in the dark might have rattled her cage, or it could be knowing the nun had just died. It was a bit much to ask anyone to be solid under the circumstances.

"Well, I guess we need to move our timeline then, don't we?" I lowered the flashlight on the floor, the thing throwing enough of a glow so we could both see. "There are going to be holy people crawling all over that place like ants. Too many eyes, it will expose us for sure."

The fact one of the other nuns had the mindset to stash Sofia out of the way was a fucking revelation. I was positive those do-gooders would have taken the first out and waited for the cops to discover her. Turns out they really are a loyal bunch, who knew? Of course she wasn't as calm as Catherine. And looked like she was about to join her dearly departed *sister* when I showed up on their back doorstep. But she told me what I needed to know and didn't make eye contact. So she was smart too.

"Did you see my father?" Sofia barely made eye contact, her hands squeezed into fists.

"Yep, and you'll be please to know he was pissed I'd burned you." Not that knowing would take the sting off your father wanting to kill you, but I hoped it might relax her a little. "I'm probably going to need to find a new president for my fan club." I couldn't help but laugh.

"What about Franco?" Her voice wavered, her eyes hitting my chest but not getting any further.

"What about him?" I took a step closer wondering why she was worried about that asshole. "He won't care as long as he thinks you're out of the picture. If Jimmy is convinced, Franco will fall into line."

"I think it's better if I go it alone, from here." She took another backward step. "I'd appreciate the documents though if you have them."

What.

The.

Fuck.

"Go it alone? Did you stroke out when the old woman's heart gave out?" Because that was the only logical explanation for the crazy talk. "Pretty sure we went through this and we agreed I would get you to the border before you channeled your I-am-woman shit."

"I have some stuff I need to take care of before I go."

"Stuff?" Maybe I was the one who was stroking out. "Sofia, need I remind you that technically you are fucking dead? You don't exist. This isn't the time to pick up the dry-cleaning you forgot about or take a freaking stroll down at Millennium Park."

"Look, I know this doesn't make sense and I know I'll have to be careful, but there is shit that has been done—"

"Oh for fuck's sake!" If the walls hadn't been solid concrete, I would have put one of my fists through one. "You want to play snitch, you do it from a secure location. That was the plan. We just went through the whole charade so you make it out of this alive, why the hell would you want to risk it now?"

"It's my decision." She tipped her chin, a fuck you if ever I saw one. "Now, do you have those documents?"

"No." I lied, not willing to hand over shit until I knew why the hell she'd lost her damn mind. "I still need to pick them up."

Total bullshit of course. Leon had delivered exactly what I needed the day after we spoke. I had a new social, driver's license and passport tucked away in my pocket, which is exactly where they were staying until I knew why she had developed the sudden need to take care of *stuff*.

"Well, can you get them to me in the next few days?" She folded her arms tightly against her chest. "You can keep the rest of the trust fund money."

"What aren't you telling me?" My eyes narrowed as I tracked her.

She was acting weird. Nervous. Evasive. And she was struggling with making eye contact. It didn't take a genius to work out that there was more to it than was coming out of her mouth.

"Something happened while you were here?" I gauged her response. "With Catherine?"

Ding, ding, ding. We had a fucking winner. Because the minute I'd strung that sentence together her eyes gave me all the confirmation I needed. She might have been trying to keep it locked down but her poker face sucked.

"No. Nothing." She shrugged, continuing to play the game.

"Fine, nothing." I smirked, stalking a little closer. "Catherine has a heart attack and you decide to go rogue. Sounds like it's been a busy few days."

I continued to move closer. Her eyes got wider as I closed the gap between us, but to her credit she didn't take any more backward steps, holding her ground.

"Let me go, Michael." She blinked, a long exhale pushing past her lips. "This is where you and I end."

Any other time, the person on the other side of that conversation would have received a middle finger as I walked out the door. But Sofia had been different from the start. And now, well fuck if I knew why I was so compelled, but walking away wasn't an option. Not until I knew why. It wasn't because I fucked her. It wasn't because I felt sorry for her either. And it sure as shit wasn't out of a sense of duty.

"I'll decide when it ends," I breathed into her face. "And it doesn't end here."

She looked like she wanted to crumble; her arms twitched at her side while her eyes got glassy, but she stayed standing.

"I promised her," she whispered. "I owe her."

"Catherine? What do you owe her?" I asked, the extra words not getting us any closer to a clearer picture. "Tell me."

"You. I need to save you."

I'd heard the words, but they didn't make sense. Like someone had given me an uppercut right to the jaw and rung my bell.

Me?

She needs to save me?

I wasn't the one whose father had sanctioned her death just to cover his own ass. There was no one out there gunning for me. Well, no more than usual given my line of work.

"Sofia, I'm not the one who needs saving."

"You do, more than you know."

There was something different in her face. Something I hadn't seen before and it made me five different shades of uncomfortable. It crawled up my skin, infecting me like a motherfucking disease as I felt whatever self-control I had shatter into a million pieces.

"Look at me." My hands grabbed her chin forcing her to look me in the eyes. "This is not someone you or anyone else can save. If there was any such thing as redemption, I'm beyond it." I squeezed harder, my fingers bound to leave a mark in her pretty skin as I pushed her back against the wall. "So, if that's the prayers you're offering up, save your breath. Ain't no one up there who's listening."

She struggled, trying to fight against my hand as I pinned her, the weight of my body holding her in place. "Now that we have straightened that out, tell me exactly what that fucking bitch told you."

Her eyes welled, her head shaking as I held her in place, her mouth clamped shut.

"Tell me."

"Your mother. She wasn't a nun." The words came out in a rush, surprising us both, her chest heaving up and down as she took big gasps of air.

"So, who was she then?"

Her existence had meant so little to me for so long I wasn't sure I wanted to know. It would change nothing. Except that now Sofia had said it, she looked like she instantly regretted it and I wasn't about to let it go.

"Sofia. Who was my mother?"

"Michael, you're hurting me." Her nails bit into my skin as she tried to loosen my grip on her face. "Let go."

"Say it." The words coming out of my mouth barely sounded human anymore as my jaw locked.

"Rose Santini!" she yelled. "Franco's first wife."

My hand let go instantly as I stepped away from her, unsure of what the hell I'd heard.

"It's true." She coughed. "You're Franco's son."

It made no sense.

No fucking sense.

It couldn't be true.

"There is no way Franco would have let her leave with his kid. The man is a sadistic asshole and he would have chained her to the bed if he had to. There's no way, especially if she was married to him."

"He didn't know." She shook her head, wrapping her arms around her middle like she was going to split apart. "She left before he found out. That's why she was hidden in the convent. Why she was dressed as a nun. It was the only chance she had.

She was trying to protect you. She loved—"

"Shut your fucking mouth." My fists white knuckled at my side, ready to UFC the wall if that was my only option. "Don't you dare."

I couldn't keep still. My nerves jangled as heat rose up my spine, making my skin feel too tight against my bones. I wasn't sure what pissed me off more, the lies coming out of her mouth or that she'd convinced herself that they were true.

"You might hate it, but it doesn't make it any less a fact." She opened her mouth, refusing to stop talking even though I didn't want to hear another fucking word. "You have people who can find out things, do some digging. The marriage was annulled after she disappeared but the records will still exist. Paper clippings, there will be proof that Rose was married to him."

"So what?" I laughed, wondering how much of the Kool-Aid she'd actually drunk. "You think there was only one *Rose* in the whole of Chicago? Don't be so naïve."

"No, but I bet there is only one Rose who fits your mother's description and disappeared about eight months before you were born." She moved away from the wall, eyeing me carefully as she put some distance between us. "What did you tell me about coincidences? You didn't believe in them."

So Catherine fucking tells me nothing—you know, the person who was actually involved—but spends five minutes with Sofia then all of a sudden spills her guts?

If she hadn't been dead, I would have killed her myself.

"It was eating Catherine alive. I could see it." Sofia filled the silence. "She didn't tell you because your mother died trying to protect you from Franco, Catherine promised her that he would never know."

"Just stop." My hands shot out, the only reason they didn't make contact with anything is because she'd been smart enough to keep her distance. "I can't fucking think."

Intellectually I agreed, assuming this checked out—the stuff about Franco's first wife—then it would be a one in a million chance that it was bullshit. Like a fucking lottery win, except instead of a truck load of cash you got syphilis. And I was just as excited at the prospect of being Franco's kid as I was at getting a sore dick and going blind.

"So even if it is true—and I'm not saying I believe this horseshit—but say it is." Pretty sure I'd prefer the sore dick at this point. "This affects *you* how?"

"Because I know what this information could do to you, I can see it in your eyes." She looked like she was carefully considering her words. Good thing too because if she mentioned the need to save me again, I wasn't going to be responsible for my actions. "And because I want to make sure that your father *and* mine never destroy another life again."

It was a little late for that. She was nothing like the girl I'd met on her doorstep. Seems like it or not, there was more of Jimmy in her than we both knew was there. And me, well I guess I'd always been a bastard, I guess it just made more sense now.

"If anyone has the right for revenge, it's me, Sofia." And she better hear the words because I wasn't joking. "You don't get to make the rules on that. I don't give a fuck how many dead nuns you promised."

I watched the lump in her neck bob up and down her throat. She might have a fairytale in her head about how this was going to play out, but she knew what I was capable of. I guess the apple didn't fall too far from the tree after all. The difference between me and my so-called dad—I had nothing left to lose.

"So, what are you going to do?" she asked, tiptoeing around the powder keg she'd just lit a match near.

"Exactly what I said I was going to do." I rolled my head to one side and then the other, fighting a losing battle against the tension in my neck. "Get you out of here and then come back for them."

"What if I won't go?"

"Why would you stay?"

"The same reason why you won't leave."

I hated that her reasoning made fucking sense. She had every right to make her own choices and if sticking a knife through her father's heart was one of them, then I didn't get to stop her. Fuck knows the bastard deserved it. But there was so much noise in my head and part of it was me not wanting that for her.

My emotional grid was all over the place. But I didn't have time or the inclination to process it, and I hated fucking feelings to begin with.

While the possible new branch to my family tree sure put a new spin on things, it didn't change that the reason I knew any of it was because of the woman in front of me.

I still wasn't sure if I was pissed off or grateful, probably both. And whatever was driving her—why she was so compelled to see this through to the end with me—it was probably the same reason as to why I hadn't put her in a body bag when Jimmy asked for it.

Like it or not, there was a fucking connection. Maybe it was just the fact we both had sadists as fathers, or maybe it was because we both didn't lie down and die. But I was confident she would be all right as long we stuck together. And then, when this was all over, she could leave like she was supposed to. Without me, because that had always been the plan.

"I know you don't want to hear it. And I can't imagine what it must be like for you. It's like everything you've ever known has been turned upside down. But even though you are Franco

Santini's son, you are not him. For once, let someone in. Let *me* in."

"Don't turn this into a tragedy, Sofia," I warned her, the words ironic considering we were halfway there already. "I'll be disappointed if you aren't smarter than that."

TWENTY-SIX

MICHAEL

It took a while before the steady stream of traffic slowed at the church. For a nobody, the nun sure did attract a lot of attention. And instead of me using that time to smash my fist against the wall, I'd calmed down a little and let Sofia tell me what she knew. Yeah, I couldn't believe I'd been so adult about it either. I may have checked my balls a couple of times just to make sure they were still there. Wonders will never cease.

The idea that I'd had actual parents—and not some random bastard—was something I gave up on a long time ago. The only comfort in finding out exactly who *they* were was that I finally had a name. Theirs. Not so I could attach it to mine, nope, that wasn't the reason I wanted it. It was so I knew whose doorstep to turn up on and unleash my anger.

"Here are the things you asked for." The same nun who'd shown me the fallout shelter in the first place held out two canvas bags. "I must go and be with my sisters."

"Go, but remember to keep your mouth shut." I eyeballed her, her gaze dropping as soon as I'd grabbed the bags.

"You know, she is actually helping us." Sofia took one of the bags from me and set up one of the kerosene lamps. "I've seen you be kind when you want to be."

"The key words there were *when I want to be*," I pointed out, going through the second bag as soon as the door was secure. "And we have bigger issues than my mood."

I wasn't talking about the ancestory.com revelations she'd dropped in my lap either. I was more concerned about the fact that she'd decided we needed to go to the house where she used to live—the place her father, mother and three brothers were holed up in—and kill Jimmy. *And she thought I had issues with my sanity.*

"Have you got a car?" She armed herself, shoving extra clips in her waistband as she multitasked and ate some of the food we'd been given. "I think we need to go over the plan one more time too."

"I have a car." Nothing as sweet as the Camaro that I'd had to ditch—sadly, last I'd heard had been impounded—but it would do the job. "And I still don't think driving to your dad's house is the way to do this."

I lifted my fingers to serve as a visual aid because clearly talking wasn't cutting it. "We'll have no advantage. No line of sight until we're in there. And have no clue as to how many guns and people holding them are inside. Not to mention security cameras that line the property and motion sensors."

"There is a side door up the main drive that has a blind stop." Her hand got busy with a pencil sketching a rough rectangle, illustrating where Jimmy's house sat on the block.

"All you have to do is park on the street and jump the fence from the left hand side." She marked an X over the front extreme corner close to the front gate. "Then as long as you keep your back flush against the metal railings, you can walk the entire length without being seen. Unless someone happens to look at the front window at that exact time, and then you're shit out of luck." She smirked, obviously having tested the theory.

"And the motion sensors positioned on the property line are at forty-five degree angles." She drew circles on the border of the rectangle, with extending lines to indicate their range. "That corner—the one you jump the fence from—is just beyond its reach." She pointed the pencil toward the heavily drawn X.

"My father was too arrogant to install a backup there because the area not covered is so small. But it's possible, and when you jump it needs to be dead center or you'll completely miss the mark. It's how I snuck out of the house when I was a teenager, and how my brothers snuck their girlfriends in. Everyone assumed the back is more vulnerable so that's where my father concentrated his efforts. He never thought anyone would be brazen enough to come from the front. And I'm telling you, it can be done."

"What's the margin? The jump onto that exact spot." I pointed to the mystical magical X that would supposedly get us in and out unnoticed.

"Three inches over and the sensors get you." She cleared her throat. "It's got to be dead on."

Three inches and we hadn't even accounted for shoe size. Yep, this was going to be a motherfucking good time.

"And you're sure he hasn't fixed the oversight? It's been a few years since you lived there." Because if I were him, I would have overhauled the system and double layered the dead zone. Hell, I'd have made sure every single one of those cameras and sensors overlapped so not even one blade of grass wasn't covered.

"Positive." She nodded. "He upgraded a few years ago but the new motion sensors kept going off. He pulled them out and went back to the old system. Same margin exists that there has always been."

"And you know this how?" Because it sounded like an awful lot of information and not any of it sounded hypothetical.

"I tested it myself three months ago." She bit her lip, her

feet doing a two-step shuffle before she stood up straight and looked me in the eye. The silent admiration for her skill set and attention to detail remained unsaid. "How do you think I got some of the information on the drive? I had to access the house and scanned some documents from his file cabinet. He hasn't changed any of the combinations or codes either. Like I said, he's arrogant."

"So, assuming we get to that side door." I resisted humming the Mission Impossible theme, but essentially that was what we were dealing with.

"We will," she shot back, zero hesitation.

"And we can get in. Not setting off the motion detectors, not getting caught on the cameras and there isn't some asshole at the window admiring the view."

"We can."

I ignored the optimism and stated the obvious. "What are you going to do once you get in there?"

"I'm going to end it."

As expected, but she still hadn't said how.

"Your brothers are in town, not to mention we don't know who else is in the house. So unless you are thinking of smothering him with a pillow, I am almost positive someone will hear a gunshot." More than likely *everyone* would hear the fucking gunshot and we'd be SOL on our exit strategy.

"My brothers won't hurt me." She got defensive, obviously forgetting it had been her father who had wanted her out of the picture in the first place. "Anyone else, I'll take the chance."

"No. You do this, you don't trust your brothers." The trio of douchebags might not be involved in the family business on paper, but the old man had been grooming them for years. "You need to get up close and personal. You use a knife and if you don't have the stomach for it then this isn't going to work."

There were so many variables and possibilities, that even

with careful execution, it could still turn into a shit storm. But there would be only one chance, and that was to get him when he slept.

Take him out quickly and with as little noise as possible. The mess, well that couldn't be helped, but I'd rather worry about bloodstains on my shirt than a bullet hole to the head.

"Can you do that, Sofia? Because if you are serious about doing this, you are going to have to look into his eyes when he dies."

"Yes." For once she didn't hesitate. Just a leveled stare that hinted she'd given it some serious thought. And regardless of whether I believed her, she looked like she'd convinced herself. "I know I can do this."

••••

The Nissan Maxima looked like every other car on the road. Which is why I had chosen it. That and the asshole I'd bought it from didn't ask too many questions when I'd paid cash for it. A whole lot of don't ask, don't tell happening on both sides of the transaction and it would be safe to say the car had questionable origins.

Even though Sofia had shoved her hair up into a ball cap and had it pulled down low in front of her face, I wasn't taking a chance in having her ride shotgun beside me. Nope, wasn't happening. Instead she curled herself into the trunk and hid until we reached the pretentious leafy 'burbs. It was where all the jerk offs had their overpriced mansions.

The car eased, coming to a stop near the curb. It was close enough that we didn't have far to walk but not so close anyone at the Amaro residence would get an eyeful.

The house was dark. No lights were on except for a couple of security beams around the periphery, with the drapes drawn tight like everyone was in for the night.

When the trunk released, Sofia's body uncoiled, her legs stretching as I helped her out of the car. She had changed so much since I'd met her. I guess we both had. I still wasn't sure if either of those changes were for the better.

"You sure about this?" I grabbed her arm, not entirely convinced she could one-eighty her decision to let the *law* bring him to justice. "Once you go down this road, there is no turning back."

"I'm already on the road, Michael." She smiled, the reaction so fucking unexpected I almost fell back on my ass.

"Okay then, let's go."

There was no further talking. No need for it either unless we wanted to sign post we were breaking in. We'd gone over our entrance a million times, our bodies moving through the dark with only the streetlights' glow thrown into the mix.

Jimmy lived in a good neighborhood. High trees, tall fancy fences—it made it easier to slip into the shades and stay out of sight. Plus most of those assholes believed no one would have the nerve to rob them with their hi-tech security systems and their *beware of guard dog* signs. Little did they know their false sense of entitlement had made them all sitting ducks.

Sofia took the lead. It's what we agreed considering she knew the way and I would be better support if I didn't stick my toe over the invisible do-not-cross-line and get us both killed. I still wasn't a hundred percent sure this shit was going to work, but we were in too deep to turn around now. And we were all in, because there wasn't a backup plan.

Her body moved smoothly in front of me, stepping into Jimmy's neighbor's front yard and pushing herself out of sight as I followed close behind.

She pointed silently to the ground a few feet in front of her. A large rock had been positioned with smaller rocks surrounding it like some fucking art installation that didn't make sense. And with a nod she took a small run up using the rock to propel her body, her hands catching the top of the fence as the inertia swung her weight around. She wasn't kidding when she'd said she done this before, the maneuver looking as smooth as an Olympic gymnast, her hands gripping the top of the metal fence without even disturbing the nearby hedge.

She hung for a second, her hands adjusting slightly and then there was a small thud as she landed on the opposite side.

Now I just had to replicate it.

Awesome.

I didn't take so much of a run but more of a step up onto the rock. I had more height and a hell of a lot more weight, and the last thing I needed was to swing too far because gravity had decided to be an asshole. It wasn't as quiet or as graceful as she'd done, but I hefted myself over and waited for her to point to my mark before I let go. A couple of dogs barked in the distance, but no one turned their lights on.

My landing was a little heavier than I would have liked, my legs bent at the knees to absorb the impact keeping me upright. Sofia gave me the thumbs up when no security lights turned on.

She wasn't kidding about keeping our backs flush against the wall. If my ass got any closer to the metal that separated the two property boundaries, it was going to fuse to the fucking bars. But we kept moving, our feet shuffling as quickly as we could while keeping out of sensor range.

Once we got in proximity of the side door, it was going to get a little more involved. There was a camera tracked right on the entrance but apparently it wasn't on. A hell of a gamble but there was no way to tell if it was just a prop or if Jimmy had stopped having his head up his ass and actually fixed the thing.

Either way we were going to find out as Sofia took a small step into its range and held her breath.

Nothing.

There was no more hesitation on her part, her hands getting busy on the keypad and gaining access like she still had a key. The door opened with a little more than a flick of her wrist.

She took a step inside the doorway, gun drawn, running point as I followed her through with twin nines gracing my palms.

Whether we stayed in the clear was yet to be determined but for now the lights stayed off and the door clicked back into place behind us. There was no time to congratulate each other as I followed her through the house, moving on the balls of my feet making as little contact with the floor as possible.

This was easy.

Too easy.

Sofia had run through the layout of the house before we'd left. She'd roughly drawn where rooms were, and the location of doors and stairs, so some of it felt familiar as we walked around in the space. All the bedrooms were upstairs though, which didn't improve our chances of continuing to be undetected.

We'd just cleared the massive marble entrance wall when we'd heard the click of a light switch.

Mother. Fucker.

I knew this had been too easy.

Sofia gestured to the large hall closet, one hand pointing wildly to the door while the other was still locked around her nine. But she had a better chance of her father rolling out a welcome mat than I did of getting into that closet. Nope, wasn't going to happen. Apart from giving us no way out, it cut off any advantage, making us completely blind.

My head gave her the it-ain't-happening shake as she moved closer. The echo of uneven footsteps traveled down the staircase as I clued up that it hadn't been the closet she'd been pointing to but the corner next to it. The edge of the wall able to provide us some cover while we still maintained some visual of the room. Good enough for me.

"James? Is that you?" A woman's voice called out as another light went on. The room on the other side of the wall flooded with overhead halogen.

Great. It was Sofia's mother.

Don't. I wanted to say it but couldn't risk giving away our position, so instead I lowered my hand to her arm and pressed my knuckles against her. It was the best I could do while juggling my nine.

Her body tensed but she didn't step out, staying where she was as we waited to see if her mother was going to go left or right.

"Elena, come to bed." More footsteps, Jimmy's voice carried down the length of the stairs.

"I'm sure I heard James."

We couldn't see a lot, but I was able to catch the corner of Sofia's mom face. She dressed for bed but her hair was a mess. It also looked like her face was melting off; the forgotten makeup probably having competed with a pillow.

"I'm right here, Elena." Jimmy stayed out of view, his voice agitated as he remained somewhere on the stairs. "And the boys are out tonight."

"Then it must be Sofia." She looked to the front door like she was expecting it to open.

I felt her body jerk at the mention of her name, but she managed to stay quiet. Both of us watching her parents interact with the limited view we had, wondering what the fuck was going to happen next.

"Elena, we've been through this before. Sofia is gone." Cue the exaggerated breath. Something told me the old lady was missing a marble or two and this sort of scenario had happened more than once. "Remember, we are burying her tomorrow."

"My little girl is gone?" The words got wavy, like she was about to cry. "Are you sure, James?"

"Yes, I'm sure. How many times do we have to go over it?" Another fucking deep breath, the asshole showing zero sympathy over the loss of his kid or that his wife was having a moment. "She's in a better place now." He tacked on like a Hallmark tagline. Father of the fucking year.

"Yes, yes a better place." Elena shook her head as she slowly ambled toward the stairs. "I'm not sure why I came down here," she muttered under her breath seeming to already have forgotten the dialogue with Jimmy.

"Let's get you back to bed. We'll get you one of those pills to help you sleep."

Something told me those pills were part of the old lady's problems.

She didn't fight him though, her feet shuffling back up the stairs and killing the lights as she went. The house went dark again as we waited to hear the closing of doors.

One.

Then two.

Sofia's parents hadn't slept in the same bedroom in years, which might be sad for their marital harmony but helped us when there was only one of them we want to kill.

And while I hadn't enjoyed the mild heart attack Elena's midnight sleepwalk had caused, it had been informative. The close call gave us some much needed recon. For now the Amaro Trio, aka Sofia's brothers, weren't in the house and Elena's freak show mask suggested there weren't any other houseguests either. Jimmy's wife would never allow anyone to see her if she wasn't at her best. And hopefully whatever drug cocktail she had taken would keep her out for the count and we could get this done without collateral damage. We also didn't know if and when Sofia's brothers were coming back so shit needed to happen ASAP.

"Wait," I whispered against her hair, her body jerking as she was about to take a step. "Give him time to settle back in and then go."

She nodded her head in understanding, her shoulders relaxing a little as she settled into her shoes.

This was the last time she would ever feel like this and I wanted for her to remember what it felt like before.

Before she'd taken that final step and crossed onto the other side.

Because once you've gone there, there was no coming back.

TWENTY-SEVEN

SOFIA

He'd killed her too.

My mother.

She might be alive in the physical sense, but who she used to be was completely gone. I barely recognized her anymore; her once perfectly coiffured hair in complete disarray. It looked like it hadn't been combed in days. The smear of lipstick across her face making her mouth look distorted, her eyes blackened by forgotten mascara.

That was not my mother; that was a woman who had given up. Beaten down by a man who hadn't loved her or paid attention to her in years, who believed as long as he kept her in diamonds and designer clothes that he had fulfilled his duty.

A man who could corrupt his sons into believing that this was the way life worked and then turned around and killed his only daughter because she hadn't *toed the line*.

I felt sick. Consumed by rage on how he had infected them all, with no regard for anyone's life or happiness other than his own.

And I'd never wanted to kill him as much as I did at that moment.

It felt like an eternity waiting, but I knew it hadn't been longer than a couple of minutes, and when everything had gone quiet again I took the first step away from Michael. He had been at my back, and I knew that as I did this, he would continue to be. And then I would do the same for him. Freeing us both from this merry-go-round.

My head nodded as I moved slowly up the stairs, Michael following me close behind. I could tell he hated not being in the lead, but it had to be me. And for once he didn't argue, his tensed jaw staying shut as I strode further and further toward my father's bedroom door.

It was dark, so dark. The house starved of light just like it had been of compassion. And every single part of my body was hypersensitive as my hand slowly pushed open the door and my foot took a step inside.

"Elena, I told you there is no one here." My father's voice was followed by a rustle of sheets, his hand hitting the lamp on his nightstand.

Michael didn't wait, stepping out from my side and getting behind my father before his feet had fully hit the floor.

"Hello, Jimmy." The gun in his right hand was pointblank at my father's temple while his left was pressed against my father's kidneys. "We've come to pay our respects."

"What the fuck." My dad's eyes got wide as they focused on me, my gun aimed at his heart. "Sofia?" he coughed in surprise.

"You look like you've seen a ghost." My feet moved me closer even though my skin prickled in repulsion at being in the same room with him. "Maybe that's exactly what I am."

His chest expanded but for a man who always had so much to say he was speechless. I'm sure he was asking the questions even if he wasn't vocalizing them, namely why hadn't Michael killed me? But in his eyes I saw that he knew that none of them mattered anymore. I was still here and I knew everything.

"Sofia," Michael hissed, reminding me I had a job to do. "Do it, or I will."

I secured the safety and holstered my weapon. It was the

first time since we'd entered the house that I didn't have it in my hand and I felt naked without it. But Michael was right about not being able to shoot my father. It would attract too much attention and could only be used as a last resort.

The sheath Velcro'd to my thigh held a hunting knife. Michael had given it to me before I'd crawled into the trunk of his car. It was heavier than it looked, razor sharp, and as my hand grabbed the perfectly balanced hilt, I felt empowered.

"You won't do it." My father coughed, his lips twisting into a smirk. "You are too much like your mother. She's weak too, but at least she learned her place."

Later I would try and remember the moment, but in the present I didn't care. My hand rose and I sliced his neck from one side to the other as the gush of blood sprayed onto my chest.

He spluttered. His eyes wide open in complete bewilderment, his body jerking as Michael held him up—the guns in his hands not helping—as the blood flowed onto the floor. And there would be no final words spoken, not from him to me or me to him.

"Good thing you're dead and they won't be able to find me in the cop DNA data base." Michael lowered my father's still-twitching body to the floor. "It will be a real head scratcher for their CSI team." He stood up, holstering one of his guns and smiled. Completely unaffected by the fact he'd just witnessed me fillet my father's throat.

"Is that it?" My eyes fell to the floor when my father's eyes were closing, everything around him being stained red.

"Yeah, if he isn't already dead, it will happen in about another minute." He looked down at my father. "I think he's already gone."

I wasn't in a white dress, but my dark blue jeans and black hooded sweatshirt were covered in blood just like in the dream. My hands were also stained, as whatever was left on the blade continued to run down my hand.

It wasn't that I regretted it, because I didn't. He needed to die and it needed to be by my hand. But there was no instant relief. Like I expected some weight to be lifted off my shoulders and that didn't happen. I guess that was because the job was only half done. There was still one more man who needed to go before I would feel free. I just wasn't sure how I was going to get to him without Michael trying to stop me.

"We need to go, now." Michael took the knife from my hand and wiped it on my father's comforter. It was mostly clean when he slid it back into the sheath on my thigh. "Just in case." He nodded, twisting my body so I was facing the door. "Now, walk."

My body clicked into automatic, my feet moving one in front of the other until they were at the doorway. Hands functioned when they were supposed to, opening the door, my legs carrying me out of the room until I was out in the hall. Michael took care of closing the door, or at least I assumed, seeing it was shut and I didn't think I had done it.

We'd only gone five steps.

Five steps before I heard the door open. No, my father wasn't the second coming like he had thought he was, his dead body not resurrecting from the bloody pile where we'd left it. It was another door.

"James?"

The light from my mother's bedroom spilled out into the hall, her slippered feet carrying her out of her room with barely a sound.

"Oh, fuck," Michael whispered behind me, his hand giving my arm a squeeze before I heard it reach for his other gun.

"No," I blew out of my mouth in a rush, praying he wouldn't hurt her. As much as I used to despise her compliancy, I realized now she had been a victim in this too. She was just doing what she needed to survive. Unlike me, she didn't have a choice to leave.

"Sofia?" My mother's kohl rimmed eyes squinted, her irises so glassy I wasn't sure she could see at all.

"Mama, it's okay." I took a tentative step forward, the open palm behind my back the only hold-on I could give Michael. "Go back to bed."

"What happened to you?" She lifted her hand to her mouth as she took in my appearance, traveling the length of my body. "Were you in an accident? There is so much blood."

"I'm fine, Mama." I moved as close as I could without touching her. "Please, go lay down and go to sleep."

Lord knows how many sedatives she'd taken, a lot given her unsteadiness on her feet and even with the limited light I could see the dilation of her pupils. With any luck she wouldn't remember a thing by morning. The encounter explained away as a weird Valium induced dream that was brought on by the grief.

"Did you die, Sofia?" She stood still, her chest moving slowly as she looked at me with pain in her eyes. "Your father told me that . . . you died."

"Yes, Mama." I struggled against the lump in my throat. "I died." My chest tightened as I fought the urge to cry, unimaginable pain ripping through my heart. "I'm sorry. I'm sorry I wasn't able to be here for you. I'm sorry you had to do this alone."

"Beautiful child, no." She opened her arms wide, inviting an embrace. But I didn't move, my heart breaking that I couldn't touch her. "Did you feel pain, did it hurt?" Her eyes pooled with tears as her arms closed around herself, the hug I'd rejected given to herself.

"No, there was no pain." I shook my head as my own eyes

started to water, the words harder and harder to speak. "There is no pain where I am." I swallowed hard and took a breath. "There is a beautiful field, full of cornflowers and the sun shines all the time. I'm free now."

"Sofia. We need to—"

"Who is this man?" My mother's eyes widened as they fixed on Michael.

He didn't get a chance to finish his sentence, her body recoiling as his large frame appeared beside mine. He had waited as long as he was going to.

"Is he the one who killed you?" Her fingers made the sign of the cross as she took a step back.

"No, he has protected me." The strangled words made their way up my throat. "He has kept me safe, Mama. This is Michael and he is a good man."

"Well thank you, Michael." She struggled a little but managed to tug the edges of her sad mouth into a smile. "For taking care of my beloved."

"You're." Michael looked at me and then my mother before clearing his throat. "You're welcome."

His head jerked to the stairs we still had to descend, calmly indicating our time was running out. He went first, carefully hiding the gun he still held in his hand under his arm as he backed away from us. And as much as it hurt to leave, I turned and followed. Muscle memory was the only thing controlling my limbs, doing what I couldn't as they carried me away. Every stride killing me that I had just convinced my mother I had died.

"Sofia," she hiccupped, making my body unable to take another step.

"Yes, Mama." I turned knowing it would be the last time I would ever see her again.

"I love you, baby." Her voice broke as the tears spilled from her eyes. One of her hands was outstretched as if to reach for me while the other rested on the nearby wall. Her ability to support her own weight exhausted as she tried to stave off her tears. "Even when you left I loved you. I know your father drove you away. I know he said terrible things, said that you weren't part of this family anymore. But he never got to take you out of my heart. I love you even now that you're gone."

"I love you too." I barely got the words out as the first tear fell, my heart literally tearing into pieces as I witnessed the pain in her eyes.

"Don't cry, my darling." She wiped her own tears before managing a crooked smile. "I'll be with you soon."

"I'll be waiting."

It was the only comfort I could give her, the only thing I could offer her as my father's blood stained my chest and the floor of the house she had to sleep in tonight. I hoped in the morning one of my brothers would take her away from here, that she would finally find some peace. That the days she spent in a medicated haze would end, and she would find some of herself again. I prayed that it wasn't too late and she hadn't been lost forever.

It should have been hard to turn around and leave. But it wasn't. And not because my heart wasn't breaking with every step I took away from her, because it was. But because unlike the first time I'd left this house, there was hope that she would make it. And if all of this had to happen for that, then it was worth whatever hell I was going through.

The stairs seemed longer on their way down, neither of us saying a word as Michael moved a step ahead of me until we were back on the ground floor. The enormous marble entranceway that sprawled out in front of us was empty and dark, just as it had been before. Or at least it was until the ornate glass panels in the large wooden front door illuminated, the rumble of an engine suggesting that headlights were the source.

"We need another way out, Sofia." Michael grabbed my arm and all but threw me into the living room, squeal of dusty brakes barely audible over the heartbeat in my ears.

"Every other way is covered by the cameras," I hissed as my panic rose. "The sensors will kick in and trigger the lights. Our best way is to head to the garage and wait it out and then go the way we came."

It wasn't a good plan. With no way of knowing who was out there and how they were getting in, it might be damn well idiotic. But it was the best chance we had of making it out undetected or without getting into a gunfight on the front lawn. While the neighbors hadn't noticed us silently breaking and entering, they would definitely call the police the minute they heard a gunshot.

His jaw tensed not agreeing with my assessment but he didn't seem to have a better one himself. And with a quick nod he followed me to the door that enabled internal access to the garage. It wasn't far from where we'd entered through the side door, the few feet hopefully able to be navigated without detection when the time came to leave.

We stepped quickly inside, closing the door behind us, our bodies crouching down in between my father's Bentley Continental and Cadillac Escalade. *Dear God, please don't let whoever is out there have the remote to the roller door,* my lips moved in silent prayer. The hope that both the cars were parked inside enough of a guarantee that no one would be coming in that way.

It smelled like Armor All and leather as I palmed my Smith and Wesson. My body leaned on the car to help me balance my weight but the slick paint of the Caddy was making it difficult for me to stay still. And while the engine of the car had stopped, there was no sound of the front door to the house opening either.

The wait made me nervous; especially since there was no way of knowing who was out there and what were they doing.

Fear shot through me as the whirl of the overhead motor hoisting the heavy door kicked in. We had literally a second to scoot from in between the cars to wedging ourselves between the grille and the wall. It was a tight fit, each of us just being able to sink to our hunches as the overhead light clicked on and the door rose higher.

Those prayers I'd been saying weren't getting answered.

And whoever it was in the driveway, was coming in.

"Michael," I whispered knowing this might be my last chance.

"Not now." He put his finger to his lips. His head turned side to side, apparently trying to form a new plan.

"It was worth it."

"What?" He stopped cold.

Our eyes connected.

"Everything."

TWENTY-EIGHT

MICHAEL

Sofia's oldest brother—James the second, or Little Jimmy as he was known by his family—walked inside with Franco Santini. Because I had wrongly assumed the night couldn't get any worse so a big steaming bowl of fuck-you had to land in our laps.

Little Jimmy was agitated, his hand holding a gun and he looked like shit. His shirt was crumpled like he'd slept in the thing, with his tie pulled loose at the neck. Franco on the other hand was his usual GQ—three-piece suit, fedora and big ass grin on his smug fucking face. He seemed to have zero concern that only one of them appeared armed. I guess considering the angle Little Jimmy was holding the revolver he had a greater chance of getting a hangnail than actually getting shot. The barrel not pointed in any way hostile.

The other Y chromosome Amaro children weren't with the duo, the two of them walking inside and lowering the door. The implications of what the hell was taking place sending my brain into free fall.

Aside from the fact that Franco hated Jimmy senior—the two assholes only working together over the mutual dissent with Sofia—Franco also didn't make house calls.

The bastard demanded you came to *him*, or at the very least met on neutral territory, so his appearance at Casa Armaro was more than a little suspect.

And there was also the situation where the last time I'd seen the piece of shit he'd jacked me from behind and drugged me in an effort to "incentivize" me. Oh and we hadn't even gotten to the part where I'd recently found out he was also apparently my father. Fucking brilliant because I didn't think I could hate the man any more than I already did.

Sofia's eyes widened as she crouched lower against the Bentley. I, on the other hand, angled my head so I was just able to see past the Cadillac's giant front bumper, just enough to be able to see the view.

They stayed at the far end of the garage, leaning against the cars like they were about to shoot the breeze while pumping gas but the look on Little Jimmy's face was anything but calm.

"You know I've known your father for fifty years." Franco looked around the walls of the garage, bastard seeming to enjoy himself. "Never once have I ever been invited to his house. Even when we were boys who played in the street together."

"Well, that's the difference between me and him." Little Jimmy yanked at the tie knot and loosened it further. The gun still not pointed at anyone in particular. "I don't care about invisible lines between neighborhoods, and who runs what. All I care about is finding the piece of shit who torched my sister and returning the favor. You know that's what I'm owed at the very least based on the agreement between the families." His hands twitched at his sides. "And my father can either get on board or step aside, because I won't rest until the animal who did that to her is in the ground."

Well well, it seems like there was a little communication problem between the two Jimmies, with senior failing to mention he'd been the one pulling the strings.

Of course, we all knew the reason I'd been tasked for the

job in the first place was because he needed a fall guy. But his assurances that shit wouldn't blow back on me weren't looking too solid now were they. Good thing he was dead already, or I would ass fuck him with my nine and watch as he vomited up the bullets.

"You talk like you're ready to play with the big boys now." Franco laughed, no doubt enjoying the fact that Jimmy's kid was looking to him for permission. "You done pretending to be a businessman in New York City?"

"I was done being a pussy when my sister ended up in an ashtray." Little Jimmy's voice got hard, guttural. And while I knew Sofia's father hadn't given a rat's ass about her, this kid definitely gave a fuck. Well, at least one of the Jimmies had a pair.

"You said I have your support on this. We agree that I get the kill on Michael. And not you, my father, or anyone else in Chicago gets to retaliate."

A *big* pair it seemed if he thought he could come after me. Pity the situation was what it was; if he wasn't so hell bent on killing me I might have shaken his hand.

Sofia's face was getting panicked, her chest moving in and out as she started to freak out.

"He has no family." Franco crossed his arms across his chest. "If you have our blessing, there is no one who would dare come after you. But are you *sure* you have discussed this with your father?"

Read that: You have no fucking idea what you are dealing with and maybe don't want to go against dear old dad. Little did both of them know *Daddy* no longer had an opinion on account he no longer had a pulse.

"I told you, it's my right."

As stimulating as the conversation was—hearing how Sofia's brother wanted to end my life and the watching the dipshit who was supposedly my father enjoy it—it was time to end their fun time.

The odds weren't great.

Secured garage, close proximity and a lot of bullets.

Had just as much chance of it going south as I did walking out alive, but there were two of us and two of them. And while Sofia was looking like a deer in headlights, I'd seen her open her father's jugular. She'd been through too much to toss it all away now.

On three. I mouthed silently raising my gun for the visual. Her head shook, as she mouthed back *no.*

I didn't give her the choice, tilting my gun as my lips counted out *one . . . two . . .*

"Asshole, I'm right here." My legs jacked up, coming the full height as I leveled a nine each at Little Jimmy and Franco. "So, let's discuss your family's *right* while you give a blowjob to my Glock."

Sofia popped up right after, her gun pointed at Franco while her brother did the whole holy-fuck-am-I-seeing-a-ghost, his face twitching like it was having a seizure.

"Sofia?" Little Jimmy ignored the nine I had pointed as his chest and focused on his sister. "How can this be?" His gun inadvertently pointed directly at her.

"Well, isn't this a treat?" Franco smirked, casually leaning back against the shiny black Caddy, his own piece palmed, pointed at Sofia. "Very efficient to have everyone here in one place."

"Lose the gun, Franco." I tilted my head to his torso to remind him he had two tracking him. Even Vegas wouldn't have backed the odds of both of us missing.

"I'm rather attached to this." He tightened his grip and smiled. "So fuck you."

"Sofia, what's going on?" Little Jimmy waved the gun in her

direction, not able to understand why his dead sister was standing very much alive in front of him. "What are you doing with this guy?"

"Jimmy, please." Sofia nodded to the barrel he had pointed at her, no doubt hoping to telepathically try and get him to lower it. "I know you don't understand, but Dad lied to you. He is the one who wanted me dead."

"No, no. He wouldn't do that." The gun stayed raised, but wavered a little like he was unconvinced of where to point it. "You're his blood. He disowned you but he'd never kill you."

"He did." She turned and looked at the man standing beside him. "Franco was in on it."

"Is this true?" Little Jimmy's head whipped to the side while trying to maintain visual on both Sofia and me. "Tell me!"

"I hate family disputes. Not my place to get involved." Franco yawned, apparently bored and not the least bit concerned we were in a four-way standoff.

"Except you *are* involved." I laughed, and as much as I hated to admit it—even to myself—I saw a family resemblance. That cold hard stare when he eyeballed, the lack of fucks he gave— it was like looking into a mirror. "And I still owe you for the last time we were together."

"Stop." Little Jimmy's voice shot out of his mouth. "Someone tell me what the fuck is going on."

"You're too late for that conversation, son." Franco smiled, his eyes remaining on me.

I'm not sure it bothered me, because fuck knows I didn't want that *son* directed at me, but I really hated how these conceited bastards threw the word around.

There'd been a time when I would have literally killed to hear it, to know that there was a part of me that belonged. But like everything in life I'd been disappointed too many times to believe it was possible. There hadn't been a place for me; I'd wandered from wake up to lights out as an outsider. And no one ever had my back. Except for a woman, the one I was supposed to kill and couldn't.

And now here he was, the guy who had no idea of my existence, or even the chain of events he set in motion all those years ago. Looking at me like I was the disappointment, the stench of entitlement suffocating the room.

An eerie calm washed over me as words I hadn't planned on saying came spilling out of my mouth. "What happened to your first wife, Rose?"

"What?" His head whipped around as his smug ass smile evaporated.

Yeah, he hadn't been expecting *that*. Just the mention was enough to jack his spine up straight.

Sofia's eyes widened, but she kept her mouth clamped. She nodded, giving me the signal she would back me up as her eyes stayed on Franco. Little Jimmy's head continued to swivel between us all trying to work out what the fuck was going on.

"Rose?" I repeated it, enjoying watching him flinch as I said it again. "The woman who you were married to? You remember her, right?"

"I divorced her, she had an affair." His jaw tensed, the words barely getting out of his tight row of teeth. "Stupid whore couldn't keep her legs closed."

Stupid whore.

How many times had I said those words?

How many times had I believed them?

But had she *actually* been either stupid or a whore? Or was that something that had been programmed into me without me even knowing. A silent legacy gifted to me by a shithead.

"What did that feel like?" I couldn't help it, wanting to scratch that itch a little bit more. "Not being able to keep your woman satisfied that she had to go elsewhere.

"That's how you want to spend the last moments of your life, talking about the dumb bitch I used to be married to?" He was searching for an answer, wondering why the fuck I'd bring it up. The mention completely out of left field.

And it was getting to him, rattling his cage so much his nice expensive suit was getting tighter in the collar. "Because I *will* fucking end you, Michael."

And I saw in his eyes that every single word of it was true.

No, not what *he* was saying. What Sofia had said.

That woman I'd spent my entire life hating had to look at Franco and know that the kid she was carrying would probably end up like that. I couldn't imagine what that would have been like for her and not giving into the urge of ending it all together.

It was easier when I believed the lie, one that in a weird way the asshole had perpetuated even without him knowing. And maybe, just maybe I didn't really hate her at all.

It was hatred in general that consumed me and I was just addicted to the burn. Those flames were easier when they had a name, when hating myself didn't cut it

"You think I care if you kill me?" It was my turn to laugh. "But you didn't divorce her, she left you when she found out she was pregnant." I watched as he fought the desire to react, failing miserably as it came double barreling at him. "And the woman you say you were so willing to get rid of was the one person who denied you what you most wanted in life—a son."

"Michael!" Sofia yelled, forcing me to look where Franco's gun was pointed.

He turned his hand away from Sofia and angled it right at me.

Good, that was a better place for it.

I'd done so many things in my life, seen so many things that could never be unseen. And I was ready for the ride to stop.

I'd welcomed the fall once before but I hadn't been ready, this time I needed to do something right for the first time in my life. Not because I suddenly believed in the bullshit lie that there was something for me after, but because I needed to give it to her.

I would save her and take those bullets, not because I'd given her my word, but because I owed her. Sofia showed me the truth even when I didn't want to see it.

And for giving me the first moments of peace I had ever had.

Even if they were going to be my last.

"Rose was my mother, you cocksucker. Which as much as I hate to admit it, makes you my father. And guess what asshole? I may not have known her but she obviously knew you. And I guess she knew me too. Because I'd rather die than continue your fucking legacy."

It was automatic, my right hand squeezing the trigger and the bullet spiraled out of the barrel.

I was sure I made contact; positive as I felt the impact of a bullet traveling in the opposite direction hit me.

It burned, the blood spilling out of me as my vision started to fade. The echo of guns firing bounced off the confined walls; the only thing louder was the screaming.

There were voices above me, but I couldn't see.

"Thank you, Sofia." I wasn't sure she had heard me, but I didn't have anything left in me to say it louder.

The darkness was coming faster than it ever had, wrapping my body like a blanket and taking me away with it.

There was no fear.

No pain.

No regret.

And as my lungs rattled in my chest, I felt it for the first time.

Freedom.

EPILOGUE

Thirty years ago there had been a storm.

The heavens had opened up and the earth had trembled, and fear had been struck into the hearts of those who had to endure it.

Not because of the relentless rain that had drowned the Chicago streets and the thunder that had shaken the walls. But because *that* storm, hadn't been the only one that had come that day.

An expectant mother was weathering her own storm. Her body failing as it fought bravely, the love for her unborn child the only thing that kept her heart going. Just holding on long enough to give birth to a son.

She knew it would be a boy; he would have his father's eyes and her smile and despite the sadness that had surrounded his creation, he would only have the best of them. There had been a time where his father had been kind and loved her, where his embrace had made her feel safe, and *those* were the things that she knew would be imparted.

And her son's heart, *his* heart, would eventually find its way back to hers. Because that was the only way she could bare it, unable to face the prospect of saying goodbye forever.

And if she had to leave before she could ever hold him—give her life for his—she would do it a million times over. Because that's what a mother did, love her baby beyond her own mortality even before he took his first breath.

Forever.

She would love him forever.

But thirty years wasn't long enough, and she would have more time to wait before she would see her son again.

Because she had indeed given the very best parts of herself to him. And the muscle in his chest continued to beat long after it should have stopped, finding its own will when it seemed that all was lost. In that moment, he had been more her son than he'd ever been, and whether he knew it or not, embraced her resilience to survive.

"Sofia," he mumbled, the oxygen mask against his face making it difficult for him to speak. "Safe?"

"Shhhhhhh." A nurse gently moved her fingers against his arm in an attempt to comfort him, hoping this time her touch wouldn't upset him. She had learned the first time she had done it that he didn't like it, and was trying to resist her instinct to soothe. "You're safe."

He heard the voice of a woman but didn't know who it was. The cadence was wrong and the pitch was slightly off, and she didn't sound like Sofia. He tried to open his eyes, needing answers as to where she was but that fog around his head hung heavy. It was an effort that seemed beyond him, his eyelids just able to stretch a tiny bit so that he could hope to see where he was.

There was too much light, the brightness burning his retinas so that he only saw shapes. He squinted, hoping to make out the owner of the voice but she was hidden by a sepia aura distorting his vision.

"Sofia?" he asked again, the muscles in his neck straining as he tried to lift his head off the pillow. "Where. Is. She?"

Each word was broken into its own sentence as they battled against his need to breathe. He wasn't going back to sleep until he knew, until he was certain that she was here too.

"Michael." He heard his name, and for a second he thought it was her. But even though her voice was kind, she was too young. "Are you coming back to us, Michael?"

He couldn't fight anymore, the effort exhausting him as he lowered his head back down on the pillow and concentrated on breathing.

In and out.

In and out.

The mask made it easier, the steady push of oxygen making him slightly dizzy, so he closed his eyes but he forced himself to stay awake.

Maybe she had escaped. Had gone before the police had come and left all of it—and him—behind. And while he hoped he would see her again, he would be glad to know she was safe. It would make him happy to know she got away. Away from her father and away from his.

"He is asking for her, the woman he was with?" The younger female moved closer to the bed, unsure as her hand hovered above his wanting to touch him.

She didn't though; instead retracting her hand and pinning a lock of her long blonde hair behind her ear. She wondered if she would get to know him, and if he would want to know her. His existence so new to her that it had only been days since they'd first met. Well, not really met, but she hoped that would come later.

"Yes, he wakes occasionally." The nurse carefully emptied a syringe of clear liquid into his cannula, the medicine seeming to settle him. "He always asks for her but no one has told him yet."

Michael stilled and not because of the sedative that was making its way into his veins. Instead he hoped the quiet would keep his brain alert just long enough to hear what they were saying. Because they sounded like they knew.

"Does he know about his father?"

The young blonde lowered herself down onto the seat that sat beside his bed. She had been there yesterday too but this time was the first time he had spoken.

"No, he knows nothing."

The nurse checked the IV machine beside him, rolling her fingers across the dial and adjusted the dosage. "Your father is getting stronger but may never regain the ability to walk. He was luckier than Michael, and while the bullet severed his spinal cord it missed most of his internal organs. But they both have a long way to go."

The nurse smiled at the girl, watching her shift awkwardly in her seat. Seeing two of her family members almost die would be hard enough for anyone but especially difficult for someone so young. She was so brave, a warrior like her brother.

And it was strange the nurse thought, that Mona Santini spent more of her time with him—her brother—than she did with her father. The man who was only a few doors away and completely conscious.

Of course the nurse had heard the whispers. That Franco had been the one to shoot the son he had never known he had, but she didn't believe any father was capable of that. People could say such horrible things, and vicious rumors weren't things she'd ever entertain. No, she was there to heal people, which is what she intended to do.

"Stay as long as you like." She stopped beside Mona and looked at the siblings side by side. Her skin was a little lighter than his and her hair of course was blonde, but it was striking how much they resembled each other. "You can talk to him too, they can hear us and it helps them to know we're here."

Michael hadn't moved, his body on his back with his limbs loose on either side but he hadn't been asleep like they had assumed.

Inside his head he was screaming, the noise so loud that it would surely drive him mad.

Franco had somehow survived.

Michael had only one wish when he'd pulled that trigger. And that was to make sure that the monster who happened to be his father had taken his last breath. Even if it meant dying with him. And he didn't know why or how the bullet that had been intended for his heart had missed it entirely, but it no longer mattered.

And even as the noise echoed inside his skull, not even a whisper passed his lips. He was still no closer to knowing what had happened to Sofia.

"Michael?" Mona asked, her hands knotting in her lap as she felt stupid talking to someone she didn't really know. "I'm Mona. We're . . . well, Dad says we're family. I'm going to stay here for awhile and just hang out, if that's okay. Maybe just talk, but I don't mind if you fall asleep." She twisted her hands nervously as he watched the faintest movement of his lashes bounce off his cheeks.

It had been isolating being Franco Santini's only child, she'd been so lonely and sheltered, and her heart had ached for a sibling. It seemed that by some miracle, God had answered her prayer and now she would no longer be alone.

"I know you are asking about Sofia and they won't tell you." She took a deep breath, hesitating before she continued.

He felt his skin prickle, wishing there was some way he could urge her to continue, but there was nothing he could do. He was imprisoned in a body that had once served him well and he would have done anything to get out.

"She's gone, and you're safe from her. She can't hurt you anymore. Dad—" Her dark almond-shaped eyes darted quickly left and then right knowing she shouldn't be talking about it.

"Dad made it so she is never coming back." She leaned closely and whispered. "He killed her; this time he made sure of it."

Mona wasn't to know that with those words she had stirred up another storm. Because she had only received one side of the story, the one carefully curated by her father. And while he'd been careful about what he said, he hadn't been with what he'd done.

It was true that his gun had been pointed at Michael when he'd been in the Amaro garage. But not even Jesus Christ demanding it would have made him shoot the son—the heir—he'd longed for. He smiled as his hand twisted, changing the trajectory of the bullet. And it was that quick change in movement that was enough to save his own life.

Little Jimmy would never have killed Sofia, and it had been him who ultimately shot Michael.

Confused and overcome with grief, he chose the closest target when the gunfire started. Sadly for him, he had chosen the wrong side. The same gun Franco had used to shoot Sofia was then turned on the other Amaro child.

And in a tragic and horrific twist of irony, they both had been buried with their father.

The machines beside Mona sounded loudly, sending medical personal rushing into the room. Her lithe frame jumped from her seat beside him, the body on the hospital gurney jerking in violent convulsions.

"Get her out of here," yelled a doctor, the kind nurse from earlier gently ushering her out of the room.

"Please, don't die," she whispered, the door closing in front of her as doctors and nurses worked in an erratic sea of activity. "I need you." She couldn't bear the thought of once again being alone.

The heart monitor flat lined with paddles being placed on his chest prompting his back to lift after each charge.

They weren't sure how much his heart could take, and whether the shocks would kick start the rhythm or end it entirely.

But they weren't to know, as they charged up the paddles one last time, that he was very much his mother's son.

And she would wait for him a little longer.

An eternity if necessary.

Because that's what mothers did.

"We've got something!" the doctor yelled, the tiniest of peaks appeared on the long flat line of the ECG. "I think he's back."

The heart that had served him so well in the past continued to beat. And while no one would know what the future would hold for it, it was clear it wouldn't stop just yet.

Some would argue that it would have been better if he died in that room. They were the same people who claimed he had no soul.

As Michael and his heart proved that day—neither of those things were true.

To keep up to date with all T Gephart's
news, appearances and releases,
please subscribe to her mailing list at
http://eepurl.com/bws5Av

ACKNOWLEDGEMENTS

The first thank you always goes to my family—Gep, Jenna, Liam and Woodley. I think I cried a little more with this book and was probably more unbearable than usual, but you loved me anyway. I love you guys so very much.

Thanks to my amazing extended family and friends. I'm sorry if I haven't seen you enough or told you how much I love you and I promise I will try and do better. I will *even* put on pants and occasionally leave the house—that's how much I care. PS. I think I owe a few of you drinks, feel free to cash in your I owe yous.

Special thanks to MK. Your insight is phenomenal and I can't tell you how much I appreciate it. Amazing. Please don't ever get too busy to read my books.

Thank you to the many authors I adore who strangely think I'm okay too. Lili Saint Germain, JB Hartnett, Monica James, Skyla Madi, CJ Duggan, Lilliana Andersen, Rachel Brookes, JD Nixon, Natasha Preston, Kirsty Mosely, Jane Harvey-Berrick, Ker Dukey, LA Casey, Tillie Cole, Abbi Glines, Chantal Fernando, Helena Hunting, Christina Hobbs and Lauren Billings, Kelly Elliot, Jay Crownover, Kim Karr, SC Stephens, Joanna Wylde, Kylie Scott and MK Harkins—and to anyone I've left out, you all rock.

Hang Le—cover artist extraordinaire and general badass! Thanks for all the pretty things.

Huge thanks and appreciation to all the bloggers and blogs who have, and continue to support me. So many of you share my covers, releases, sales without even so much as a word from me. It is a massive job and see the incredible effort you put in. I'm sorry if I miss your shares or posts, but every single one of you is amazing.

Thanks to the T Gephart Entourage, #InsertInsanity. I promise one of these days we'll talk books. LOL

Thanks to my Penny and Angela #WhereISUnimpressedCat? Those messages and GIFs make my day.

Thank you to my editor, Nichole Strauss, from Perfectly Publishable. This one was a challenge for me but I knew you would be honest if it was shit. Luckily for both of us it wasn't. LOL Thanks for walking this road with me even when I'm freaking out, saying fuck too much and Power Station-ing my way through my drafts.

Thank you to my proofreaders Marie and Rosa for picking up pesky Typ0s LOL.

Massive thanks to Max Henry from Max Effect—Fantastic formatting yet again.

And the biggest thank you is of course to YOU, the readers. This was a different book for me to write and I didn't want to insult you by giving you a half-assed effort. You trusted me and allowed me to do what I do. It means everything. Thank you.

ABOUT THE AUTHOR

T Gephart is an indie author from Melbourne, Australia. T's approach to life has been somewhat unconventional. Rather than going to University, she jumped on a plane to Los Angeles, USA in search of adventure. While this first trip left her somewhat underwhelmed and largely depleted of funds it fueled her appetite for travel and life experience.

With a rather eclectic resume, which reads more like the fiction she writes than an actual employment history, T struggled to find her niche in the world.

While on a subsequent trip the United States in 1999, T met and married her husband. Their whirlwind courtship and interesting impromptu convenience store wedding set the tone for their life together, which is anything but ordinary. They have lived in Louisiana, Guam and Australia and have traveled extensively throughout the US. T has two beautiful young children and one four legged child, Woodley, the wonder dog.

An avid reader, T became increasingly frustrated by the lack of strong female characters in the books she was reading. She wanted to read about a woman she could identify with, someone strong, independent and confident and who didn't lack femininity. Out of this need, she decided to pen her first book, A Twist of Fate. T set herself the challenge to write something that was interesting, compelling and yet easy enough to read that was still enjoyable. Pulling from her own past "colorful" experiences and the amazing personalities she has surrounded herself with, she had no shortage of inspiration. With a strong slant on erotic fiction, her core characters are empowered women who don't have to sacrifice their femininity. She enjoyed the process so much that when it was over she couldn't let it go.

T loves to travel, laugh and surround herself with colorful characters. This inevitably spills into her writing and makes for an interesting journey - she is well and truly enjoying the ride!

Based on her life experiences, T has plenty of material for her books and has a wealth of ideas to keep you all enthralled.

CONNECT WITH T

Website
http://tgephart.com

Facebook
www.facebook.com/tgephartauthor

Goodreads
www.goodreads.com/author/show/
7243737.T_Gephart

Twitter
https://twitter.com/tinagephart

BOOKS BY T

The Lexi Series
Lexi
A Twist of Fate
Twisted Views: Fate's Companion
A Leap of Faith
A Time for Hope

The Power Station Series
High Strung
Crash Ride
Back Stage

The Black Addiction Series
Slide
Sticks
Stand

Standalones
The Fall
#1 Crush (coming soon)

Made in the USA
Columbia, SC
07 March 2018